W9-COH-781

THE FURTHER CHRONICLES
OF
SHERLOCK HOLMES
VOLUME 2

DENIS O. SMITH

LUDINGTON
PUBLIC LIBRARY & INFORMATION CENTER
5 S. BRYN MAWR AVENUE
BRYN MAWR, PA 19010-3406

First edition published in 2018
© Copyright 2018
Denis O Smith

The right of Denis O Smith to be identified as the author of this work has been asserted by him in accordance with the Copyright, Designs and Patents Act 1998.

All rights reserved. No reproduction, copy or transmission of this publication may be made without express prior written permission. No paragraph of this publication may be reproduced, copied or transmitted except with express prior written permission or in accordance with the provisions of the Copyright Act 1956 (as amended). Any person who commits any unauthorised act in relation to this publication may be liable to criminal prosecution and civil claims for damage.

All characters appearing in this work are fictitious. Any resemblance to real persons, living or dead, is purely coincidental. The opinions expressed herein are those of the author and not of MX Publishing.

ePub ISBN 978-1-78705-324-3
PDF ISBN 978-1-78705-325-0
Paperback ISBN 978-1-78705-323-6

Published in the UK by MX Publishing
335 Princess Park Manor, Royal Drive,
London, N11 3GX
www.mxpublishing.co.uk

For Penny, Dorothy and, especially, Harriet, who have all, at various times, read and commented on previous collections of stories, in the hope that they will find something to enjoy in the present collection.

CONTENTS

THE MAN IN THE GREEN TWEED SUIT

MY MORNING MEDICAL ROUND being finished earlier than usual, I had called upon my friend, Mr. Sherlock Holmes, on a pleasant day in October and found him lounging full-length on the sofa in his old mouse-coloured dressing-gown, apparently staring at the ceiling. On the floor beside him lay crumpled heaps of newspapers, like so much flotsam washed up against the sofa by some unseen tide.

He acknowledged my presence with a slight wave of his hand, but did not move, and, aware as I was of his occasional weakness for artificial stimulants when he found life too boring to contemplate, I feared for a moment that he was in the poisonous grip of some powerful narcotic. But, abruptly, he swung his legs to the floor and sat up, with a sparkle and clarity in his eyes which told me that my fears were groundless.

"My dear fellow!" said he. "Do forgive my rudeness! My thoughts were elsewhere. It is always a pleasure to see you here, Watson, as I'm sure you know."

"I take it you have no case in hand at present," I remarked as I sat down in my old arm-chair.

"On the contrary," he responded, as he reached for his pipe and the slipper in which he kept his tobacco, "I have a singularly puzzling business to consider. Our old friend, Inspector Lanner, called round last night to consult me on the matter."

"Were you able to help him?"

Holmes shook his head. "Not in any very decisive way. Of course, I have my own theory – one cannot help but form a preliminary hypothesis, even against one's own better judgement – but I cannot prove it, and did not feel inclined to trouble Lanner with it. I was just running over the facts of the matter again in my mind, when you entered."

"I would be very interested to hear about it," said I, "if it would be helpful to you to repeat it aloud to someone."

"Very well," said he. "It's the Wentworth case. You have perhaps read something of it in your newspaper."

"Very little, other than the barest outline. I have been kept very busy lately with my professional duties, and have not had time to study the papers in the way I used to."

"All the better!" cried my friend, as he put a match to his pipe. "Then your judgement will not be biased by what you have already read. As I have often remarked to you, one cannot hope to solve a case merely from reading an account of it in the daily press. Such accounts are generally lacking in the very details one wishes most to know about. In this case, we have, at least, Inspector Lanner's account, which is a little more detailed than that in the papers. Indeed, because of the nature of the case, Lanner's account may be all the material we shall ever have, so we must make the most of it.

"The case, Watson, as you probably know, is one of murder, the murder of a gentleman by the name of Piers Wentworth, of Links House, Woodside Lane, Bickley, a man well known in the more Bohemian circles of London Society, who was found shot dead in his own study."

"One of the papers," I interrupted, "the *Daily Chronicle*, I think it was, reported that when the body of the unfortunate man was discovered, all the doors of the house were found to be locked on the inside."

Holmes chuckled. "That is true," said he, "but the fact is of no significance. That item of information represents, I take it, an attempt by the *Daily Chronicle* to add a little more mystery to a crime which is in no need of such embellishment. The back door of the house, and the French window which gives directly from the study onto the back garden were indeed both locked on the inside. The front door, however, has a sprung latch, so that anyone leaving the house that way merely has to pull the door shut behind him and the lock is engaged. It is therefore practically a certainty that the murderer left the house by the front door, but the point is of no importance. Of somewhat greater interest is the question as to how he had entered the house in the first place – but I shall come to that in a moment.

"Now, to give you a little more general information about the victim of this crime: He seems to have been moderately well off; not what might be described as significantly wealthy, but, still, sufficiently comfortably placed that he was not obliged to pursue any particular profession. He did, however, have an interest in a couple of commercial enterprises, one a brokerage house in the City, the other a wholesale drapers in Holborn, at both of which he spent one day a week.

"He was not married, and lived alone in a fairly isolated house near Bickley, which, as you are no doubt aware, is in Kent, just the other side of Bromley. His sole domestic servant was an elderly widow, Mrs. Barnham, who acted as cook, housekeeper and maid-of-all-work, although her duties, according to her own testimony, were not very exacting.

"Wentworth's recreation seems to have consisted chiefly of two activities. The first of these was golf. He was a very keen golfer and was able to indulge his fondness for the game without difficulty, as his house adjoins the local golf course. There is in fact a gate at the bottom of the back garden which gives directly onto the course. Except in bad weather, he played most days of the week, save those days he was obliged to go up to town on business.

"His second great interest in life and probably the more important, both from his point of view and from ours, was the fair sex. Of course, most men have an interest, to a greater or lesser degree, in the opposite sex, but Wentworth seems to have been one of those in whom this interest has become the ruling passion of their lives. He was, in short, something of a Don Juan, and, by all accounts, a very successful one. For this information, as with the rest of what we know, we must thank the indefatigable researches of Inspector Lanner. Wentworth had never been married, he had never even been nearly married, and seemed unlikely ever to be so. It is said that he valued his independence and his bachelor establishment at Bickley too highly for that. But the chase, the pursuit and conquest of whichever female he had set his sights on at any given moment, that, it seems, was the source of the very greatest pleasure for Wentworth, and the mainspring of his life.

"He was no longer a young man – he was not far short of his fortieth birthday – but the passage of the years does not seem to have brought any noticeable alteration in his habits. He would go up to town, to a theatre or music-hall, at least once a week and often more frequently than that, where he would endeavour to strike up an acquaintance with some pretty girl or other and invite her to dine with him. He was also a member of Tilbury's Club, in the Haymarket, where he would call in at least once a week, to play cards and the like. He was well known there, and had a fairly large circle of acquaintances, but does not seem to have had any really close friends.

"And that," said Holmes after a moment, "gives you the main points of the antecedents to the case." He leaned over, struck a match on the hearth and put it to his pipe, which had gone out while he was speaking. "Is that clear so far, Watson? Do you have any questions?"

"Clear enough," I replied, "but I do have one question: Did the murdered man have any other place of lodging, an apartment in town, for instance?"

Holmes shook his head. "He had had such a place when he was younger, a small *pied-a-terre* in Knightsbridge, but had sold it about ten years ago. The train-journey from Victoria down to Bickley is a fairly quick one and the service is frequent, so I imagine Wentworth found it just as easy to go home at night as to stay in town. He did occasionally stay at his club, but not very often, and if the evening had got late, he sometimes put up with one of his cronies. He had also been known to borrow someone else's apartment in town for a few days when the owner was away.

"Now, on the day in question, which was just over two weeks ago, on the twenty-fifth of September, Wentworth did not come up to town. He had played a round of golf in the morning with Colonel Stockley, another member of the local golf club, who states that there was nothing in either Wentworth's speech or manner which was at all unusual. He had then spent the rest of the day at home, reading, attending to business correspondence and so on. That day being a Wednesday, Wentworth's housekeeper had the afternoon off, as was usual, but before she left to visit friends, at about twelve o'clock, she had prepared a cold luncheon, which she had left, under covers, on the dining-room table. The weather all that week was pleasant and mild, and when Wentworth had informed her, a few days earlier, that he was expecting a visitor on Wednesday, he had mentioned that they might take lunch in the open, at Frog's Heath, a popular spot locally for walking and taking picnics. But he seems to have dropped this idea, as he did not mention it on the Wednesday. Nor did he mention who the visitor he was expecting might be. The departure of Mrs. Barnham, by the way, was the last time that Wentworth was seen alive. She was just going out of the front gate when he called to her, then he followed her down the path and they exchanged a few words by the gate concerning what she had left for luncheon. The nearest house is some considerable distance away, but it has a very large garden which comes close to that of Links House, and at that time a gardener was working there. He overheard the brief conversation between Wentworth and his housekeeper and states that it was as Mrs. Barnham describes, and that there seemed nothing unusual in Wentworth's manner.

"The housekeeper returned at about half past five, and let herself in with her latch-key. After hanging up her coat, she went into the study to inform her master she was back and to ask if there was anything he required. There, she was shocked to find Wentworth lying on his back upon the floor, the front of his clothes soaked with blood. She at once ran to fetch the local doctor, who pronounced him dead, shot through the heart at close quarters about four hours previously with a small-calibre pistol.

"The police were quickly notified of the crime, and Inspector Lanner was assigned to the case. The first significant fact he discovered was that there was a considerable sum of money on both the desk and table in Wentworth's study; not a huge amount, but certainly enough to tempt a thief. That this had not been touched suggested, therefore, that the motive for the crime had not been theft, but something else. There was also no indication that a struggle had taken place in the study, which suggested that Wentworth had been taken by surprise by his assassin. The question then arose as to how the murderer had gained entry to the house. There seemed to be two possibilities here: either Wentworth himself had admitted him at the front door, or the French window of the study had been standing open when the murderer arrived and he had gained entry to the house that way. If the former, then Wentworth probably knew the identity of his murderer; if the latter, then the inference is not so clear.

"Energetic enquiries were at once instituted in the district, to try to learn if anyone had seen this assassin, but these enquiries largely drew a blank. None of Wentworth's immediate neighbours had seen any strangers on the road that day, and nor had they seen anyone at all entering Wentworth's property by the front gate. However, two members of the local golf club – a Mr. Ould and a Mr. Poulter – had been playing a round that afternoon, and they state that at about one o'clock they had seen a man crossing the golf course from right to left some distance ahead of them. He was about fifty yards away – too far for them to give a very accurate description of him, but close enough for them to be sure that it was no one that they had ever seen before. He had a beard, they say, was wearing a green tweed suit, with a soft, wide-brimmed felt hat upon his head, and was carrying a light-brown overcoat folded over his arm. They had just finished the third hole at the time, and were about to tee off on the fourth when they saw him, and as the man was crossing the fairway ahead of them, one of them called 'fore' to warn him. He turned, raised his arm and waved in acknowledgement of the warning.

Then he paused, glanced up at the sky, slipped on his overcoat and proceeded on his way. The last they saw of him was when he passed behind a clump of bushes to the left of the fairway. As the path he was on leads directly to Woodside Lane, passing the back garden gate of Wentworth's house as it does so, they assumed that that was where he was going, and gave him no more thought. They never saw him again.

"As the only person seen in the vicinity of Wentworth's house on the day he was murdered, the man in the green tweed suit naturally became the focus for all the police enquiries, but he proved somewhat difficult to track down. No one seemed to have noticed him as he passed along the road from the centre of Bickley towards Wentworth's house, and no one at the golf club had noticed him either, save only the two men I mentioned before. Enquiries at the railway station proved a little more fruitful, however. There, a porter, who was busy on the platform during the afternoon, recalled seeing a young man in a green tweed suit sitting on one of the platform benches, smoking a cigarette. A light-brown overcoat was flung over the back of the bench beside him. The porter says he did not give the man much consideration. He did think, however, that with his well-cut clothes and the languid way he was lounging on the bench, the young man seemed something of a 'swell.' When the train for Victoria rolled in, the young man rose to his feet, slipped on his overcoat, although he didn't bother to fasten it, and made his way to a smoking carriage.

"From the description of the young man, the police understandably thought it more likely that he would have been returning to the West End, rather than anywhere in the suburbs, and, accordingly, concentrated their enquiries at Victoria station. Here, however, they again drew a blank. None of the officials there could recall seeing such a traveller on the day in question. The police then widened their enquiries to Ludgate Hill and the other stations on the City branch, thinking that the young man might have changed trains at Herne Hill, but with an equal lack of success. They also asked Wentworth's housekeeper if her master had ever had a visitor answering to the description given by the two golfers and the porter at Bickley station, but she could not think of anyone.

"Now, as the young man seen on the golf-course had also been seen at the railway station, it seemed a reasonable assumption that he had arrived in and left the district by train, but the police were puzzled at first as to why he had chosen the route he did from the station to Wentworth's house. You see, the road from the railway station towards Links House forks as it comes away from the centre of Bickley. The left-hand branch, Woodside Lane, has a number of houses on it before passing the front of Wentworth's own house. The right-hand branch, Links Lane, which goes up to the golf club-house, is much narrower, has no houses on it, and is little frequented save by those bound for the golf-course. The left-hand branch is the shorter, more direct route from the station to Wentworth's house. The right-hand branch is longer, but much quieter. That the gentleman in the green tweed suit had chosen the latter route therefore suggests certain conclusions. First, that as he was familiar enough with the district to know that it was possible to get to Wentworth's house by going up Links Lane and then crossing the golf-course, he had almost certainly visited Wentworth's house before, or had been instructed by someone who had. Second, that as he had chosen the way which was longer but quieter, it must be supposed that his intention was to avoid being seen. This in turn suggests that the murder was not an accident or the result of a spur-of-the-moment decision, but had been planned in advance.

"There the matter rested for a couple of days, until one of the officials at Bromley station – which is, of course, the very next station on the line towards London after Bickley – came forward with a fresh piece of information, having read of the crime in his newspaper. No enquiries had up to then been made at Bromley, it being the almost universal belief that the murderer – if that is what the young man was – must have travelled from Bickley to Victoria, or somewhere close to it. The idea that he might have travelled just one stop on the line before alighting had been assumed to be so unlikely as to be not worth considering. That, however, is precisely what the railway official's information suggested. The official in question, a man by the name of Badger, had been in charge of the left-luggage office at Bromley station on the afternoon of the day of the murder. He states that a young man in a light-brown overcoat and a soft brown hat called at the office at about half past three in the afternoon to collect a medium-sized carpet-bag which had been deposited there earlier that same day. As to the green tweed suit, he can't be certain, as the young man's overcoat was buttoned up. But, aside from that, he has provided the best description so far. The man, he says, was certainly young, of medium height, with light brown hair and a sandy, almost gingery beard. He also states that the young man did not say very much, seeming preoccupied as he handed over the ticket relating to the carpet-bag. Mr. Badger says that he himself made some remark about the fine weather, at which the other smiled in a pleasant enough fashion, nodded his head in agreement, and made some observation in a quiet voice, which Mr. Badger did not catch. After collecting the bag, the young man simply walked away, and was not seen again by anyone. He may have caught the next up train, he may have caught the next down train, he may have left the station altogether: no one knows."

"As he had a travelling-bag with him," I interjected, "could it be that he was not going home, but was on his way to somewhere else, perhaps in Kent or Sussex?"

"The police certainly considered that a possibility."

"He may even have been making for Folkestone or Dover," I added, "to take a boat to the Continent."

"That, also, was considered possible. However, although enquiries have been made at all the ports, they have met with no success. The man in the green tweed suit has become somewhat like the 'x' in algebra – the unknown quantity. Do you have any further observations?"

"I have at least some questions," I responded. "First of all, is it known who deposited the carpet-bag that the young man collected on the afternoon of the murder?"

"No. All that is known for certain is that the bag was deposited on the same day as it was collected; the time and date are on the ticket. But a different official was on duty there in the morning, someone not as observant as Mr. Badger, and he cannot recall who it was that left the bag there."

"It seems to me," I remarked after a moment, "that even if these three sightings are all of the same person, as seems more than likely, we still cannot say for certain that he is definitely the murderer of Piers Wentworth."

"Why do you say that?" asked Holmes, a note of curiosity in his voice.

"It seems to me possible," I replied, "that even if the young man crossing the golf-course was indeed making for Wentworth's house, as appeared to be the case, he may not have committed any crime. It is possible that when he reached the house he found that Wentworth had already been shot dead by someone else. Then, seeing that there was nothing he could do for the dead man, and fearing that he himself would be accused of the crime, he decided to make himself scarce and deny ever having been there."

"That would certainly be possible," conceded my friend, "although no one else was seen in the vicinity of Wentworth's house on that day, and it is difficult to see why, if he is innocent, he should fear being accused of the crime unless (a) he had a good motive for committing it, and (b) he had arrived armed with a pistol of his own. Still, I am glad to see that you are keeping an open mind on the subject. You are becoming a more careful reasoner in your mature years, Watson!"

"I don't know about 'mature years,'" I returned with a chuckle; "but all the years I spent lodging here with you have no doubt had an effect upon my investigative abilities."

"Any other questions?"

"Yes. What of Wentworth's luncheon guest? You have said nothing about him. Was that the young man in the green tweed suit, or was it someone else? Surely that person, if not the murderer himself, was more likely than anyone else to have seen the murderer."

Holmes shook his head. "The person Wentworth was expecting may have been the man in the green tweed suit or it may not. No one knows. The fact is that no one else came. The meal which Mrs. Barnham had laid on the dining-room table remained perfectly undisturbed when she returned at half-past five. However, what *is* known is who the luncheon-guest was originally supposed to be. One of the performers at the Frivolity Theatre in the Strand, a singer and dancer who goes by the name of Belinda Lee, came forward the day after the murder – when news of the crime was in all the morning papers – to say that she had been invited to Links House for lunch on the 25th. There is no matinee performance at the Frivolity Theatre on Wednesdays, and she had often visited Links House on that day, although not for several weeks. On the day before, however – that is, Tuesday the 24th – she had arrived at the theatre in the early afternoon to find that among the letters which had come for her that morning was one from Wentworth, expressing regret that their Wednesday luncheon appointment would have to be postponed, as he had had notice that someone else proposed to call on him that day and he could not get out of the arrangement. He said he was very sorry about this, and he looked forward to seeing her on another day."

"Did he mention who this other visitor might be?"

"No, he didn't. In Wentworth's study, Lanner found a diary or appointment-book. On the page for Wednesday, 25th September, a single letter – 'B' – is inscribed. This probably refers to Miss Lee, her first name, as I mentioned, being Belinda, but we can't say for certain. It might also be someone else's initial."

"I suppose if he had just heard, on the Monday, say, that someone else intended to pay him a visit, he would be unlikely to forget it, and there would thus be little point in recording the fact in his appointment-book."

"That is certainly possible," said Holmes. "It is also possible, however, that he had some other specific reason for not wishing the appointment to be recorded."

"Such as?"

"I don't pretend to know. I am merely stating that it is a possibility."

"And Wentworth's housekeeper could shed no light on the question of his likely visitor?"

"None whatever. Apparently, it was only rarely that he told her who he was expecting, and she, like the good, discreet housekeeper she was, never asked. That illustrates one of the problems of this case: although Wentworth's habits were, in a general sense, well known to everyone, no one really knows any details, particularly of what he intended to do on the day he was murdered. Without such details, it is very difficult to solve a case such as this, and I fear that Lanner is finding it an uphill struggle."

"Is that the end of the matter, then, from your point of view?"

"Not quite. Lanner is calling round this morning, to conduct me to interviews he has arranged with some of Wentworth's associates. He has questioned them all already, without eliciting any information of interest, but thought it might be worthwhile for me to see them for myself and form my own opinion of them. Having nothing better to do, I agreed to accompany him, although I shall probably take no part in the questioning. Will you come? You can leave your medical case here."

I had opened my mouth to reply when there came a peal at the front-door bell. A moment later, Inspector Lanner was shown into the room. There was a look of anxiety upon his features, but his expression brightened up considerably when he saw me.

"Why, Dr. Watson!" he cried, greeting me like a long-lost friend. "It seems a long time since our paths have crossed! You are coming with us, I take it. It will be good to have another opinion on the matter."

I had been about to tell Holmes that I could not spare the time, partly, I admit, because I could not see that we were likely to learn anything fresh if Lanner had already questioned all the people we were going to see; but the policeman appeared so pleased that I might accompany them that I didn't have the heart to disappoint him. "I should be delighted to come," I said, and a few moments later, the three of us set off.

"I imagine Mr. Holmes has given you an account of the case," said Lanner to me as we walked along. "You will understand, then, that we have believed right from the start that Wentworth's murderer was someone known to him."

"That must have narrowed the field down considerably."

"Yes, but it was still a large one. Wentworth seems to have had a very wide circle of acquaintances. However, we have managed to eliminate from our enquiries all those people he knew at the golf club, and most of those connected with his business activities, too. He did have a quarrel, the week before he died, with someone at the stockbroking firm in which he has an interest, but that doesn't seem to have amounted to much. In any case, the whereabouts of all these people on the day of Wentworth's death are all accounted for. With his personal friends and acquaintances it has been a different story. We have had the devil of a job trying to establish their movements on that day. In the last few days, however, we have eliminated most of them, leaving us with just three young men whose account of their activities cannot be satisfactorily verified – George Redfearn, Alexander Wychwood and Albert Maitland. As these three men were also three of Wentworth's closest acquaintances, had visited his house several times and knew his habits well, they are, in my opinion, our chief suspects – but I can get no further than that. It is they we are going to see this morning. We shall also pay a visit on Miss Belinda Lee, who knows these three particularly well, for a view from the other side of the fence, as it were."

Our first call was at a modern apartment building in New Cavendish Street, near the corner of Marylebone Lane. This was, Lanner informed us, the residence of George Redfearn. He had been a regular crony of Wentworth's in the last two or three years, although they had apparently fallen out over a woman, and had not been so close recently as they had been before.

Our ring at the bell was answered by a middle-aged woman in the uniform of a housekeeper, who showed us into a light and airy drawing-room, Lanner having introduced Holmes and myself as consulting detectives. For several minutes we sat waiting in silence, before Redfearn himself at length appeared, clad in a dressing-gown, unshaven and bleary-eyed.

"Well?" he demanded in an aggressive tone, as he dropped into an armchair. "What do you want? I've already told you all I know."

"We simply wish to clarify one or two points, sir," returned Lanner placidly.

"Clarify? I should have thought it was clear enough already – as far as I am concerned, anyway. The rest of it may be as clear as mud for all I know, but I neither know nor care. Somebody's shot Wentworth and it wasn't me: that's all I know."

"It doesn't sound as if the thought of it troubles you very greatly," observed Lanner.

"It doesn't" returned Redfearn.

"You didn't care for Wentworth?"

"Not particularly. I wouldn't have shot him, if that's what you're driving at – that's a pretty drastic step to take – but I'm not going to grieve about it. He wouldn't have shed any tears if the boot were on the other foot."

"Do you own a pistol?" Lanner asked after a moment.

"No, I don't," returned Redfearn. "You have already asked me that."

"But I have learnt since that you are a member of the 'Sharp-shooters' Society at your club."

"That's true. We have a range in the basement. But I use one of the society's pistols."

"I see. Can you suggest who might have shot Mr. Wentworth?"

"No, I can't. You might do better to ask Sandy Wychwood or Albert Maitland that question."

"Are you suggesting that either of those two gentlemen might have had something to do with the crime?"

"Certainly not. Please desist from trying to twist my words. I simply mean that they have had more to do with Wentworth in recent months than I have."

"Is there anyone you can think of who might have had a grudge against Mr. Wentworth?"

"Not really. It depends what you mean by a grudge. I mean, everyone has enemies of some sort or another, don't they?"

"I'll give you an example, to show you what I mean," said the policeman, ignoring the other's question. "I understand that you were very friendly at one time with Miss Belinda Lee, but that she subsequently became somewhat less friendly with you and more friendly with Mr. Wentworth. That's the sort of thing a man might bear a grudge about."

"I suppose he might, in certain circumstances, but it's hardly a shooting matter. In any case, your example is not entirely accurate, Inspector. Any connection I had with Belinda Lee ended a long time since – several months ago. And it wasn't Wentworth who relieved me of her, either, but Albert Maitland. I do believe that Wentworth later extended the same courtesy to Maitland, but by then it was a matter of complete indifference to me."

I glanced at Sherlock Holmes. He had remained silent throughout this exchange, but I could see from the expression on his face and frown of concentration, that he was taking in all this information and carefully docketing it somewhere in his brain.

"On the day of Mr. Wentworth's death," Lanner continued after a moment, "you were, you informed us, with your brother, Lewis."

"That's right," replied Redfearn. "As I told you, he had come up to London from the depths of Shropshire. He doesn't get up very often, so I felt obliged to give him a guided tour. We wandered about town for a while, then took a boat down the river to Greenwich, where we had something to eat. Afterwards, we meandered slowly back. But I've told you all this already."

"Yes, sir; but we have not been able to find anyone, either on the boat or at the restaurant in Greenwich, who definitely remembers you and your brother."

Redfearn snorted. "You can hardly blame me for other people's poor memories, Inspector. That's not my problem."

A few minutes later, Holmes, Lanner and I were making our way along New Cavendish Street.

"Despite Redfearn's protestations of indifference," said Holmes to the policeman, "I rather fancy that your reference to Miss Lee stung him – and more than a little, too."

"I had the same impression," I remarked. "Do you think that Redfearn's ill-feeling might be what lies behind this crime?"

"We cannot yet say, Watson. Let us wait until we have heard the testimony of all the others in the case before we draw any conclusions. One thing we can say with confidence, however, is that human nature does not change. For all the affectations of careless indifference by those such as Redfearn – and, no doubt, all his cronies, too – there remain few things quite so mortifying as being deserted for a rival by a member of the opposite sex."

A walk of twenty minutes brought us to Bloomsbury and the address of Alexander Wychwood's lodgings in a pleasant house in Montague Street. He was seated at a writing-table as we were shown in, but he put down his pen, stood up and greeted us cordially.

"I was just writing a letter to my mother," he volunteered with a wry smile. "Mothers always want to know what one is doing, down to the last detail! Now, gentlemen, what can I do for you? I assume it's about the Wentworth business."

"Just a few more questions for you, sir," said Lanner, nodding his head. "I wondered – now you've had more time to think about it – if you could think of anyone who might have had a grudge against Mr. Wentworth."

"No, absolutely not. I still think it's most likely that the motive for the crime was robbery."

"That is always possible, of course, sir; but there was money in Mr. Wentworth's study which was not touched."

"Then perhaps the gun went off accidentally, and the robber lost his nerve and fled when he realised that Wentworth was dead."

"Yes, but on the other hand, if anyone did have a grudge against Mr. Wentworth," Lanner persisted, "that also might explain the crime."

"I suppose so," Wychwood conceded, "but it would have to be a pretty strong grudge. I can't believe that of anyone I know."

"But one or two people perhaps did have a grudge against Mr. Wentworth? I understand he wasn't the most popular man in London."

Wychwood paused, ran his hand through his hair and sighed. "That can't be denied," he said at length. "Wentworth was always very popular with the ladies, but somewhat less so with the men."

"Indeed, so I understand. I've heard that this was part of the problem, that Wentworth was a little too popular with the ladies."

"What do you mean?"

"I understand, for instance, that Miss Belinda Lee had been particularly friendly with George Redfearn for some time, but later switched her affections to Mr. Wentworth."

"That's not quite true, Inspector. She certainly switched her affections: not to Wentworth, though, but to Albert Maitland. However, you're right in a sense, as her dalliance with Maitland didn't last long, and then she did fall in with Wentworth. That's some time ago."

"Miss Lee seems a very popular woman," Lanner remarked after a moment in a dry tone. "Did you ever harbour hopes in that direction yourself, Mr. Wychwood?"

"Me? Hardly, Inspector. Belinda Lee has been popular for some considerable time, and not just with Wentworth and his cronies, either, but with the general public, too. She is altogether too grand for me, I'm afraid, even if I were interested, which I'm not. Besides, I have other irons in the fire, as it were, irons that are more approachable and unlikely to burn one's fingers so badly."

"Without wishing to seem too inquisitive about your private affairs," Lanner continued after a moment, "might I enquire who these other 'irons in the fire' might be?"

"Certainly," Wychwood replied in a careless tone, although he appeared a little embarrassed at the question. "There is no secret about it, though I must say I can't see the relevance to your enquiries. I have recently been paying court, as you might say, to a young lady by the name of Maria Monkley. You may have heard of her."

"Is she also employed at the Frivolity Theatre?"

"Yes, she is a singer and dancer there, although she is a more recent arrival there than Belinda Lee, and her name is not yet so well known. Apparently, she was very popular in Liverpool, and I am sure she will soon become so in London, too. She is a very attractive girl."

"I don't doubt it. It would not be surprising, then, if you had had rivals for Miss Monkley's favour."

"That is true. but I think I have seen off the competition – for the present at least."

"Would George Redfearn be one of your rivals?"

"Yes, I suppose that is so. I think that – whatever he might say – he was a little bitter at losing out in the case of Belinda Lee, and tried to make up for it by buzzing like a bee around Miss Monkley. But all to no avail, I am pleased to say, as she seems to prefer me."

"And Albert Maitland?"

"The same applies to him."

"And Piers Wentworth?"

Wychwood paused. "Look, Inspector, I know you're looking for someone with a strong grudge against Wentworth, so you can close your case, and move on to something else, but, speaking for myself at least, I can assure you that that doesn't apply in this case. Any annoyance I might have felt in his direction was only temporary and has been quite expunged by the fact that if it had been a challenge competition – which it wasn't – I would have won."

"So Mr. Wentworth *did* annoy you then?"

"Yes, he annoyed me. He annoyed everybody."

"He tried to push himself forward with regard to Miss Monkley?"

"Yes, of course he did. With a man like Wentworth, it would have been surprising if he hadn't. She had scarcely arrived in London from Liverpool when he began making obvious overtures to her. Apart from trying to elbow me aside with his fatter pocket-book, speaking to her in my presence as if I were not there at all and as if he knew her much better than I did anyway, he also invited her down to his house at Bickley."

"Did she go?"

"Yes, eventually. She went twice, both on Wednesday afternoons, the first time four weeks ago and then again three weeks ago."

"That must have been annoying for you."

"Yes, of course it was," Wychwood responded quickly. "I wouldn't deny it." He paused a moment, then continued at a rush. "Under normal circumstances, I wouldn't repeat the content of a private conversation, but on this occasion I'll make an exception, so you will understand the situation clearly. Miss Monkley said to me after she had visited Wentworth that she found his attentions both unwelcome and boring. She said she had at length accepted his invitation to go down for lunch to Links House just so that he would stop badgering her about it in the future.

"'I must have been a great disappointment to him,' she said to me, 'as I resisted all his overtures to me, and told him I was not interested. On both occasions, we had lunch, we discussed the musical theatre, and then he read me some poetry. This was obviously meant to put me in a romantic mood, but I just found it stupid and tedious, like having a love-song read out by the man who shouts out the train-times at the railway station.'

"She laughed when she was telling me, and said that Wentworth seemed old enough to be her father and she thought he ought to be pensioned off. So you see, Inspector, I had no reason to hold a grudge against Wentworth."

As we made our way down to Holborn, I considered what Wychwood had told us.

"Wychwood was certainly somewhat more forthcoming than Redfearn," I remarked to Lanner. "What do you think about his testimony?"

The policeman shook his head. "I don't know, Dr. Watson," said he. "He seems a pleasant enough young man. But he's no fool, and quite capable of lying if it suited his purposes to do so. I'm not sure I entirely believe him, and not sure he entirely believes Miss Monkley – if she did say what he claims she did. What do you think, Mr. Holmes?"

"I am simply watching and listening for the moment, Lanner," responded Holmes, "and should rather not pass any detailed judgement on what any of them say, until I have seen and heard all of them."

The traffic in High Holborn was dense, but we managed at length to thread our way through it, and plunged at once into the warren of streets which lies on the south side. Left and right and left again we turned, until I was quite lost, but eventually we stopped before a small cobbler's shop just round the corner from Drury Lane.

"Maitland has rooms above this shop," said Lanner, giving a sharp rap on the door-knocker. This was answered by a maid, who conducted us up a narrow and steep staircase to the first floor. There, in a pleasant if cramped sitting-room, Albert Maitland was waiting for us. He was a pale-faced, thin young man, who stood very erect in the middle of the room.

"I assume this visit is something to do with the death of Piers Wentworth," said he, as he waved his hand vaguely in the direction of some upright chairs which stood by the wall. "I hope it will not take too long. I have a number of things to do this morning, and several important appointments."

"We just wished to clarify a few points," returned Lanner.

"I'm sure I don't know anything other than what I have already told you."

"That may be so, sir, but we are re-interviewing everyone connected with the matter, in case they have remembered anything which might be helpful to us."

"I haven't."

"Perhaps not, sir, but I wonder – now that you've had time to give the matter more thought – if you can think of anyone who might have borne a grudge against Mr. Wentworth?"

"No," returned the young man with a firm shake of the head.

"Not anyone?"

"No."

"Had anyone, to your knowledge, quarrelled with Mr. Wentworth recently?"

"No."

"I understand that your cousin, William Maitland, has a position at the stockbroking firm in which Mr. Wentworth had an interest."

"Indeed he does. What of it?"

"Nothing, sir. I am merely verifying the fact. You are familiar, I believe, with Mr. Wentworth's house at Bickley."

"That is so. I have stayed there on one or two occasions and he stayed here with me once or twice."

"I have in my notes that you are the owner of a small revolver," said Lanner, consulting his note-book.

"That is surely hardly surprising, Inspector, considering that I myself gave you that information."

"Quite so, sir. Have you lent it to anyone recently?"

"No."

"Do you know if anyone else has borrowed a revolver – from the club, say?"

"No. I am not in the habit of monitoring the actions of my friends and acquaintances."

"I am aware, from the information you provided before, that you do not possess a green tweed suit, but I wonder now if you can think of anyone else who does?"

"No, I can't. You asked me that before."

"Finally, Mr. Maitland, I wonder if you could tell us something of your relations with Miss Belinda Lee?"

"I don't see why I should. What the devil has that got to do with you?"

"Just this, sir, that Miss Lee was associated with you in the eyes of others for some time, but was subsequently associated with Piers Wentworth."

"What of it? You might as well point out that prior to being 'associated' with me, as you so quaintly put it, she had been 'associated' with George Redfearn for some time. This all proves nothing whatsoever, except, I suppose, that Miss Lee has always been very popular and that Piers Wentworth always got what he wanted in the end."

"And Miss Maria Monkley? Do you have an interest in that direction, sir?"

"Not particularly. As far as I understand it, she was making some sort of decision between Wentworth and Sandy Wychwood. You know what they say, Inspector: a man can put all the effort he wants into his wooing, but in the end it's the woman who will make the decision, usually for reasons the man doesn't even understand."

"Indeed, sir. I suppose that Mr. Wentworth's death clears the field in that respect for Mr. Wychwood."

"Yes, I suppose it does."

As we made our way down Drury Lane towards the Strand, Lanner and I discussed the case, but neither of us could reach any worthwhile conclusions. Holmes took no part in the discussion, appearing lost in his own thoughts.

The doorman at the Frivolity Theatre admitted us without demur, and we were shown in to Miss Lee's dressing-room. She turned as we entered, but did not rise, being busy at her dressing-table, in front of a very large mirror, assisted by a small, middle-aged woman.

"You must excuse me, Inspector Lanner," said Miss Lee. "I had expected you a little earlier. We have a matinee performance this afternoon, and I must begin to get ready now. But I am all ears, and I am sure if I can help you I will. You may go and get yourself a cup of tea, Alice," she added, addressing the other woman. "I shouldn't think we'll be more than five or ten minutes. Now, Inspector, what is it you wish to know? I'm sure I've told you all I can think of."

"I simply wish to clarify a few points," replied Lanner. "In the first place, about visitors to Mr. Wentworth's house at Bickley. You yourself had paid visits there, I understand."

"Yes, numerous times."

"Were you by yourself on these occasions, or were others present at the same time?"

"Both. Sometimes there was quite a crowd there, some of whom had to stay overnight at the Station Hotel, as Links House was not very big. At other times there were just one or two other people there, and sometimes I was there alone."

"When was the last time you were there?"

"Towards the end of August."

"About a month before Mr. Wentworth's death?"

"Yes, that would be about right."

"Did you happen to observe, Miss Lee, on those occasions when there were others present, if any of them approached the house by way of the golf-course?"

Miss Lee considered the question for a moment. "No," she replied at length, "I don't believe so. On some occasions, though," she added, "when he had invited his friends down for a game of golf, I think they would meet up at the clubhouse and I suppose when they had finished their game they would walk back to Links House across the golf-course."

Lanner nodded. "Now," he said: "about three gentlemen in particular: George Redfearn, Alexander Wychwood and Albert Maitland: did Mr. Wentworth ever fall out with any of them?"

"I really have no idea," returned Miss Lee. "He may have done, for all I know. They could all be a little quarrelsome on occasion, when they had had too much to drink."

"Are you aware that any of them ever fell out over *you*?"

"Absolutely not. Well, not in my presence, anyhow. What they may have done at other times, I really couldn't say, but I never had any indication of anything like that."

"You don't think that any of the gentlemen I named might have had a grudge against Mr. Wentworth for any reason?"

"I doubt it. I don't think they are the grudge-bearing kind. Well, George Redfearn might be, but I don't think he'd ever bother to do anything about it, even if he did bear someone a grudge. Sandy is a lovely boy, but he's an incurable romantic, and sees the world through a prism of romantic ideals. I don't think he could possibly bear a grudge against Piers, especially as – so I understand – he'd recently come out on top in a tussle with Piers for the affections of Maria Monkley."

"Miss Monkley is also employed here, at the Frivolity, I understand."

"Yes, that's right. She's a sweet girl, but another one who's a hopeless romantic, like Sandy Wychwood – so I think they were probably meant for each other."

"What about Albert Maitland?"

"What, Bertie? He wouldn't hurt a fly. He puts on a very stiff front – frightfully correct, and all that – but behind that front he's as soft as a brush, really. He does have rather strong views on what's right and what's wrong, but they are just his own personal views, and I don't think he'd ever try to impose them on anyone else."

"I see," said Lanner. "Finally, then, Miss Lee, as to the note you received from Mr. Wentworth the day before he died, which I have here." He took a folded slip of stiff, cream-coloured paper from an inside pocket and opened it out. "It says 'Very sorry, Belinda, but our plan for tomorrow will have to be postponed. Someone is coming here that I can't put off. Will see you at the end of the week as usual, when we can make a fresh arrangement. Yours as ever, P.'"

Lanner handed the note to Miss Lee. "Are you sure," he asked, "that that is Mr. Wentworth's hand?"

For a moment she studied the note. "I believe so," she responded at length, looking up. "Of course, when I received it I had no reason to suppose it wasn't from Piers. The possibility that it might not be from Piers never even crossed my mind. And now I see it again, I feel much the same. I'm sure it's his hand. Do you have any reason for supposing it might not be?"

"Nothing in particular," returned the policeman. "The stationery certainly seems the same as some blank sheets we found in Mr. Wentworth's study. It simply occurred to us that although the letter appeared to be from Mr. Wentworth, it might not have been. If, for instance, someone planned to do harm to Mr. Wentworth, and was aware that you were due to go down that particular day, he might have sent this letter to put you off from going, to leave the field open for himself. Had you ever had letters of this sort from Mr. Wentworth before?"

"Yes, a number of times."

"Did he always sign himself simply with the initial 'P'?"

"Not always. Sometimes he would put 'P W', and, on rare occasions, 'Piers'. There didn't seem to be any significance to this, one way or the other. Piers was a very discreet man, who had a horror, I think, of his correspondence falling into the wrong hands. So his communications were always fairly anonymous, if you know what I mean."

Lanner nodded, as he took back the note from Miss Lee. "Thank you for your help," he said. "I think that that is all for the present."

"Have you made any progress with the case?" she asked as we prepared to leave.

"A little," the policeman returned. "We are still looking into one or two possibilities."

Outside, Holmes, Lanner and I stood for a few moments on the pavement in the Strand, as the unbroken stream of traffic rattled past us.

"And that, gentlemen, is that," said the policeman with a sigh. "You see the difficulty? We have so little evidence upon which to found a solution to the mystery. We cannot narrow down who had an opportunity to commit the crime, and nor can we establish who might have had a motive. Unless some new information comes to light, I fear we may never solve the case."

"So," I said, "your remark to Miss Lee about looking into one or two possibilities was, I take it, the merest humbug."

Lanner looked abashed. "I should not have put it so bluntly myself, Dr. Watson," he returned, "but, yes, I admit it. As a young man in the police force, I was instructed by my superiors to always answer enquiries from the public in a positive, optimistic manner. 'Negativity upsets people,' they said, 'and achieves nothing.' I can certainly see the point of that as a general rule, but it's hard sometimes to be optimistic when there's nothing but negative thoughts in your head."

"What of your enquiries at Bickley?" I asked. "Have you had any success in your search for the young man in the green tweed suit?"

Lanner shook his head. "None whatsoever," he replied. "He has disappeared without trace. And, of course, I still do not know for a certainty whether he had anything to do with the crime or not. He certainly doesn't resemble any of our chief suspects very closely. What do you think about it all, Mr. Holmes?" he continued, turning to my friend. "If I may say so, I have never known you so silent in all the time I have known you. Do you have any insight into the matter? Or are you as puzzled as the rest of us?"

"One could postulate several hypotheses," returned Holmes, "but, as you say, the solid evidence for any view is somewhat lacking. I regret that I cannot yet give you a conclusive solution to the problem."

With that, we parted, Lanner returning to Scotland Yard, and Holmes and I to Baker Street. My friend was as uncommunicative back in his lodgings as he had been earlier, and after a little while I abandoned my efforts to try to get him to discuss the case, picked up my medical bag and prepared to leave. As I had my hand on the doorknob, however, he looked up and spoke.

"I should like to bring the Wentworth case to a close," he remarked in a matter-of-fact tone. "To that end, I intend to make a few more enquiries this afternoon and, I hope, interview Wentworth's murderer. If you wish to know how I got on, pray feel free to drop by this evening and we can discuss the matter."

"What!" I cried. "I thought you told Lanner that any number of hypotheses were possible and you could not venture an opinion as to which might be correct."

"That's not quite right," returned my friend. "Of course, it is always possible to suggest different possible solutions to any problem, and that is what I said to Lanner. But that does not mean that I do not have a theory of my own. In fact, I do have such a theory, which I hope to put to the test this afternoon."

"Then why did you not inform Lanner? Why give him such a misleading impression?"

"You know how much I dislike indulging in idle speculation, Watson. It would have gained us nothing. Besides, I cannot yet prove my own hypothesis, and may never be able to."

With that unsatisfactory conclusion, I left him then and made my way home, but I was determined to return later and learn more of my friend's theories. The unfathomable nature of the case fascinated me, and having had so many years' experience of my friend's successes, I could not doubt that if he had formed his own theory of the matter, it was very likely to be the correct one, or, at least, very close to it. Lanner was convinced that Piers Wentworth had been murdered by someone known to him, and could see no other motive for the crime, but did Holmes agree with him or did he see some other possibility?

I was intrigued, also, by the note Miss Lee had received, the day before the murder. She seemed fairly sure it really was from Wentworth, as it purported to be. If so, the clear inferences were, first, that Wentworth was expecting someone to call; second, that this was someone he knew; and third, that it was this person that shot him. If, however, the letter was a forgery, and had not been written by Wentworth, then he must have still been expecting Miss Lee to call on the Wednesday, and must have been taken by surprise by the arrival of the other visitor. In either case, it seemed to me, we were brought back to the man in the green tweed suit. Did Wentworth know this man, or was it someone he had never met before? It was impossible to tell, and although I wasted some considerable time in considering the matter, I got precisely nowhere with this conundrum.

Keen though I was to hear Holmes's conclusions on the case, various tasks, both professional and domestic, delayed me, and it was not until a quarter to eight that I reached my friend's lodgings that evening. I found him busy at his chemical bench, and although he acknowledged my presence with a nod of his head and a murmured word of greeting, he appeared preoccupied by what he was doing.

"Well?" I demanded at length, unable to contain my curiosity any longer. "Any success to report?"

"Hardly," he replied in a dry tone, as he measured some dark liquid from a small glass bottle into a test-tube. "I have only just begun. The fact is, I misplaced my small stock of silver nitrate. You will never guess where I found it, Watson. In my sock drawer, of all places!"

"Never mind that," I said. "What about the Wentworth case? You said you would have something more to tell me about it this evening."

"Oh, *that*," said he in a dismissive tone, as if I were raising some long-forgotten and unimportant issue. "I have been trying to put that out of my mind."

"Have you solved the case?"

"Yes. I thought I had made that clear."

"No, you didn't. Is the villain under arrest?"

Holmes paused, put the test-tube in the rack and came over to where I was standing by the fire. "Do take a seat, Watson. Your standing about in that fashion suggests that you have only called in for a minute or two in order to upbraid me!"

I laughed as I seated myself in my old arm-chair. "I simply wish to know the results of your enquiries, Holmes. The Wentworth case seems such an unfathomable puzzle!"

As I spoke, my friend flung himself into his own chair, then leaned over and took his pipe and tobacco from the hearth. "It is not really such a puzzle if one understands human nature," said he as he filled his pipe. "There were clear indications from the very beginning for anyone prepared to read them. However, building a case which could stand up in court is another matter. But I shall tell you in order what steps I took, and you can then compare my views with your own – and upbraid me if you wish."

"I very much doubt I shall wish to," I responded.

Holmes shook his head. "I think you should reserve your judgment on that point until you have heard my report, Watson," said he. "I fear I have not handled the case well." He put a match to his pipe, and I settled back to listen to his account.

"I decided after we spoke earlier that the first thing I would do would be to go and interview Miss Belinda Lee again. Apart from any other consideration, it was clear that she was a central figure in the case, for she was the one actor in this little drama who had intimate knowledge of all of the others – their characters, habits, propensities and so on."

"I did think, when we spoke to Miss Lee earlier," I remarked, "that she could have said more if she would. Although, to be honest," I added, "I think I thought something similar about all of them."

"You are probably right," said Holmes with a chuckle. "When questioning the actors in a drama such as the present one, you must always remember that although they will answer your questions – with a greater or lesser degree of honesty – they tend not to volunteer information which is outwith the scope of your questions. Therefore, the questions you ask are as important as the answers they give to them. Anyhow, having managed to catch Miss Lee in the short interval between the matinee performance and the evening one, and having little time at my disposal, I decided to omit all preliminaries and get straight to the point.

"'You will have heard, I imagine,' I said to her, 'about the man in the green tweed suit.'

"'Of course,' she returned. 'Who can have read anything of the case who hasn't also read about that mysterious gentleman? It has been in all the papers. But, as I understand it, it is not yet clear whether he had anything to do with the death of Piers Wentworth or not.'

"I nodded. 'And yet,' I said, 'despite all the publicity the matter has had, no one has yet come forward to state that he is that man, and to explain what he was doing at Bickley that day, which would have cleared him of all suspicion and enabled the authorities to eliminate him from their enquiries.'

"'Yes, that is true,' she said, 'but perhaps he has gone abroad and has heard nothing of the case: I understand that on the day of Mr. Wentworth's death, the man in the green tweed suit was seen in the district with a small travelling-bag of some sort.'

"'It is possible; but two weeks have now passed. You would think he would have heard something of the matter by now. Besides, if he had nothing to do with the crime, and was not making for Wentworth's house when he was seen crossing the golf course, then where was he going? For the police have interviewed all Wentworth's neighbours, and not one of them saw such a man on the day in question.'

"'Then it is a mystery. But I do not quite understand why you are discussing this man at such length with me; I thought you had come back to ask me some more questions.'

"'I thought perhaps the young man's description might put you in mind of someone.'

"She frowned. 'Well, it doesn't,' she said. 'Why did you think it might?'

"'Because it puts me in mind of someone – not so much what the young man looked like, as what he did. However, let us leave that for the moment. Do you know of anyone who possesses such a distinctive tweed suit – perhaps someone in Wentworth's circle of acquaintances?'

"'No,' she replied with a firm shake of the head. 'The police have already asked me that, more than once.'

"'But I suppose it might be possible to hire such an outfit for a day or two?'

"She looked surprised. 'I wouldn't know,' she said. 'I suppose it might be. But I think the gentlemen's dress-hire establishments deal mainly in formal wear, rather than tweeds.'

"'But tweeds might be available somewhere else,' I persisted, 'somewhere such as a theatrical costumiers, or the costume department of a theatre.'

"'Perhaps,' said she, 'but, again, I wouldn't know. I believe that most of the big costumiers only hire out complete sets of costumes, rather than odd ones, as you are suggesting. And I don't think that most theatres ever hire out their own costumes at all.'

"'No, but if someone were employed at a theatre, or had some other regular connection with it, he might, I suppose, be able to borrow such a costume – "unofficially", as it were.'

"'I suppose he might. I really wouldn't know.'

"'Is there such a green tweed suit in the stock here, at the Frivolity?'

"'I have no idea. There may well be, but I can't recall seeing any of the actors wearing such an outfit.'

"'I see,' I said. I had hoped to shake her composure a little, and extract a little more information from her, but she remained perfectly calm and self-possessed, so I decided to take a yet more direct route to my destination. 'Very well,' I said. 'I will now make a conjecture, Miss Lee. I believe, despite what you say, that there is indeed such a green tweed suit in the costume stock here. Yes, and a wide-brimmed brown hat and light-brown overcoat, too, not to mention materials for making up a gingery beard. I believe that, in a sense, the man in the green tweed suit both started and finished his journey here, at this theatre.'

"She frowned again. 'If that is what you believe, should you not inform the police?'

"'Perhaps I should. What would you do then?'

"'I? Why should I do anything?'

"'Because, Miss Lee, you yourself were the man in the green tweed suit, a disguise you adopted for one day only, in order to murder Piers Wentworth. Having arrived at Bickley and made your way up Links Lane, you crossed the golf-course – where, unfortunately for you, you were seen by two golfers – passed up the back garden of Links House and entered the study directly through the French window which, it being a fine day, was standing open. No doubt Wentworth sprang to his feet in surprise, not recognizing who you were, but you raised your pistol and shot him through the heart before he could make any further move. You then closed and locked the French window, left the house by the front door, and returned the way you had come.'

"'What nonsense!' she cried, although her voice faltered a little. 'If you have come here only to make these wild and absurd accusations, I must ask you to leave at once!'

"'An accusation it may be,' I returned, 'but there is nothing absurd about it. You and I both know it is the truth.'

"For a long moment we sat there, looking at each other in silence.

"'I repeat,' said she at length, 'that what you say is complete and utter nonsense, and is moreover a gross slander which I'm sure is actionable at law. However," she continued, a little smile playing about her lips, 'I am intrigued as to why you should be advancing this ridiculous theory. What do you hope to gain by it?'

"'The truth.'

"At this, she laughed out loud. 'Well, if that is your aim I rather fancy you will be disappointed,' said she. 'And if you hoped for celebrity as a great reasoner, I am sorry to tell you that you will only gain celebrity as a pitiable eccentric.' There was a gleam of triumph in her eye now, and I could see that she thought she had me at a severe disadvantage. 'Let us examine your ludicrous theory, then, Mr. Holmes. Why, to start with, do you think I would wish to murder Piers Wentworth?'

"'I was hoping that you might tell me that,' I returned.

"'Well, I can't, because I didn't. Besides, it was undoubtedly a man who went to see Piers that day, a man wearing the green tweed suit. Everyone is agreed upon that point.'

"I shook my head. 'No, they are not,' said I. 'I do not agree. What anyone else might think is of no importance. It was a woman who went to see Wentworth that day, a woman dressed as a man.'

"'You are forgetting,' said she, 'that I received a note from Piers, the day before he was killed, postponing my own visit to him, as he was expecting someone else.'

"'I am not forgetting that,' I said. 'You wrote that letter yourself, Miss Lee.'

"'Nonsense! The letter was written on his own notepaper, and in his own hand.'

"'The hand would not be difficult to imitate for someone who had received numerous letters from Wentworth in the past, as you mentioned earlier. As to the stationery, there is no difficulty there: you simply took a sheet of it from Wentworth's study.'

"'But how could I?' she demanded. 'I hadn't been to Mr. Wentworth's house for a month or more before that day, before the week he was killed – unless you are going to claim that I planned his murder far in advance, and took the paper months ago.'

"'Such a claim is unnecessary, and the solution to the problem is simpler, if a little more subtle: you took the sheet of notepaper from Wentworth's study *after* you had killed him. You wrote the letter to yourself later, at your leisure, and subsequently claimed to have received it in the post on Tuesday.'

"'That is a clever theory,' said Miss Lee after a moment with a little smile, 'but you have still not explained why, if you were correct in your reasoning, I should have committed the crime at all.'

"'Perhaps you were annoyed that Wentworth had dropped you in favour of Maria Monkley,' I suggested.

"At this, Miss Lee threw her head back and laughed loudly again. 'So,' she said, 'you are not so clever as you imagine, Mr. Holmes. Piers got nowhere with Maria, that I know for a fact. Not only that, but she told him in no uncertain terms that she never wished to see him or visit his house again.'

"'Perhaps so,' I responded. I could see from her expression and the look in her eye that what she said was almost certainly true, and it also accorded with my own view of the matter. 'But, still,' I ventured, 'he treated you badly.' I watched her face closely. She was trying to conceal her emotion, but I could see that I had touched a nerve. 'Ah!' I said. 'I think I see now. When Miss Monkley came along, Wentworth dropped you abruptly, without ceremony and without any thought for your feelings. This was a blow to your pride, but was perhaps bearable. But then, when Miss Monkley rebuffed him so firmly, told him, in effect, to 'sling his hook elsewhere,' as they say in some parts, he turned once more to you, and expected you to simply take up where you had left off before, as if nothing had happened. This, I imagine was an insult you could not bear, this treating of you as a disposable commodity, and perhaps expecting you to show gratitude for another invitation to Links House, despite all that had happened.'

"Again we sat in silence for some time. Then Miss Lee stood up, opened the door of her dressing-room and looked out into the corridor. Evidently satisfied that there was no one there who might be listening, she closed the door again and resumed her seat.

"'Perhaps you do have some perception after all, Mr. Holmes,' she began in a tone of amusement, although there was a wary look in her eye, 'and what they say of you is true. You are right to use the word "gratitude" in connection with Piers Wentworth. I admit nothing, but I shall tell you something now, something you do not know. Piers Wentworth was an odious and obnoxious man. Of course, no one is perfect, and in his case there were, at least, some compensations. He was wealthy and could be quite free with his money when he wished to be. But always, underlying his apparent open-handedness, was an unpleasant expectation that the recipients of his largesse should show gratitude. This was a constant irritation and annoyance, for it cost him little to spend his plentiful money, and, moreover, he himself never showed the slightest shred of gratitude for anything that anyone else did for him. It was as if, having spent his money, he considered it his right to expect such generosity from others.

"'Yes, he treated me badly, very badly, in many ways which you cannot imagine, and which I shall not go into. He made promises to me which turned out to be like pledges written on water. And all the while, as he continued to humiliate and disparage me, he expected me to show gratitude that he was seeing me at all. His treatment of me over the last month or two was not an isolated incident, but was, rather, the latest in a chapter of such incidents. I do not blame Maria Monkley; she is, as I mentioned to you earlier, something of a romantic, and decidedly naive in the way she perceives the world; all the blame lies with Piers Wentworth.'

"'So you killed him.'

"For a moment, her eyelashes flickered, and, almost imperceptibly, she nodded her head in silence. Next moment, this mute admission of guilt had vanished, and she spoke in a firm, defiant tone.

"'My tongue will never confess to such a charge,' said she. 'Should the police make any further enquiries of me, I shall say the following: I know nothing of Piers Wentworth's death, I have no idea who might have killed him, I have never known any man who possessed a green tweed suit, I do not own a revolver and I have no knowledge of anyone who does.'

"'And the carpet-bag?' I interjected.

"'What carpet-bag?'

"'The carpet-bag which the man in the green tweed suit collected from Bromley station and took away with him.'

"'I know nothing of that. I myself once owned such a bag, but that has gone to glory some time ago. I think it was burnt on the fire.'

"'Then there is nothing more you can tell me?'

"'No.'

"'I think you have made a mistake, Miss Lee.'

"For a brief moment there was a flicker of alarm in her eyes, but when she spoke, it was in a defiant tone. 'I think not,' said she, but then added 'What did you have in mind?'

"'Not in the execution of your plan; that, for all I can tell, may be flawless; but in your decision to commit the crime at all. Wentworth may, as you say, have been odious, or worse, but you could have found some other way to drive him from your life, and put distance between the two of you.'

"'Such as ?'

"'You could have simply told him, as Miss Monkley did, that you did not wish to see him again.'

"'It would not have been sufficient. You do not know what he was like. He would not leave me alone. He would spread foul, vindictive rumours about me, as he had done in the past when I would not do as he wished'

"'Well, then, you could have moved away from London. With your reputation, you could have secured employment at any theatre in the country.'

"'No doubt, but for a much-reduced fee. Where I am now is at the very summit of the English musical theatre. To go anywhere else would be to drop far, far lower in every conceivable way. People would think I had gone mad.'

"'So, instead of that slight blow to your pride, you have sentenced yourself to a lifetime of guilt, self-recrimination and remorse.'

"'I think not.'

"'Perhaps not now, but in the years to come. You have taken a man's life, which was not yours to take, however unpleasant he may have been. Your conscience will not let you forget that. And unlike Piers Wentworth, your conscience cannot be destroyed, for it grips you not from without, but from within.'

"'We shall see, Mr. Holmes, we shall see.'

"I left her then, Watson, certain that I had solved the case, but equally certain that I would never be able to bring Wentworth's murderer to justice."

For some time we sat in silence. I confess I was shocked at what my friend had told me, shocked at the violence which seemed to lurk just beneath the glittering surface of London society.

"Have you informed Lanner?" I asked at length.

My friend shook his head. "There would seem little point."

"What!" I cried. "You know who it is that has committed this terrible crime and you are not going to do anything about it? I find that almost as shocking as the crime itself, Holmes! Where is your sense of justice?"

"My dear fellow! You interrupted me. I was about to say that there would seem little point in telling Lanner my theory, as I cannot prove it, and he would probably give it no credence, anyway, but of course I must do so. However unpleasant Wentworth may have been, he cannot now defend himself. It is therefore the duty of anyone who claims to uphold justice and truth to act on his behalf. But I fear it will be a fruitless task."

"Is there nothing you can do to prove your case?"

"It is difficult to feel optimistic, Watson. Had I been consulted earlier, I might have searched through the costumes at the Frivolity Theatre until I found the green tweed suit – for I am sure it is there – and examined it for any threads or other traces upon it which might suggest who had worn it most recently or if, for instance, the sleeves or trouser-legs had recently been shortened. I might also have examined the pockets to see if any of them showed traces of gunpowder where a pistol had been carried."

"What about the carpet-bag that you mentioned to her?"

"She is not stupid. Her planning of the crime seems to have been exceptionally thorough. If she now says that her old carpet-bag has been burnt on the fire, then I am sure that that is so. Similarly, I have no hope now of discovering the pistol that was used in the crime. You know how much I hate to guess at anything, Watson, but if I had to guess, I should say that the pistol is probably at the bottom of the Thames."

"What was the point of the carpet-bag, anyway?" I asked. "Was she simply hoping to suggest that the murderer had gone abroad, as we wondered earlier?"

Holmes shook his head. "Not at all. The bag, which she had deposited at Bromley station earlier that day, was a crucial part of her plan, for it contained her change of clothes. It is what enabled the young man in the tweed suit to vanish so completely after leaving the station, and enabled Miss Lee to journey unsuspected back to town."

"What do you mean? She could hardly change her clothes in Bromley High Street."

"Of course not. But if you were to study the map, as I have done, you would see that between Bromley and Shortlands, the next station on the line, from where I believe she caught a train back to town, there are several rural areas, including a small wood, where she could easily have slipped out of sight and changed her appearance in a matter of a minute or two."

"Surely it would take longer than that."

"Not at all. She would have had a large skirt in the bag, which she could have slipped on over what she was already wearing. That would have taken scarcely thirty seconds. Another thirty seconds to remove the suit jacket and replace it with a smaller, lady's jacket, thirty seconds more to exchange the man's hat for a more feminine item, letting her hair fall more loosely about her head, and she would be practically finished. Then, into the bag would go the tweed jacket, the overcoat and the hat, together, of course, with the false beard. She may even have had a large folded canvas bag with her, to conceal the carpet-bag itself from public view. All done in less than two minutes, and then she could walk on to Shortlands, to catch the next train unnoticed."

"I suppose you are right, Holmes. But what was it that made you suspect Miss Lee in the first place? You seem to have been very sure of it, but I cannot imagine why."

"The actions of the supposed man in the green tweed suit rather gave it away."

"His actions? But I can't recall that he did anything very notable, except lounge on a bench on the platform at Bickley station and stroll across the golf-course waving to the golfers there."

"But in both cases, if you remember, Watson, he put on his coat. It was a mild, pleasant day. We know this from the weather records, and from the testimony of witnesses, but even if we didn't, we could infer it from the fact that the young man was not wearing the coat he had brought with him. On the golf course, he was carrying it over his arm, and at the railway station he had placed it over the back of the bench. Yet when the golfers made their presence known to him by calling out, he slipped it on – his glance at the sky, as if he thought it might rain, was, I take it, the merest humbug – as he did when he stood up on the railway platform to walk to the train which had just arrived. What does that suggest to you?"

"Nothing whatever, unless he was simply tired of carrying the coat."

Holmes shook his head with a chuckle. "As I considered the matter, I was convinced it was a question of anatomy. You, as a medical man must surely appreciate the point, Watson. The fact is that a woman may readily pass for a man with suitable clothes and a little cosmetic attention to the hair and facial features. But she will only ever be entirely convincing when she is sitting down or standing still. As soon as a woman begins to walk – or run – she will almost always give herself away, unless she is completely covered up – with a large overcoat, say. Or perhaps you have never noticed that a woman's swaying gait is somewhat different from that of a man?" he added with a twinkle in his eye.

"Yes, of course I have," I responded with some heat.

"Very well," said Holmes. "You will understand, then, why I was convinced that the supposed 'young man' in the green tweed suit was in reality a woman. There was simply no other satisfactory explanation for the putting-on of the overcoat only when he was walking under the observation of others. It only remained for me to discover who the woman might be. Lanner's interviews with Wentworth's acquaintances this morning clarified that question considerably. Wentworth had invited Maria Monkley down to his house at Bickley on two consecutive Wednesdays. I think we may take it that if he had made the progress with her that he had been hoping for, he would have invited her down again the following week. However, he didn't, so I think we are justified in assuming that Wychwood's account of the matter was correct, and that Wentworth had not got anywhere with her. In that case, I judged, Miss Monkley, having rebuffed Wentworth in no uncertain terms and being apparently fond of Alexander Wychwood, had no real motive for the crime, but Belinda Lee certainly did. She had been intimate with Wentworth for some considerable time, but had been pushed unceremoniously aside when Miss Monkley appeared on the scene. That must have been a severe blow to the pride of a woman who had no doubt revelled in the general popularity she had enjoyed for so long. Then, on top of that, when Wentworth was snubbed by Miss Monkley, he seems to have expected Miss Lee to be grateful for another invitation to his house at Bickley, an invitation she must have known she would never have received if there had been any prospect of his getting Miss Monkley to visit him there again. How that knowledge must have embittered her!"

Sherlock Holmes duly notified the authorities of his view of the case, and his reasons for holding that view, but despite extensive enquiries, and despite their questioning Miss Lee closely several times, no conclusive evidence was ever found which might link her with Wentworth's murder. Acting on Holmes's suggestion, the police questioned the officials at Shortlands station, and one man there thought he remembered seeing Miss Lee at that station on the day of the murder; but she flatly denied that she had been there and, as several weeks had by then passed, the man's testimony was not given with any great conviction. Clothes which might have been the tweed suit, the overcoat and the hat worn by the murderer were indeed found in the costume department of the Frivolity theatre, as Holmes had predicted, but as the theatre's wardrobe was a very large one, that was not so surprising and proved nothing. From the perspective of the police, then, the matter remained unresolved and the case was never closed. Although I was convinced that Holmes's analysis of the matter was correct in every respect, it could not be proved, and Miss Lee was never arrested for the crime. Much to my regret, therefore, I was unable to include the Wentworth case in that series of sketches of my friend's professional career which I laid before the public some time ago.

A year or two later, however, I chanced to see a small item in the *Globe* which described how Miss Belinda Lee had fallen out acrimoniously with the management of the Frivolity Theatre, as a result of which her employment there had been terminated. Some months after that, I read somewhere that she had sailed for Australia, in the hope, it said, of rekindling her career in the antipodes. After that, she passed quite out of my knowledge and had not crossed my mind for several years when a brief paragraph in the *Telegraph* one morning caught my eye. Under the heading "Mysterious death of former 'Frivolity' singer", it described how Miss Belinda Lee had been shot dead in her dressing-room at a theatre in Sydney. She had apparently had a very wide circle of male acquaintances in Sydney, many of them disreputable and suspected of criminal activities, but, despite extensive enquiries among these men, the police had been unable to make any progress in the case. Of course, I knew nothing of the matter other than the bare outline I have indicated here, but I could not help but think as I read the account that in that mysterious way which does sometimes occur, a sort of blind justice or retribution had been meted out to Belinda Lee for the terrible crime she had committed in the Wentworth case.

AN UNUSUAL INTERVIEW

I HAD KNOWN SHERLOCK HOLMES, the well-known criminal investigator, for some years at the time of those incidents associated with Henry Barton and the *Dulwich Weekly Post*. During this time, I had become so accustomed to his every pronouncement on a case being precisely correct that the thought of his making a mistake had ceased to enter my head. It came as a surprise to me then, when, on this occasion, my friend revealed himself to be as fallible as the rest of mankind, and not immune, as I had supposed, from reaching a hasty and unwarranted conclusion. Fortunately, this uncharacteristic lapse did not prevent the truth of the matter from being discovered, as I shall describe.

It was boisterous, blustery weather in the early part of October when Mr. Henry Barton paid a visit to the chambers I shared with Holmes in Baker Street. He was a young man, no more than two-and-twenty, I judged, well dressed but with a somewhat dishevelled air about him, as if the strong autumnal winds had blown him along the street and into our rooms just as they were whirling and scattering the leaves from the trees.

We had finished our lunch and Holmes had returned to his commonplace book, into which he was pasting a heap of newspaper cuttings he had amassed over the preceding two weeks, but now he put down his pasting-brush and addressed our visitor.

"What can we do for you, Mr. Barton?" he asked, waving the young man to a chair by the fire.

"I have heard that you can extricate people from difficulties," said Barton as he sat down, "and free them from false charges."

"I try," returned Holmes. "Have false charges been made against you?"

"Not yet, but I strongly suspect they will be," Barton continued in a rush, his voice almost breathless, his chest heaving with emotion. "If anyone was ever in difficulties, Mr. Holmes, then I am."

"Very well," said Holmes in a calming tone, "take a few deep breaths and recover yourself, then tell us precisely what has occurred to discomfit you in this way."

Barton did as Holmes suggested, and, a few moments later, began the following account:

"You should know first that I am a junior reporter on the *Harrow and Wealdstone Telegraph*, one of the weekly newspapers in that district. It is a comfortable enough lay and in general I have no complaints in that direction. As I am the most junior member of staff, though, it means that I am given all the jobs that no one else wants, and I seem to spend half my working life reporting on flower shows. I sometimes think I could write the reports in my sleep. Indeed, I have even dreamed about flower shows at night recently – Mrs. Blenkinsop winning the prize for best dahlias for the third year in a row, Mr. Rogers winning the prize for biggest sunflower after being beaten into second place last year by Mr. Smithers, and so on. I may be wrong, but I feel I have the talent to go on to somewhat greater things." He paused and shook his head.

"Fortunately," he continued after a moment, "my mother's cousin, Mr. Wilfred Langwith, has always been involved with local newspapers in and around London. Indeed, it was partly as a result of his help and advice that I secured my present position. I therefore went to see him last week, to tell him of my boredom with having to do flower shows and the like, and to see if he had any suggestions to make.

"He greeted me very cordially, I must say, and listened sympathetically to my complaint before responding.

"'Do not dismiss flower shows out of hand,' said he with a chuckle. 'They are very important to some people, my boy, and the experience you have gained from reporting on them will be very valuable to you in the future. However, I can see that you are now ready to move on to greater things. As it happens, I believe that a friend of mine, Thurston Withers, who owns the *Dulwich Weekly Post*, is looking for a bright young man to add to his staff there. I think, Henry, that you might be just the sort of person he is looking for! The newspaper business in south London is extremely competitive, you know, and any advantage old Withers can gain over his rivals would be like finding gold dust to him. Of course, as you know, the papers make a certain proportion of their income from the commercial advertisements they contain. The competition for this advertising is very intense, especially with the recent launching of one or two new, upstart papers, such as the *Streatham Star*, the *Wimbledon Courier* and others, all fishing from the same pool. But local businesses will only advertise in a paper if the circulation is strong, and the circulation will only be strong if the standard of reporting is high and the reports consistently interesting. So, ultimately, a paper's prosperity depends on people like you, Henry. But apart from these considerations, there is also a strong family rivalry in south London.'

"I asked Mr. Langwith what he meant and he explained:

"'Mr. Withers's grandfather used to own two newspapers in those parts, both of which he had founded, the *Dulwich Weekly Post* and the *Dulwich and Norwood Echo*. His two sons assisted him, but they could never agree on anything and were constantly quarrelling, so when he died he stipulated in his will that his newspaper "empire" was to be divided up – somewhat like that of Alexander the Great – and his two sons were each to have one of the papers. Later, these papers passed to his grandsons, Thurston Withers having ownership of the *Dulwich Weekly Post* and his cousin, Seymour Withers, the *Dulwich and Norwood Echo*. The rivalry between the two of them is just as fierce now as it was between their respective fathers. Thurston Withers has the better paper, I believe, but his cousin has recently raised queries about the interpretation of their grandfather's will, and claimed that the *Post* should rightfully belong to his side of the family, a claim which

Thurston Withers hotly disputes. All in all, it has been a worrying time for Withers, and the last time I saw him, his nerves seemed very much on edge. He told me that the stress and worry of the business was upsetting him so badly that he had scarcely been able to sleep at night, and had recently begun taking some kind of sleeping-powders prescribed for him by his doctor. So you will appreciate, Henry, that Thurston Withers will only want to take you on if he is convinced that you show real promise. He only wants the very best! Anyway, leave the matter with me, my boy, and I'll arrange an appointment for you to see old Withers as soon as possible.'

"A few days later, I had a letter from Mr. Langwith, informing me that he had made an appointment for me to see Mr. Withers at his home, at ten o'clock on Friday the tenth."

"Today, in fact," said Holmes.

"Precisely, Mr. Holmes. Mr. Langwith said he would come with me, to introduce me and support my case, which I thought was jolly decent of him. 'However,' he said, 'we must not be late, for there is nothing old Withers hates more than poor time-keeping.' He gave me Mr. Withers's address, but said we should meet outside the front of Dulwich railway station at a quarter to ten, from where we could walk together to Mr. Withers's house, which was not far away, and prepare ourselves for the interview as we went.

"You can imagine how pleased I was at this, Mr. Holmes. This morning I rose earlier than usual, to make myself as smart as I could and put my best suit on. Unfortunately, I spent so long getting ready that I ran out of time and had to hurry off without any breakfast. Still, that is not so unusual an occurrence for me and I did not give it a thought. I was too excited at the prospect of meeting such an important man as Mr. Withers to care about breakfast, and all the way down to Dulwich in the train I practised the answers I should give to his questions.

"I was a little early reaching Dulwich, and there was no sign there of Mr. Langwith. This did not trouble me, however, and I passed the time usefully by continuing to rehearse answers to the questions I expected to be asked. All the time, as I paced back and forth before the station, with my 'Not at all, Mr. Withers', 'I could not agree more, Mr. Withers', and all the rest of it, the station clock was ticking towards ten o'clock. Another down train had called at the station since the one I had arrived on, but I looked in vain for Mr. Langwith among the passengers who alighted there.

"As the clock reached the hour, I became seriously concerned, bearing in mind what Mr. Langwith had said about Mr. Withers's dislike of people being late, and I decided I could wait no longer. I could not think what had happened to Mr. Langwith, and wondered if he had arrived earlier than I had and had left the station just before I got there. Fortunately, I had studied a map of the Dulwich area the evening before, and was confident I could find Mr. Withers's house by myself. I set off at a smart pace, and, about seven minutes later, arrived, somewhat breathless, before Banstead House, the address which Mr. Langwith had given me.

"It was a large house, surrounded by its own garden, in a quiet, tree-lined road. When I had recovered my breath and ordered my thoughts a little, I marched up to the front door and gave a couple of bangs on the large brass door-knocker. Even as I did so, I heard sounds of movement in the house, and a moment later the door was opened, not by a housemaid as I had expected, but by a tall, broad-shouldered and well-dressed middle-aged man. He was clean shaven, save for a dark, waxed moustache, and had a pair of dark, piercing eyes. His whole expression was one of thrusting impatience, as of one used to issuing orders and having them obeyed, and altogether he was a very imposing figure.

"'Yes?' he enquired abruptly. 'What is it?'

"'Mr. Withers?' I asked, somewhat taken aback by his forceful manner.

"'Yes. What do you want?'

"'May I enquire if Mr. Langwith is here?' I asked.

"'Yes, you may, and no, he isn't.'

"I quickly explained to him who I was and my connection with Mr. Langwith.

"'I thought you weren't coming,' said he, in a voice full of annoyance.

"'I'm sorry I'm a bit late,' I returned, and started to tell him how I had waited for Mr. Langwith at Dulwich station, but he cut me short.

"'That doesn't matter,' said he in a peremptory tone. 'You may as well come in now you're here. You'll have to excuse the disorder,' he continued, as I followed him in and along the hall. 'The whole house has recently been re-painted. They did the outside last month, and in the last couple of weeks they have been doing the inside.'

"In fact that was already apparent to me, for the smell of fresh paint was so strong as to be almost overpowering. 'I'm afraid the servants are all lodging elsewhere this week,' Mr. Withers continued, 'as I am myself. I only came back to collect something, so you're fortunate to find me here. However, I'll put the kettle on and make us a cup of tea. If you just wait in here,' he continued, pushing open a door at the end of the hall, 'I'll be back in a moment.'

"The room into which he ushered me was some kind of drawing-room. The painting appeared to be finished in this room and the curtains had been re-hung, although some of the furniture was still covered with dust-sheets. I perched myself on a sofa in the centre of the room and waited, somewhat apprehensively, for Mr. Withers to return. As I did so, I heard doors banging and what sounded like a violent oath from Mr. Withers, as if he was intensely annoyed about something or had banged his head on a cupboard door or something of the sort. All in all, my appointment was proving a somewhat surprising one.

"Abruptly, the door opened and Mr. Withers strode into the room.

"'The tea will be ready in a minute or two,' said he. 'We may as well get on with it. You are a reporter on the *Harrow and Wealdstone Telegraph*, you say?'

"'Yes, sir,' I responded smartly.

"'But you now wish to spread your wings, and think the *Dulwich Weekly Post* might be a suitable next step in your career?'

"'Precisely.'

"'Hum. As it happens, we are in need of another reporter at the moment – a fresh pair of eyes and a fresh pen.'

"My heart rose at this promising information. 'What might the new man's duties be?' I enquired.

"'To begin with,' he replied, 'you – or whoever we took on – would be the chief reporter of flower shows and the like.'

"My heart sank heavily at this, and my face must have betrayed my disappointment, for he hurriedly continued:

"'Of course, that is not all you would be responsible for. There are many other things which would fall within your remit – vegetable shows, for example.'

"'I see,' I said, trying to look interested.

"'Yes,' he continued. 'You'd be amazed how obsessed some people are with growing the largest marrow in the district and that sort of thing. Lord knows why!' he exclaimed with a harsh laugh. 'I can't stand marrow myself! Then there are the general "nature notes" columns – there is one every week, describing the wild flowers to be seen at that time of the year, and so on. Of course, it's all humbug, really. Most gardeners in Dulwich regard these things as weeds, and spend all their time pulling them up. Incidentally, you don't need to concern yourself with the wild-flower illustrations. They are done for us by a nun at the local convent – Sister Euphorbia – who has a gift for that sort of thing. As a matter of fact, there is another one, too, who sometimes stands in for Sister Euphorbia when she is indisposed. That's Sister Gonzaga,' he added. He shot me a keen, penetrating glance. 'You don't have any objection to working with nuns, I suppose?'

"'No,' I said, 'not at all. To be honest, Mr. Withers, it's not something I've ever really thought about.'

"'Good. Only you know how it is, Mr. Barton. Some people get beaten by nuns when they first start school, and after that they can't see a nun without a feeling of bitterness overcoming them.'

"'I assure you I don't harbour any such thoughts,' I insisted. I certainly did not want to lose the job on account of a supposed antipathy to nuns.

"'Very well,' said Mr. Withers, 'but you will appreciate that I have to ask these questions. One can't be too careful! Now I'll go and see if that kettle has boiled yet. While I'm away you can be thinking of any questions you wish to ask me.'

"I let out a very deep breath when Withers had left the room. My interview was not proceeding quite how I had expected, but, on the whole, it seemed more positive than negative. I tried to think of some intelligent-sounding questions to ask him, but I had not got very far when the door was flung open again with great force and Mr. Withers entered with two cups on a small tray.

"'You're not a tea fanatic, I hope,' he said as he put the tray down on a low table by the sofa.

"I shook my head, unsure as to his meaning.

"'That's good,' said he, 'because I've made a pot of coffee instead. The milk has gone off, so I've had to use some tinned muck, which I always think is disgusting in tea, but just about acceptable in coffee.'

"I took a sip from my cup. It was recognizable as coffee, although it was not very good, and it certainly had an odd flavour.

"'Now, about your questions,' said Mr. Withers in an impatient tone: 'Have you got any?'

"'Yes, sir,' I returned promptly, and proceeded to put to him what I hoped would strike him as intelligent and knowledgeable queries. He answered me in a very brief and brusque manner, I must say, his responses to my involved and careful questions sometimes consisting of only one or two words, after which he would say 'Next question?' We proceeded in this way for a few minutes, the rapidity of the questions and answers so great that I began to feel quite exhausted. Indeed, I was so overcome with mental weariness that I had the irresistible urge to yawn, which I managed to disguise by pretending to cough.

"Presently, Mr. Withers rose to his feet. 'I think that that just about covers everything,' he said with an air of finality. 'I like a young man who asks sensible questions.' he added, although I had become so muddled by the rapid questions and answers that I could scarcely remember anything I had asked, or the answers he had given. 'I've got something to do for a minute or two,' he continued. 'You just sit here and finish your coffee, and I'll be back in a little while.'

"When Withers had left the room and closed the door behind him, I sat for some time staring at the carpet. I was glad the main part of the discussion was over. I felt so exhausted that I really didn't feel I could carry on with it any longer. I looked down at the coffee-cup I was holding in my hand. I had drunk very little of it and didn't much fancy drinking any more. I glanced round the room. In a corner, in a raised stand, was some kind of large green plant with thick, leathery leaves. I struggled to my feet, made my way unsteadily over to the plant-stand and tipped the remainder of my coffee into the plant-pot. Then I resumed my seat on the sofa, supported my head on my hand, and—"

Our young visitor fell silent then.

"And?" prompted Holmes after a moment.

"And nothing," returned Barton. "That's just it. I can't remember anything else. Incredible though it seems, at eleven o'clock in the morning, or whatever it was, I think I must have fallen asleep. I've never felt quite so exhausted in all my life."

"What happened next?" Holmes enquired.

"I woke up abruptly. I don't think I'd been asleep very long. I looked at my watch. It was just after half past eleven. The house was in complete silence, although I was conscious of a faint hissing noise, and there was a smell of gas in the room.

"I rose to my feet, wondering where Mr. Withers was. I hoped he hadn't come in and found me asleep – that would hardly have done much for my job prospects. I decided the best thing to do was to go and find him – at least that would show a bit of initiative. I shook my head to try to clear the cobwebs away, and made to open the door. To my great surprise, the door would not move, and it was clear that it was locked.

"'Mr. Withers!' I called out, and banged on the door, but there was no answer and I could hear no sounds of movement anywhere in the house. I called again, several times, but to no avail. I thumped on the door, I pulled at the door-knob with every ounce of strength I possessed, but it was no use: I was locked in. Meanwhile, the smell of gas was becoming stronger by the minute, and, as soon as I stopped banging on the door, I could hear again the hissing noise.

"There were two gas-jets in the room, one on the wall by the window and one on the wall opposite that. The latter was properly turned off, and was not the source of the hissing or the escaping gas, but when I examined the one near the window, I could see at once that it was slightly turned on. I made to turn it off, but found that the tap was jammed. A closer examination revealed that it was stuck fast with paint. I put all my force into twisting the tap off, but made no impression on it whatsoever. In desperation, I took off my boot and, using it like a hammer, thumped the tap with it. This achieved nothing, so I tried again and again, hitting it harder each time. Suddenly, with a snapping noise, the gas-tap broke off completely and fell to the floor with a clatter. At the same moment, the sound of the gas escaping from the jet increased tremendously. It was clear that there was only one thing to be done. I must light the gas or I should die of gas-poisoning within a few minutes.

"With some trepidation, I struck a match just in front of the gas-jet. I had expected that it would flare a little at first, but I was not prepared for what in fact happened. The instant I struck the match, there was an almighty flash and bang in the air all around me and the distinctive smell of singed hair assailed my nostrils. Not only that, but the explosion had extinguished the match without lighting the escaping gas. Somewhat dazed, I quickly struck another match, and applied it to the gas-jet. To my horror, this resulted in a huge flame licking up the wall, half-way to the ceiling. I should have to find the main gas-tap in the house and turn it off as quickly as I could. but how could I get at it, prisoner as I was in that room? No sooner had I posed this question to myself than the obvious answer presented itself: if I could not get out through the doorway, I should have to get out through the window.

"The window in the room was a large one, of the sash-cord variety. I quickly opened the catch, and, for what seemed an age, struggled with the window, trying to push the bottom half upwards or pull the top half downwards, but I couldn't move it even a fraction of an inch, and it was clear that, like the gas-tap, it was stuck fast with paint. There was only one thing for it: I picked up my boot from where I had flung it onto the floor, and attacked one of the panes of glass with it.

"There was a terrific smashing noise as the glass splintered and fell to the ground outside, and a strong gust of cold, fresh, air rushed into the room. That was certainly an improvement on the foul air I had been breathing before, but my problems were hardly over. I could not possibly squeeze through the single broken pane. I should have to smash a second pane and try to break the wooden bar which separated them.

"With a heavy heart – I loathe wanton destruction of this sort – I struck the second pane with my boot-heel and smashed it to smithereens. then, replacing the boot on my foot, I kicked with all the strength I could muster at that part of the window-frame which separated the two broken panes of glass. It was only a slim-looking piece of wood, but was surprisingly sturdy, and resisted my efforts for some time. At length, however, with a loud crack, it snapped off at the top and I was able to remove it completely. I then spent several minutes picking out the jagged shards of glass which remained embedded, like dragon's teeth, in the hardened putty round the edges of the broken panes, until I thought it safe to attempt to climb through the gap. As I was doing so, being careful to avoid lacerating my hands on the many shards of glass which littered the window-sill, I saw that there was a housemaid in the next-door garden. She had been beating a carpet which was flung over a washing-line, but was now standing with mouth agape, staring at me over the low fence which separated the two gardens.

"'I have been trapped in the house,' I called out to her, by way of explanation for what no doubt struck her as extraordinary behaviour. She did not respond, but remained by the fence, staring at me. I had no time to give any further thought to her, however, as it was imperative I got back into the house as quickly as possible, to turn off the gas supply.

"Re-entering the house proved every bit as difficult as getting out of it. I ran round the whole building, but could find no easy way in. The front door was locked, the back door was locked, and all the windows were firmly closed. There was nothing for it: I should have to break in just as I had broken out. I made a quick survey of all the ground-floor windows. Some of them were too high for me to be able to scramble into them, and I eventually selected the window to the left of the front door, which gave on to what looked like a study. Again I took my boot off and began smashing the lowest panes of glass. As I did so, I glanced over to where the next-door housemaid had been standing, but she was no longer there. By the time I had snapped off the wooden frame and cleared the glass, however, and was about to climb in through the gap, the girl had returned, accompanied by a tall, distinguished-looking man with white hair and moustache. He called something to me as I clambered into the house, but I didn't stay to listen, as I could think of nothing but that great flame roaring up the wall in the back room.

"I made my way out of the study, which appeared to be in a state of great disorder, ran down the hall and glanced into the kitchen, but there was no smell of gas there. All the gas-taps were evidently turned off correctly. I then found the cellar door and clattered down the stone steps in the dark. It was almost pitch black down there, the only illumination coming from a small grating high in the wall ahead of me. I struck a match and lit a candle which was standing on a shelf below the grating. There were two chambers in the cellar. To the right was a coal-cellar, with a huge heap of coal beneath a large grating. To the left was a chamber for provisions with a stone table in the middle of the floor. I glanced about, and at once saw where the main gas pipe came into the house and where the main tap was. Having turned this off as tightly as I could, I ran back upstairs and made my way to the drawing-room in which my meeting with Mr. Withers had taken place.

"The key was in the lock. I turned it and pushed the door open. The gas-jet near the window was no longer alight, thank goodness, but I gave little thought to that, as the window-curtain was now on fire, and blazing away. It was clear that the strong gusts of wind through the broken window had blown the curtain into the flame from the gas-jet. I tried to extinguish the burning curtain by smothering it with a chair-cushion, but it was not easy, and I only succeeding in burning my hands. In a blind panic, I leapt up and grabbed the curtain above where it was burning, to try to pull it down, so that I could stamp on it on the floor. I pulled with all my weight at it, and suddenly, with a terrific crash, the whole curtain-rail came down and struck me a terrific blow on the head. Oblivious to the pain, I stamped furiously on the burning curtain, grinding the smouldering remains of it into the carpet, until I was satisfied that all the flames were out and the charred fabric held no heat.

"I had returned to the hall, and was making my way towards the front door when I heard voices. The door to the study was ajar, and I peeped through the crack between the door and the frame. A large group of people had assembled outside the window which I had broken to re-enter the house, among whom I saw the distinguished-looking man from next door.

"'It must be one of those window-smashing lunatics,' he was saying. 'He'll probably climb onto the roof next – that's usually what they do. I'm sure the constable will soon have the matter sorted out when he gets here.' As he spoke I saw a policeman approaching in the distance, in the company of the housemaid I had seen earlier.

"For a second I considered explaining to these people what had happened, but only for a second, because I got the distinct impression that they would not believe me and I should undoubtedly be arrested by the policeman and taken off in handcuffs to the nearest police station. I hesitated no longer. I ran to the back door, unlocked and opened it as quietly as I could, then slipped out into the back garden. I took the key from the lock and re-locked the door from the outside, taking the key away with me so that they should think I was still inside the house and spend time looking for me there while I made my escape. Then I ran like a hare in a straight line down the back garden, pushed my way through a thick hedge and found myself in the large garden of a house which I could see was on a different road altogether.

"As unobtrusively as I could, I made my way round the edge of this garden, out through a gate and into a quiet, tree-lined road. Up this road I set off at a fast rate. I had no idea where I was or where I was going to; I just wanted to put as much distance between Mr. Withers's house and myself as I could. Up roads, down roads, round corners I ran, and did not stop until I came to a small railway station, which turned out to be Lower Norwood. Quite where this station was situated, relative to Dulwich or anywhere else, I hadn't the faintest idea, but I was able to buy a ticket there for Victoria, which is all that I wanted, and forty minutes later I was back in town. From Victoria I came straight here to seek your advice and assistance, Mr. Holmes. That is my story, and here I am!"

Sherlock Holmes sat in silence for some time when our visitor had finished speaking.

"Your account is a fascinating one, Mr. Barton," he remarked at length. "It raises many questions, and I would not have missed it for the world! But I feel you may have made a mistake."

Barton looked surprised. "I cannot think what else I could have done at any stage in the day," he returned. "Did you have anything particular in mind?"

"Your fleeing the scene of these upsetting events may make it more difficult to convince those concerned of your innocence."

"Perhaps so, but I could see from their faces and hear from their words that they had already decided that I was as guilty as any villain could be, and that the only mitigating circumstance they would allow me was that I was probably a lunatic."

"I appreciate the point – I have been in similar situations myself – but you have certainly convinced me of your veracity, so perhaps you could have convinced others, too. Still, what is done is done, and we must work from the situation in which we find ourselves."

"You will take my case, then?" asked Barton, an imploring look in his eyes.

"Most certainly," replied Holmes. "What I propose is that we return to Dulwich at once. Do not fear, Mr. Barton," he added, as our visitor's face fell. "I shall act as your defence counsel, and I am confident we shall quickly get the whole business straightened out. Let us postpone any further discussion of the matter until we are on our way," he continued, as Barton made to speak. "Will you accompany us, Watson?"

"I should be delighted to," I replied. "I am keen to see how you propose to 'straighten out,' as you put it, such a very odd affair."

Five minutes later, the three of us were in a cab and rattling along through the crowded streets towards Victoria station.

"The surprising and alarming events at Mr. Withers's house," said Holmes, "have had the effect of eclipsing and putting out of consideration what should really be the first mystery in this business."

"What is that?" queried Barton in surprise.

"The failure of your cousin, Mr. Langwith, to turn up as arranged."

"That's true," said Barton. "I wonder what can have become of him."

"We can only speculate," said Holmes. "Perhaps he fell ill, or suffered some kind of accident on his way to meet you at Dulwich station. But both of those explanations would require a singularly unfortunate coincidence to have occurred. More likely, as it involves no such coincidence of events, is that he simply learned in the last few days that the appointment with Thurston Withers could not take place as arranged after all, and there was thus no point in his going."

"Then why did he not write and tell me of this?" objected Barton.

"Perhaps he did, and you did not receive his letter," replied Holmes. "You left home in a great hurry this morning, without taking any breakfast. Does your landlady usually place your post on the breakfast-table?"

"Yes, she does. It is always beside my plate."

"Then perhaps there was a letter from Mr. Langwith there this morning, which, in your haste, you failed to see."

Barton clapped his hand to his head. "Of course!" he cried. "That must be it! But," he added after a moment, "the fact that Mr. Langwith was not present does not even begin to explain why Mr. Withers acted and spoke so strangely to me – he was not at all as I had expected him to be – nor why he left the house so abruptly, leaving me locked in the drawing-room with a leaking gas tap which I could not turn off."

"It is certainly a singularly absurd and confused affair, although I don't imagine it struck you that way at the time. But some aspects of it seem clear enough: first of all, that the man you met in Dulwich was not Thurston Withers."

"I suppose that that is possible," remarked Barton after a moment, "but how can you be so sure? He was, after all, in Mr. Withers's house, and when I first arrived there and addressed him as Mr. Withers, he did not appear at all surprised. It is true that some of the questions he asked me were a little eccentric, but I put that down to his strong, forceful character."

"'Eccentric' is not the word I would choose to describe him," returned Holmes. "I think if we described him as an accomplished liar we should be nearer the truth. In any case, consider for a moment the point you yourself raised, that he left you locked in the drawing-room when he disappeared from the house: It is surely inconceivable that the real Thurston Withers would have done such a thing; for if it really were his house, he should have to return to it at some time, when you would still be there. It seems to me much more likely that the man you saw had no right to be in the house at all. I imagine he only answered your knock at the door because he thought it might be a neighbour of Withers's who had seen him enter the house and he did not wish to arouse suspicion. But when you first addressed him, he would at once have realised that you did not know Thurston Withers by sight, and he probably judged that the best course of action for himself was to continue the pretence of being Withers for a short time until either he could get rid of you or make his own escape. Mr. Langwith had mentioned to you that Thurston Withers had been suffering from insomnia recently, and had had recourse to some kind of sleeping-powder. It seems likely from your account that this stranger had come across this in the kitchen and had added a dose to your cup of coffee, obviously thinking that you would fall fast asleep and he could leave the house and be far away before you woke up again."

Barton nodded his agreement to this analysis. "Fortunately for me," he said, "I drank very little of the coffee, on account of its odd taste. Had I drained the cup, I might have slept for an hour or two, I suppose, and might very well have died from gas-poisoning. The mere thought of that makes me feel quite ill," he added with a shudder. "Do you think this strange man intended to murder me?"

Holmes shook his head. "I think that very unlikely. I imagine that what happened was this, that when he went to boil the kettle, he discovered there was no gas available in the kitchen, so he turned on the main gas-tap in the cellar, not realising that it had been turned off deliberately because of the leaking tap in the drawing-room. As he did not stay for long in the drawing-room with you after he brought in the coffee, he probably did not notice the smell of gas there."

"That may be true. He drank his own coffee quickly while we exchanged a series of rapid questions and answers, as I mentioned to you, then he left, saying he had something to attend to. The smell of gas was not noticeable then; it only became so when I awoke from my nap."

"I wonder who this person could have been," I remarked, "if it was not, indeed, Mr. Withers?"

"Of course we cannot say for certain," said Holmes, "but I suspect we need look no further than Thurston Withers's own cousin, Seymour Withers. We have heard that the two men are, as their fathers before them, bitter rivals in the newspaper business. We have also heard that there was some dispute over which of the two newspapers each son should have inherited. No doubt Seymour Withers learned that his cousin and his domestic staff would be absent from the house while it was being redecorated and thought to take advantage of that fact to rifle through his cousin's private papers in the hope of finding something of benefit to his own cause."

"But how could he have got into the house?" I objected.

Sherlock Holmes shook his head dismissively. "Pooh!" said he. "I see no great problem in that, if a man is determined enough. Cousin Seymour may have purloined a key during some previous visit to the house; he may have had a duplicate key made at some time; he may, for all we know, have entered the house through the coal-cellar grating. But, here we are at Victoria, so further speculation will have to wait!"

A stopping train for Bickley was just about to leave as we dashed onto the platform, and we sprang aboard as the guard blew his whistle. Twenty minutes later, we had alighted at Dulwich, and were making our way down a tree-lined avenue towards the house in which Holmes's client had had such a strange experience.

As we approached, we saw that there was a small group of people, including a policeman, in front of the house, watching two workmen affixing a piece of plywood over a broken window.

"There is Mr. Langwith," cried Barton: "just to the left of the constable."

The man in question, a tall elderly gentleman, turned at that moment and saw us.

"Why, Henry!" cried he. "Here you are at last! Where on earth have you been?" A large, stout man, standing by his side, turned to follow his gaze, and Langwith addressed him. "This is the young man – my cousin's son – that I mentioned to you, Withers," he explained. Then he turned once more to our companion. "You won't believe what has been happening here, Henry! Mr. Withers has had a lunatic in the house, who has gone round smashing all the windows and setting fire to the curtains!"

Before Holmes's client could respond, a distinguished-looking man, standing just behind Langwith, let out a cry of surprise and recognition. "That's him!" he cried. "That's the villain I saw trying to destroy the house! Constable! Arrest that man at once!"

"One moment," returned Holmes in an authoritative tone, as the policeman took a step forward. "So far from arresting this young man, you should consider giving him an award. His quick thinking and decisive actions undoubtedly saved the house from burning down or being utterly destroyed in an explosion, as a result of a serious gas leak."

The stout man beside Langwith shook his head, a look of great annoyance on his face. "I am Thurston Withers," said he in an angry voice, "this is my house, and I know all about the gas leak, thank you very much! A plumber is coming tomorrow to deal with the matter. Until then, I have had the gas turned off at the mains."

"But what you don't know," returned Holmes, "is that someone turned the main tap back on again. This young man is Mr. Henry Barton, who arrived this morning for an interview with you, and managed to save your house."

"Did you not receive my note, Henry?" Langwith interrupted in a tone of surprise. "I wrote to tell you that Mr. Withers was otherwise engaged this morning and that our appointment was therefore postponed until this afternoon."

Barton shook his head. "I came at ten o'clock, as we had previously arranged, and had an interview with someone who pretended to be Mr. Withers. But he put some kind of sleeping potion in my coffee-cup and locked me in a drawing-room where the gas was leaking."

"What!" cried Thurston Withers in a tone of disbelief. "What a preposterous and unbelievable story!"

"At least hear Mr. Barton's account before you dismiss it," said Holmes. "You are an experienced newspaperman, Mr. Withers, so you, if anyone, must know that every man must be given the opportunity to state his own case."

There came a grudging assent to this observation from Withers, and, at a sign from Holmes, his client launched into a brief account of all that had happened to him since he left home that morning.

"Can this really be true?" exclaimed Withers, as Barton finished speaking.

"Every word of it, Mr. Withers," returned the latter.

"But who could this stranger be?" asked Withers.

"I think," said Holmes, "that taking everything into account, including the fact that the intruder seems to have been well informed about you, and that he rifled the private papers in your study, which are, I take it, more concerned with personal affairs than business matters, the chief suspect must surely be your own cousin, Seymour Withers."

At this, a small man with a grizzled moustache who had been standing beside Thurston Withers, but who had not previously spoken, stepped forward, a look of great anger upon his features.

"How dare you!" he cried. "How dare you accuse an honest man of such deceitful behaviour! It is an outrage! I am Seymour Withers, and I know nothing whatever of this business!"

There was a moment's uncomfortable silence, during which the workmen behind us banged nails into their sheet of plywood.

"Describe the man you encountered this morning," said Holmes to Barton, "and let us see if anyone recognizes the description."

"He was a tall man," began Barton, "broad-shouldered and powerful-looking, with very penetrating eyes. He had very dark hair and eyebrows, and a black, waxed moustache. He was a well-spoken gentleman, but very abrupt and impatient in his manner."

Thurston Withers looked at his cousin, who nodded his head. "That sounds very much like Lancelot Woodhouse," said Seymour Withers.

"I agree," said Thurston Withers. "It must be he. The description is exact."

"Who on earth is Lancelot Woodhouse?" asked Barton.

"I believe, Henry," said Langwith, "that he is the owner and editor-in-chief of the *Streatham Star*. Is that correct, Withers?"

"Yes, and a more ruthless fellow you are never likely to meet. He has put a lot of energy recently into trying to persuade many of our commercial advertisers to switch their allegiance to his paper. I have become increasingly concerned of late about leaks from our newspaper office of confidential correspondence on the subject, and have taken to keeping such correspondence here at home. No doubt Woodhouse has learned of this and his intention this morning was to find something among my private papers which he could turn to his advantage. I wonder how the devil he got into the house?"

"Has he paid you a visit recently?" asked Holmes.

"Yes," replied Thurston Withers, "as a matter of fact he has, although I wasn't in at the time. The foreman of the painters who have been working here told me that Woodhouse called one day last week. They informed him that I wasn't at home, but he said that he had reason to think I would be returning shortly – which, incidentally, wasn't true – and that he would wait a little while for me. He sat on a chair in the hall, but, after about ten minutes, he called to the painters and told them that he had decided not to wait any longer after all. What he wanted, I do not know, as I have not spoken to him since."

"I think that explains how he gained entry to the house today," said Holmes. "No doubt when the painters left him alone in the hall for ten minutes, he removed the key from the front door and made an impression of it in softened wax or something of the sort, so that he could have a duplicate made. He has evidently been following the progress of your redecoration closely, and was aware that the house would be quite unoccupied this morning. Had Mr. Barton not arrived when he did, Woodhouse would probably have finished his survey of your private correspondence and left the house as he had found it, and no one would ever have known he had been here."

"I am sure you are right," said Thurston Withers in a determined voice. "I shall speak to my solicitor tomorrow with a view to commencing legal proceedings against Woodhouse."

"What of my cousin here, Withers?" asked Langwith. "I know it has been an upsetting business for you, but could we possibly make another appointment for Mr. Barton to see you?"

"No," said Withers, shaking his head in vehement fashion. "There will be no interview. It is not necessary. I have heard your recommendation, Langwith, and Mr. Barton himself has just given a first-class demonstration of his ability to give a report in a pithy and convincing way. That is enough for me." He turned to Barton then, and held out his hand with a smile. "The position is yours, my boy, if you want it. Whatever you were getting at the *Harrow and Wealdstone Telegraph*, I'll give you twenty per cent more. What do you say?"

Barton seized the other's hand and wrung it vigorously. "I accept your offer, Mr. Withers," said he. "I am sure you will not regret it."

Holmes was silent as we walked back to the railway station. "It is something of a relief to me," he remarked at length, "that the circumstances – Barton's being offered the position he desired and so on – had the effect of erasing my own lamentable error with regard to Seymour Withers."

"I shouldn't worry about it, Holmes," I returned with a chuckle. "Everyone makes a mistake occasionally. I shouldn't dwell on it if I were you."

"But I must dwell on it, Watson," said my friend in an emphatic tone. "One can learn more from one blunder than from a hundred successes. I must therefore concentrate all my thoughts upon the blunder in order to reap the full benefit of it."

And that was the last word my friend spoke on the subject, as we made our way back to Baker Street.

THE ZODIAC PLATE

"POISON," SAID SHERLOCK HOLMES, pushing back his chair from the supper table. I looked up from the medical journal I was reading, and watched as he took his old clay pipe from the mantelpiece. "Poison," he continued, "is, in its many and varied forms, one of the greatest benefactors of the human race. We have indeed much for which to thank the poisons."

"I hardly think that many could be found to agree with you," I replied in some amusement.

"Nevertheless, it is true. If you would consider the matter for but five seconds, Watson, you must agree. Where, to take the most obvious example, would medicine be today, but for poisons?"

"I believe I see what you mean. It is true that there are certain substances which would commonly be regarded as poisonous, but which in regulated doses may be useful in the treatment of certain ailments. In some instances, indeed, the physician will deliberately administer one poison in the knowledge that it will drive out another poison which is already present in the body – as in the case of nicotine and strychnine."

Holmes waved his hand impatiently. "Yes, yes; of course, this is true; but it is a trivial point, of little interest to the theorist: that a substance can be found that will drive out another is not so very surprising, and that either of these two, taken in isolation, would have a deleterious effect upon the human system is surely no more than experience might lead one to expect. The point I wish to make, however, is a somewhat more profound one: that it is the chance occurrence of poisons, unfortunate as their effects may be upon the individual, that has given mankind the great knowledge it now possesses. When a poison causes an upheaval of the normal, everyday run of things, it reveals to us as it does so something also of the system it has affected. In this way, little by little, our knowledge has increased. Without such revelations, on the other hand, we should really know very little of the workings of the human body. And it is not only to the realm of medicine that this observation applies: in the sphere of our mental life the situation is the same. As Kant argues in the book I was looking at this afternoon, many of the paradoxical and perplexing notions with which we are inclined to ensnare and befuddle our own minds are in a sense poisons, which, by defeating our intellects, demonstrate to us our own limitations."

"You have been reading Kant?"

"Time has been hanging somewhat heavily upon my hands just lately," replied my friend, "and the *Critique of Pure Reason* is good light reading at such a time."

"Light reading!" I cried. "I understood that Kant's *Critique* was one of the most difficult books ever written!"

"Really? You surprise me; I find it most congenial and refreshing. I suppose it is a question of temperament. There are distinct parallels between the work of the expert philosopher and that of the expert detective. In both employments, the talents of imagination, observation and deduction form an absolute prerequisite. In both fields, too, the admission of exotic poisons into the commonplace progress of life is apt to produce effects which could not have been foreseen."

"As to the philosophical aspects of your thesis, I should not care to advance an opinion," I remarked after a moment; "but upon the medical side of things I think I see a flaw in your argument. For if no poisons existed, then surely, in such a perfect world, we should simply have no need of the knowledge that, on your account, we should thereby be denied. We might not, it is true, have so full an understanding of the complexities of the human body, but we should be not one whit disadvantaged as a consequence, for there would simply be no call for such knowledge."

"Ha!" cried Holmes. "I really cannot believe that that is your considered opinion, Watson. It seems to me a quite fallacious piece of reasoning, to conclude from the fact that our knowledge, whether medical or otherwise, is often of practical use to us, that that is therefore the reason for its existence. You may as well argue, from the fact that the ocean winds have proved of the utmost use to mariners, that the winds owe their very existence to that employment. The situation in my opinion is quite the other way about: Man has an unquenchable thirst for knowledge, which leads him upon an endless quest for answers and explanations, irrespective of whether they will materially affect him either one way or the other; the fact that some of his knowledge proves to be of practical use is simply a bonus. But we will perhaps have an opportunity to take a third opinion upon the matter when my visitor arrives, for he is a medical colleague of yours, a Dr. James Saunders."

"Dr. James Saunders of Harley Street?" I cried in surprise. "He may indeed have an opinion upon the matter, for he is by all accounts one of the most brilliant men in London, and in the very van of medical research. Why, he has a monograph in the journal I have in my hand at this moment! He gives it the title 'Not a Door but a Window'."

"The reference being – ?"

"To the epidermis. He argues that it is an area of study which has been lamentably neglected and misunderstood in recent years, and one which could make a far greater contribution to general diagnosis than has hitherto been supposed. He is undoubtedly one of the foremost authorities upon the subject – I wonder what on earth he can want with us?"

"Your thirst for knowledge upon the point should be satisfied in just five minutes," remarked my friend drily, with a glance at the clock. "His appointment is for half-past-eight."

Our visitor was punctual to the minute. A tall, upright man, a little over forty years of age, he had a broad, intelligent face, in which his dark and thoughtful eyes seemed to gleam with intellectual power. A greying of the hair about the temples was the only sign that the famous specialist was as susceptible to the passage of the years as the rest of his human brethren. He took a seat by our cheerily-crackling fire, and rubbed his hands gently together in the warmth.

"Well, sir," said Holmes after a moment. "What brings Dr. James Saunders from Harley Street to Baker Street on so dark a night as this? It has meant your going without your supper, I perceive. May we offer you a sandwich and a glass of wine?"

"Thank you, Mr. Holmes," replied the other, "but I have a cold chicken waiting for me at home – but how on earth do you know that I have not yet eaten this evening? I should not have thought that my appearance would strike anyone as especially undernourished!"

"I observed that your overcoat is suffering from a swollen pocket, occasioned by the medical instruments which I see protruding from the top. You have evidently not come here direct from home, then, but have been out upon a professional call. At this time of day, and upon an evening when you already have one engagement, it seems likely that your journey was not premeditated, but the result of an unexpected summons. It has certainly occupied you some time, for the fresh mould adhering to your boot is peculiar to the Surrey side, and is found there only in certain parts. Would I be correct if I were to suggest that you have been out to Norwood?"

"As near as makes no difference," our visitor replied, a look of amazement upon his face. "I have heard of your powers, of course, Mr. Holmes, but I hardly expected to receive a demonstration of them so promptly! You have, also, a reputation for discretion," he continued after a moment, "which, if one considers it, must be so difficult an achievement as to be almost a contradiction in terms." He smiled slightly at his own jest, his eyes sparkling, and Holmes bowed his head in acknowledgement of the compliment. "It is this that brings me here tonight; for I require something to be done which may be both difficult and unpleasant – yes, and perhaps shameful, too."

"Pray be explicit."

"Very well. My sister, Winifred, who is some years older than I am, is the widow of Sir Douglas Harford Joyce, who, as you will probably recall, was our ambassador at the time of the Bucharest incident. She has one son, my nephew, Robert. He was just eighteen years old when his father died, and, to speak perfectly frankly, has sorely missed the influence of a father since that time. It is not that he is a bad lad, but he is wild and undisciplined, and shows no sign of taking any particular direction in life. As his only near relative, I have felt some responsibility in the matter of his upbringing and education, but my own work keeps me so continuously occupied that I have not always been able to devote the time to the task that I should have wished. His mother naturally thinks the world of him, and wants only what is for the best; but just as he has only one parent, so she has only one child, and she has as a result, I am afraid, tended to concede every point of contention which has arisen between them. This has not, as you will appreciate, been conducive to the formation of those manners which society expects of its members, and Robert has thus tended to gravitate to the company of those whose behaviour is as reckless and unprincipled as his own. I have done my best to arrest this downward progress, but have succeeded only in making myself a figure of stuffiness and gloom in his eyes, if not, indeed, a figure of derision.

"About a year ago he began to gamble heavily, which threw a further strain upon the already stretched resources of the allowance he receives under the terms of his father's will. Since that time he has continually approached me in my capacity as a trustee of his father's estate and begged for advances on the money he can expect to inherit upon his twenty-fifth birthday. I have, I regret to say, acquiesced more often than I have refused. When he came to me last week, however, and demanded five hundred pounds to pay off some money-lender or other, I flatly refused.

" 'You must learn to curb your excesses,' I told him. 'You cannot expect simply to do as you wish, and then presume that someone will always come along to settle your account for you.'

" 'I shall not need to, after September,' he retorted. 'When the money is under my own control you will have no further opportunity for these sermons you so enjoy delivering, Uncle James; that is something I can promise you. Now, as there is so little time remaining for you to get upon my good side, perhaps you had better reconsider, and let me have the money after all.'

" 'I shall not give you a penny!' I cried. 'In seven months' time you will be free to do whatever you wish with the money. You may gamble it away, drink it away, or throw it in the river if it pleases you to do so, and I shall not be able to stop you. But until the time I am obliged by law to relinquish control of your financial affairs, I shall not be a party to such profligate and reprehensible waste. You will not, I repeat, get another penny out of me until the appointed day, on the first of next month.'

" 'You may regret it, Uncle,' said he, with a hard, bitter look upon his face, such as I had never seen there before.

" 'You are the one that will know regret,' I responded, but, with a foul oath by way of farewell, he left the room, slamming the door hard behind him. I worried afterwards lest I had been too severe upon the young man – I have all along sought to strike a balance between guidance and friendship – but events since have convinced me that I have not, in the past, been firm enough.

"I received a note yesterday morning from Lady Harford Joyce's butler, Milner, a man who has been in the family's employ for over a score of years, and upon whose discretion and good sense one could pledge one's life. He informed me that – well, that the very worst thing I could have conceived has taken place."

"Pray be specific," said Sherlock Holmes impatiently. "What, precisely, has happened, and in what way can I assist you?"

"I must tell you first of the Harford Joyce Plate," replied the great specialist. "It is the family's one great heirloom, and has been in their possession for generations. It is approximately twelve inches wide and eighteen in length, and is roughly oval in shape, although the corners are squared off. It is quite a heavy piece, for it is fashioned of solid silver. In the centre, depicted in relief, is a representation of the sun; and in a circle around it, also in relief, are the various traditional creatures of the Zodiac – crabs and scorpions and rams, and so on. Inset into the metal, representing the stars whose configurations first inspired men's minds with the idea of the Zodiac creatures, are scores of precious and semi-precious stones. While these certainly have a considerable intrinsic value, they are not, so I understand, of the very finest. It is rather the skill of the setting, the remarkable craftsmanship which has gone into the execution of its unique design, which gives the plate its value."

"Which is?" interjected Holmes.

"At a conservative estimate, twelve thousand pounds. A few years ago, my late brother-in-law had it valued, for insurance purposes, and I believe that the figure agreed upon was of that order. It may be worth considerably more now, for all I know. In one sense, of course, it is priceless, for there is not another like it in the world. To my sister, also, it has a value far greater than any price which it might fetch at auction; for, since Sir Douglas's death, the things which attached to him and to his family have become most dear to her; and the Zodiac Plate is, of course, of all such things, the very *non plus ultra*. Indeed, she has become almost obsessive about it: only last year she turned down an invitation from the British Museum for the Plate to be included in an exhibition of such artefacts which they were mounting, giving as her reason the wish of her husband that the Plate remain forever in the family home."

"And your nephew has threatened to sell this plate unless you advance him the money he requires?"

"Worse than that, Mr. Holmes; he has already given it into the hands of the money-lender he had mentioned to me, as security against the loan which is still outstanding. This was the news which Milner conveyed to me yesterday."

"I am not quite clear why it fell to the butler to be your informant," remarked Holmes, a note of curiosity in his voice. "Is Lady Harford Joyce ignorant of this recent transaction?"

"She has been in ill-health for some years, Mr. Holmes," replied Dr. Saunders, with a shake of the head, "and has been virtually bed-ridden this last nine months. She knows nothing of what occurs downstairs, other than what she learns from her son or from her domestic staff. In this case, Robert of course told no one what he was about, and Milner, having discovered what had happened, thought it wiser not to break the news of her son's idiocy to his mistress unless he was obliged to do so. With this judgement, I agree: The shock of such a disclosure might very well have appalling consequences upon her precarious state of health. Instead, he at once sent a note to me."

"Your intention, then, is to get the Plate back without your sister's knowing that it has ever left the house?"

"Precisely."

"Who has legal ownership of the Plate?"

"At present it is held in trust, the trustees being my sister, her solicitor in Gray's Inn and myself. When Robert attains the age of twenty-five, in seven months' time, it becomes his property absolutely."

"But your object, I take it, is less to remedy a legal wrong than to protect your sister, Lady Harford Joyce, from distress."

"That is correct; and, also, I might add – although he would sneer if he heard me say it – to protect my nephew from future remorse at the foolish actions of his youth. I do not imagine for one moment that his coming of age will mark any great change in his character, but I feel sure that something will one day bring him to his senses. Then, if he has inherited but one scrap of the dignity and sense of honour of his parents, he must surely hide his head in shame at the recollection of the life he is leading now. My only wish for him is that his memories should not be unbearably painful."

"Quite so. I can understand the scandal which would be aroused if it became generally known that the family's chief heirloom had been pawned to pay gambling debts. But the situation does not seem so very serious. Have you had a word with your nephew?"

"I spoke with him yesterday afternoon, and pointed out that if he had intended by his action to spite me, then he had badly misjudged the matter, for it was he himself he would hurt most. At this he only laughed. Eventually, seeing that there was no other way out of it, and with his mother's condition at the forefront of my mind, I offered him the five hundred pounds he had asked me for last week, on condition that he use it to redeem the Plate. At this he laughed still louder.

" 'It will take more than that to get the Plate back now,' he cried, a jeering note in his voice. 'I have already borrowed another thousand on the strength of it.'

"I was aghast at this, for I realised at once his intentions."

"To continue borrowing against the plate until September, presumably," observed Holmes. "Did you offer him any further money?"

Dr. Saunders nodded his head slowly, a defeated look upon his face.

"But he turned you down?"

"He did. It is evident that no amount short of his full inheritance will persuade him to alter his plans. I could see as we spoke that he felt that he had scored over me, and this only made him more obdurate. Then, in the heat of the moment, I said a foolish thing."

"You threatened him with legal action of some kind," said Holmes with a sigh, resting his chin upon his hand.

"I am afraid that I did, Mr. Holmes. Of course, the very idea is ridiculous. A legal suit would be guaranteed to stir up precisely the sort of scandal that I most wish to avoid – "

"And would likely enough not reach the courts before September in any case," interjected Holmes, with a grim smile.

"At any event," continued our visitor, "all that my threats achieved was to harden my nephew's heart yet further, and turn his cold scorn into hot anger. His response to my threat was swift:

" 'The Harford Joyce Plate is mine, to do with as I please,' cried he angrily.

" 'Not until September,' I returned, attempting to speak calmly and thus remedy the damage my unconsidered threat had caused.

" 'It is morally mine now,' retorted Robert, 'and you know it. There is no other male Harford Joyce alive but me, so whose else could it be?'

" 'But your father, in his wisdom – '

" 'Leave my father out of it, if you please.'

" 'Very well, Robert: if you will not consider your father's wishes, consider at least your mother's feelings.'

" 'She need know nothing of it,' replied the young scoundrel with a smirk of superiority, ' – unless, of course, you tell her yourself. And now, Uncle, I really must be off; I promised some fellows that I would meet them at Gates' this afternoon.' With that he left the room and our interview was at an end."

"If he is losing money at Gates' Club, then he is undoubtedly losing a great deal of it," observed Holmes after a moment; "and the arrangement with the money-lender regarding the Plate will of course only encourage him to lose yet more." He paused for a moment, his brows knitted with thought. "Tell me," he said at length; "to which of the Society parasites is he indebted?"

"A man by the name of Oscar Morley."

"Ah! That is bad, very bad! He is the most odious man in London. We can hope for little assistance there, I am afraid. Indeed, his involvement raises the possibility of a yet greater calamity."

"Whatever do you mean?" asked Dr. Saunders quickly, a note of alarm in his voice.

"I have no desire to raise fears unnecessarily," replied Holmes gravely, "but it is my duty as an expert in these matters to apprise you of all the possibilities, however unpleasant. Oscar Morley has no principles but one, the principle of ruthless self-interest. Should he judge that his interests were best served by selling the Zodiac Plate to some third party, and pocketing the proceeds, then no consideration on earth would weigh against it."

"Good God!" cried our visitor, clapping his hand to his head. "I had no idea our position was so perilous! But, wait! Surely you exaggerate the danger? Surely he cannot sell the Plate without exposing himself to criminal charges? For by no interpretation of the circumstances could he claim that the Plate was his; it is merely in his keeping as a temporary security."

Holmes shook his head, the severity of his expression offering no comfort to the imploring eyes of the other. "Unfortunately," said he, "it is not so simple as you imagine. These things are rarely arranged with full legal propriety. He has given your nephew five hundred pounds – or fifteen hundred, as it now is – and your nephew has given him the Zodiac Plate. That is all there is to it. Should anything happen to the Plate, neither your nephew nor anyone else would have the slightest legal recourse – unless, of course, you are prepared to demonstrate in a court of law that your nephew had no right to take the Plate in the first place."

"But surely there must be some signed documents, some record of the transaction between the two of them?" Dr. Saunders persisted.

Again Holmes shook his head. "If there is such a record, whom would you expect it to favour? The man who has recourse to such a transaction but once or twice in his life, in moments of desperation, or the man whose every day is spent in such dealings? But very likely there are no papers in existence at all, save a couple of simple, bald and unconditional receipts. To the lawyers it is known as a debt of honour, and, as such, outwith their purview."

"A debt of dishonour, more like!" cried our visitor, thumping the chair-arm with his fist.

"However that may be," said Holmes after a moment, in a measured tone, "it is imperative that the pledge be redeemed, and redeemed as quickly as possible. You have approached your nephew without success, so I take it you wish me to approach Morley directly."

Our visitor nodded his head. "It is a task, I readily confess, for which my education has not well fitted me."

"Very well, then," continued Holmes; "but I cannot promise success. I tell you now that Oscar Morley has not an atom of decency in his whole being, and that he is susceptible to no persuasion but that which is withdrawn from a bank vault."

For answer, the eminent specialist reached deep within the recesses of his coat and produced a thick brown leather purse, which he tossed across to my friend. "There are bank-notes there to the value of fifteen hundred pounds, which I withdrew this afternoon."

"It will not be enough."

"I shall also give you a blank cheque. Please keep it locked in your desk. When you have fixed a price with this vile man, fill in whatever amount is necessary, up to five thousand. My bankers are Drummond's, at Charing Cross. They will pay over the counter there without question." He took a cheque-book from his pocket, I passed him a pen, and he wrote out a cheque upon his knee.

"You had best give me a fuller description of the Harford Joyce Plate," said Holmes, as he took the cheque and placed it in his drawer. "I would not put it past Morley to attempt to swindle us in some way."

"I can do better than that," replied Dr Saunders, glancing at his watch. "At the time my brother-in-law had the Plate valued, an extremely good photograph was taken of it, showing its every detail in great clarity. This photograph hangs in the family home; if we go along there now, the chances are that my sister will be asleep and will thus not know that we have called. I sent a note to Milner earlier, to say that such a visit might be made, so we should be able to get in quietly enough."

"Excellent!" cried Holmes, springing from his chair. "You appear to have anticipated our every need!" He disappeared into his room, but was back again in a few seconds, his heaviest overcoat in his hand. "Are you up to a trip through the fog, Watson?" he called to me.

"Certainly," I replied, "if my presence would be of any value to you."

"Good old Watson!" said my friend with a dry chuckle. "Your presence is always of value, old fellow. Where does your sister reside, Dr. Saunders?"

"In the Campden Hill area. It should not take us more than half an hour."

The night was cold and dark, and the dense and swirling fog deadened all noise and hid all but the faint glimmer of the streetlamps from our view, so that, for all our senses could tell us, we might have been the last men in London. Indeed, so silent and deserted was the dismal, dripping world through which we passed that night, that were it not for the muffled clatter of the horse's hooves and the constant silvery jingle of the harness, one could have believed that the four walls of the cab marked the very bounds of existence itself. No word passed between us to dispel this gloomy monotony, and it seemed a long half-hour indeed before our cab finally halted. But at length the driver reined in his horse, and we stepped down into a broad road, lined with stark, leafless plane trees, which loomed up like sentinels out of the fog as we approached, only to vanish once again a moment later, as the fog wreathed its ghostly fingers about them. Beyond the trees lay the dark, solid masses of the large houses, dimly seen through chance rifts in the greasy brown curtain.

"This is Campden Hill Crescent," said James Saunders, clapping his gloved hands together vigorously. The words were scarcely out of his mouth, when there came the crack of a whip, the shrill whinny of a horse, and, with a sudden and startling rattle and crash, a carriage emerged at a rush from a gateway a few yards ahead of us. An iron-faced driver sat upon the box with his coat collar turned up; and as the carriage passed us with a clatter, I saw a frowning face within. For a second our eyes met, and I had the impression of a young and arrogant face, the thin line of a moustache above a curling, disdainful lip; a moment later and the carriage had vanished from sight into the dense and silent fog-bank.

"This is most annoying," remarked our guide with chagrin, as we stepped forward once more. "That was my nephew, Robert, and he evidently saw us. I had made arrangements with Milner for the side-door to be left unlocked for us, that we might enter in as unobtrusive a manner as possible, to lessen the chance of our presence becoming apparent to my sister; but as Robert may well mention to his mother that he has seen us, perhaps we had best appear like honest men and use the front door after all."

The butler, a tall, spare figure, whose bald head gleamed in the bright lights of the hall, directed us in silence to a large warm room at the rear of the house, and turned up the gas. The fragrant aroma of Turkish tobacco which hung in the air there told me that Robert Harford Joyce had only recently quit the room, and in the hearth I observed a number of dark cigarette-stubs. Upon the white cloth of a small table was a broad red stain, in the middle of which stood a bottle of wine and a half-emptied glass. Dr. Saunders stepped at once to a tall lacquered cabinet beside the fireplace and took from the top of it a large silver-framed photograph.

"The Harford Joyce Plate," said he, holding the picture for us beneath the light. It did indeed appear a splendid example of the silversmith's art, its surface embossed with gentle, graceful curves and lines, and set with a great number of gems, in its exquisite depiction of the mythical creatures of the Zodiac.

"Of course, the real thing is far more impressive," remarked our guide after a moment. "The stones were chosen for their purity of colour, and are extremely well matched. They say – "

The door opened abruptly, and we were joined by the butler. "Her Ladyship has heard you and would speak with you, Dr. Saunders," said he. The two of them left the room together, but scarcely a minute had passed before Milner returned to inform us that our presence, too, was required. We ascended the broad, thickly carpeted stairs, and followed him into a warm and stifling bedroom, where a frail, sickly looking woman was sitting up in bed, propped up on pillows. What little of her was visible, above the mound of blankets, was swathed in thick plaid shawls, and there was a woollen bonnet upon her head. Her brother was seated upon a chair beside the bed, but rose to his feet as we entered.

"Allow me to introduce you," said he. "Lady Harford Joyce, this is Dr. John Watson, a medical colleague of mine, and his friend, Mr. Sherlock Holmes. I was just telling my sister, gentlemen, of your interest in her collection of Ming vases. It is an excellent collection, is it not?" We nodded our heads and murmured our assent, and he continued, addressing Lady Harford Joyce. "I feared to disturb you, Winifred, and knew you would have no objection to my showing these gentlemen your collection."

We then exchanged a few pleasantries about pottery in general, the London museums and the weather, and it seemed that the interview was about to end, when Lady Harford Joyce spoke suddenly in a different, agitated tone.

"Why are you telling me these lies?" she demanded abruptly, addressing her brother with all the power of her faint, weak voice. He took a step backwards in surprise, and did not reply. "I have heard Mr. Holmes's name," she continued. "He is an enquiry agent or lawyer of some kind; he was involved in the settling of that unpleasantness at Delvoir Castle, the year before last. Furthermore, you have not so much as glanced at the Ming since you entered the house – your movements have been perfectly audible to me, and I am well aware that you have entered no room but the drawing-room."

There followed a long moment during which no one spoke. Dr. Saunders cleared his throat, and seemed about to reply, but then lapsed once more into silence. Evidently the story of the Ming vases had exhausted his powers of invention for the present. I shot a swift glance at Holmes, but it was evident from the expression upon his face that he was disinclined to take any active part in the deception being practised upon Lady Harford Joyce.

"Madam," said I, almost before I knew what I was doing; "permit me as a medical man to express my pleasure at the fact that both your sense of hearing and your memory for names remain unaffected by your bodily infirmity. You are perfectly correct in all your observations. Your brother naturally did not wish to alarm you, but the fact of the matter is this: there has been a spate of burglaries in the Notting Hill area recently, and he was concerned that these premises were not as secure against intruders as they perhaps ought to be, especially in view of the numerous objects of value which are kept here. I therefore recommended that he take the opinion of my friend, Mr. Holmes, who is an acknowledged expert in this field. Our intention was to make our survey of your doors and windows without your knowledge, in order to spare you anxiety upon the matter."

As I finished speaking, I realised that I had hardly taken a breath since I began, and I stood with heaving chest as Lady Harford Joyce replied. Fortunately, she addressed herself to James Saunders, and did not observe my discomfort, nor the flush which I felt burning upon my cheeks.

"Is this correct?" she asked her brother.

He nodded his head. "Theft is, indeed, the subject of our visit," he replied.

"How like you it is, to be concerned on my behalf," she remarked. "Dear James! I do not know what I ever should have done without you since Douglas's death!"

Five minutes later the three of us were descending the front steps of the house.

"You demonstrated a remarkable turn of speed in your thoughts, there, Watson," said Holmes, in an appreciative voice. "I must congratulate you; I thought for a moment we were undone. But you do not look very happy, old fellow!"

"I have never lied to a woman before."

"It is all in a good cause," remarked Dr. Saunders, but there was little enthusiasm in his voice.

"I only hope that that proves true," I replied.

"And I," remarked Holmes, "that what little reputation I now possess is not forever destroyed by the enterprise of some thoughtless and inconsiderate burglar!"

At breakfast the next morning, Holmes was uncommunicative. It was clear enough from his brisk manner that he had formulated some plan of approach to the money-lender, Oscar Morley, but what it might be, I could not guess. As he was donning his hat and coat, however, he turned and addressed me.

"How is your leg, today, old fellow?" he enquired. "Is it up to an hour's standing about on the pavement, would you say?"

"I imagine it could manage that," I returned with a smile, my egg-spoon poised half-way to my mouth. "Is there something you wish me to do?"

He nodded. "I shall give you the details later. I should be back at lunchtime. *Au revoir!*"

As it turned out, my friend returned well in advance of lunch, his features crestfallen.

"You have seen Morley," I remarked, looking up from my newspaper, "and he would not agree to your terms."

"Such an outcome would have been a relative success," replied Holmes sardonically. "He refused even to see me."

He tossed off his hat and coat, poured himself a glass of beer, and stood before the fire in silence for several minutes.

"I should derive a quite singular degree of pleasure," said he at length, "from completing this commission successfully. Do you know this man, Morley, Watson?"

"I have heard the name; that is all."

"He is a man who lives off the folly of youth – aye, and lives handsomely off it, too. Each year a fresh complement of young men reaches the age at which the attractions of gambling and general high-living seem irresistible, each year a fresh complement spends more than it should, and is forced to borrow to remain active in these wastrel activities. After a season or two of living in this way, the majority of these young men discover that there is more to life than spending money and rendering oneself insensible with alcohol, and they drift away into other pursuits, generally with little regret. But by this time a fresh complement has arrived to take their place. Thus, while the cast is constantly changing, the play runs continuously – and waiting in the wings each year to claim his share of the profits is one of the managers, our friend Oscar Morley. His presence is constant, his influence malign. Without his encouragement, his ready offers of money, the folly and the waste would be decidedly less, and the all-too-frequent tragedies of which one reads would very likely not occur at all."

Holmes drained off the glass of beer and banged it down upon the mantelpiece. "Do you know," he cried angrily, "there are men of forty who now live quietly and studiously in respectable homes up and down the country, whom one would take for the very models of propriety and sensible decorum – as indeed they now are – but who are yet paying off the debt which Morley encouraged them to run up in a few months of madness, twenty years ago. I am not a vindictive man, Watson, but I tell you that the satisfaction of knowing that I had discomfited Oscar Morley would last me a long time indeed!"

"You have a plan of some kind?"

"I have. It is risky and uncertain, but I see nothing better. This morning, when I called at his house in Hill Street, I was obliged to give a preliminary account of my purpose to his servant – a man who seemed every bit as odious as his master – and was then kept waiting for half an hour in the morning-room, until the reply came back from upstairs that it was not convenient for Mr. Morley to see me today."

"The nerve of the man!"

"Unfortunately, he holds the best cards at present, Watson, and there is little we can do about it. I made it perfectly clear to his man that I acted at the request of the family, and that I was prepared to pay a considerable sum for the return of the Plate, but the response was nil."

"I cannot understand why such a man should turn down the opportunity to make a fat profit so quickly and at so little trouble to himself," I remarked.

"It may be simply that he prefers to curry favour with the younger Harford Joyce, no doubt seeing that as likely to be the more profitable line of business in the long run; or it may be that he has other plans – which brings me to this afternoon: it is vitally important that a watch be kept upon Morley's house, and as I shall not myself be free to undertake the task, I should be most obliged if you would stand in for me."

I readily agreed to this request, for I welcomed any opportunity to escape for a while from the confines of our chambers. When I asked if there were anything in particular for which I should watch, Holmes nodded his head.

"A man, Watson, a specific visitor to friend Morley. What other callers he may have, I neither know nor care, but there is one man in London at present whose appearance upon the scene can only spell trouble, and I have good reason to believe that he may show himself this afternoon."

"Who, then?"

"His name, when last I heard, was Dmitri Theokritoff, but that may not be what he is calling himself at present; for it is not the name he was born with, and he is a man who has in the past shown a distinct aversion to retaining any one name for very long. He is an Armenian by birth, but lives everywhere and nowhere. He is an international dealer in works of art, curios, antiquities and so on, most of which find their way into his hands by means which would not pass muster at Sotheby's or

Christie's. Indeed, he is wanted for questioning by the authorities in at least three countries on the Continent, in connection with certain transactions in which he was involved last year. He has been lying low of late, but the Zodiac Plate is just such a prize as might tempt him to emerge into the open once more. If he does come, as I strongly suspect he will, it would be greatly to our advantage to have some knowledge of his whereabouts. But, come, let us take lunch now, and I can give you a description of the fellow as we eat."

At two-thirty that afternoon, I was standing beside a lamp-post near the corner of Hill Street and South Audley Street. The day had brightened up a little since the morning, but there was a damp heaviness in the air which made me hope that my vigil would not be a long one. From where I stood I was able to observe anyone who might call at Morley's house, which was on the opposite side of the road and about twenty yards to the east. In the first half-hour he had two callers, a fashionably dressed young man, and a tall woman dressed in black, her face concealed behind a veil. Neither of them stayed for very long. At ten past three I took a walk along the street in the direction of Berkeley Square, in order to give some exercise to my leg, which was beginning to throb painfully from the old wound I carried there. When I had gone perhaps a hundred yards, I chanced to glance back along the street, and it was fortunate that I did so, for there upon the step of Morley's house was the very man whose description Holmes had given me. Even at that distance there could be no mistaking the dark, oily complexion and the stoop to the shoulders. He was clad in a heavy overcoat, of an unusual shade of dark olive green, and upon his head was an uncommonly tall hat. I began to retrace my steps, but before I had gone ten yards the door had opened and he had passed inside, and out of my sight. I returned to my former position, reasoning that as he had evidently entered the street from the Park Lane end, he would very likely return that way, also, and, if so, I should be able to observe him more closely as he passed me.

For fully half an hour I waited, feeling the cold more keenly with each minute that passed. The throbbing in my leg had settled to a dull, persistent ache, and my mind had wandered far from the matter in hand, when Morley's front door opened suddenly and Theokritoff stood once more upon the step. He glanced swiftly up and down the street, then set off at a brisk pace towards Berkeley Square, tapping his cane upon the pavement as he went. I waited until there were thirty or forty yards between us, then set off after him. Holmes's instructions were that I should follow him as far as I could, in the hope of discovering his present abode. As I drew level with Morley's house, the door opened again, and a small, sharp-faced man emerged, clad in a top hat and a heavy black coat which reached almost to the ground. He, too, looked about him in a furtive manner, then abruptly bent down and began to adjust the laces of his boots. Ahead of me, my quarry had increased the distance between us, so I lengthened my own stride. Along Hill Street I followed him, across the angle of Berkeley Square, and up Berkeley Street to Piccadilly. At the corner he paused a moment, looked this way and that, and then turned to the east and set off once more at a brisk rate. When I reached the corner he was some distance ahead, but although the pavement was thronged with passengers, the unusual colour of his coat and his tall hat made it less difficult than it might otherwise have been for me to keep him in view.

We had gone some three hundred yards when Theokritoff abruptly stopped, and stared with great intensity across the street. I followed his gaze, but could see nothing there which might account for his sudden interest. A moment later, I was disconcerted to see that he was staring back the way he had come, and I feared for a moment that my pursuit had been discovered. As I looked again, however, it seemed, so far as I could determine, that his attention was not fixed upon me, nor upon anything in my immediate vicinity, but on something, or someone, much further back down the street. I did not turn, but put my head down and continued walking. When I looked up again, I was just in time to see him turning quickly into Sackville Street.

There seemed something more rapid and determined in his movements, and, fearing that he might give me the slip, I hurried forward to the corner. To my surprise I saw that he was already three-quarters of the way to the other end of the street. I quickened my stride, but had not succeeded in reducing the distance between us to any appreciable extent before he had reached the corner and turned left into Vigo Street. Cursing myself for my carelessness, I increased my pace still further. His route was certainly an odd one, I reflected as I hurried along: unless he altered his direction drastically, he might very well end up back in Hill Street.

I was quite breathless by the time I reached the corner. There, my worst fears were realised: there was no sign whatever of my quarry. He had evidently perceived that he was pursued and taken deliberate steps to escape. Fool that I was to have let him get so far ahead of me! I almost shouted aloud in my annoyance, as I hastened to the corner of Savile Row, and desperately scanned the pavements there, and along Burlington Gardens to the west. It was no use; Dmitri Theokritoff had demonstrated that guile which my little knowledge of his past career should have led me to expect. Once more he had sunk without trace in the very centre of this vast metropolis, once more we had no resource but to watch and wait patiently for him to reappear of his own volition.

But, no! I could not give up my commission so easily. I ran back along Vigo Street to see if there were any doorway or shop into which he might have slipped. Perhaps even now he was standing in the shadows, waiting for me to abandon my search; perhaps I had passed him without seeing him, and he had then slipped from his hiding-place and returned the way we had come, back down towards Piccadilly. At the corner of Vigo Street and Sackville Street I ran straight into a man who was hurrying in the opposite direction. I apologized, although the fault was as much his as mine, and, as I did so, I recognized him as the man who had been attending to his boot-laces outside Oscar Morley's house. My courtesy was wasted upon him, for he answered it only with a vile oath, as he pushed his way past me. Down towards the south end of Sackville Street, I descried a man with a tall hat, and with a sudden uprush of hope I hastened forward. But I had not gone ten yards before I saw that it was not the man I sought. Utterly dejected at my failure, I made my way down to Piccadilly and caught a cab home, wondering what Holmes would say when he learnt that I had found Theokritoff only to lose him again.

My colleague returned at half-past-five. He seemed in good spirits, and I hesitated to inform him of my own failure.

"My plans go as well as I could have hoped," said he in answer to my query. "You have been back some time, I see – the teapot is distinctly on the tepid side. I'll chance a cup, nevertheless, and you can tell me how you fared this afternoon."

"I have failed you, Holmes," said I.

"Oh? How is that?" said he in an unconcerned manner, as he stirred his tea.

"I watched Morley's house, as you directed, saw Theokritoff, and followed him half-way round the West End, but he gave me the slip, I am afraid to say, and I am no wiser now as to his whereabouts than I was this morning."

"Do not be concerned; you have done very well," said my friend, to my great surprise.

"I would rather you reserved your praise for those occasions upon which I have earned it," I remarked.

"But you most certainly *have* earned it," he returned with emphasis. "You identified your quarry and you followed him, which is all that I had asked you to do. You followed him well – along Hill Street, up Berkeley Street, along Piccadilly and into Sackville Street. No man could have done better, and some not so well."

"Holmes!" I cried. "This is amazing! How on earth? – Holmes, you were following me!"

"On the contrary," replied my friend in a languid and careless tone: "It is you who were following *me*"

I sprang from my chair in anger, as I perceived the meaning of his words.

"Holmes! Do you mean to tell me that Theokritoff was simply another of your wretched disguises?"

"But a reasonably effective one, would you not say?" he replied, a chuckle in his voice.

"This is unworthy of you, Holmes!" I protested. "What purpose you may have in deceiving Oscar Morley in this way, I do not know; but it seems a mean trick to play upon your oldest friend, I must say, to have him standing about in the cold all afternoon to no purpose whatever."

"My dear fellow!" cried he, a look of anxiety upon his face. "Pray calm yourself! Your presence this afternoon was absolutely vital, of that I can assure you. I should not even have considered subjecting you to this dank and dismal weather under any but the most compelling of circumstances."

"Forgive my obtuseness," I retorted, "but I fail to see what could possibly be vital about such a fool's errand as I have been sent upon! As for your assurance, I seem to remember your assuring me that it was vital we discovered Theokritoff's hiding-place, which, considering that he exists nowhere but in your own head, must rank as the most futile and pointless commission ever given by one man to another!"

"I can see that it must strike you in that light," said Holmes after a moment, in a quieter tone.

"We are agreed upon one thing, then, at least."

"I do apologize, Watson. I have been so absorbed in my own plans that it did not occur to me that what was clear to me would not be clear to you; but if you will permit me to describe to you how matters stand, I am sure that you will see the worth of it all."

I sat back down in my chair, crossed my legs and lit a cigar. "You have my full attention," said I.

"In the first place," said he, "Morley would not deal with me this morning. This was no more than I had expected, and merely confirmed my opinion that it was only upon the side of his bank account that he was accessible. Unfortunately, the funds at my disposal are limited, and incapable of taking the trick. My only chance, therefore, lay in pretending to greater wealth than I in fact possessed. Clearly I could not do this with any conviction as myself, and it was therefore necessary that I assume a fresh identity. Now, I happen to know that Dmitri Theokritoff – whose career was approximately as I sketched out for you at lunchtime – was stabbed to death in Marseilles, two years ago, and thus I could see no objection to my assuming for a short while his identity, which is precisely what the occasion required."

"Will Morley not be aware of his death?"

"Not unless he is a student of foreign criminal reports, which is so unlikely a possibility as to be beneath consideration."

"You intend, then, to offer him a large sum of money, in the hope that he will hand over the Plate," I suggested. "You will give him a worthless cheque, perhaps?"

"Hardly that, Watson. Friend Morley is no fool. He may be the most odious man in London, but he is also one of the smartest. As a matter of fact, I have offered him the crown jewels of one of the independent Arabian tribes."

"You have offered him *what!*" I cried incredulously.

"The prize must be a large one to tempt him. I have given him a dark account of how I acquired my treasure, and stressed that were it not that there are agents all over Europe actively pursuing it at this very moment, I should not even consider parting with it for less than twenty-five thousand. Under the circumstances, however – so I informed him – I am prepared to trade it for a certain object which I have reason to believe has recently come into his possession."

"What a preposterous story! Surely you invite disaster by such an overblown tale?"

"On the contrary, it is very often the biggest lies which enjoy the greatest success. Human nature is an odd thing, Watson, and does not always operate in the most perfectly logical manner. Morley showed considerable interest in my proposition, so it seemed to me, and intimated that he might not be averse to parting with the Zodiac Plate if the terms were right. However, it does not really matter whether he believed me or not, for it is my intention that he be informed tomorrow that the story of the crown jewels is, indeed, a complete tissue of lies."

My face must have betrayed the utter bewilderment I felt at Holmes's complex, and, as it seemed to me, nonsensical scheme, for he chuckled as his eyes met mine.

"All will become clear!" said he, with a broad smile upon his face.

He pulled a handful of tobacco from the old slipper in which he kept it to dry beside the fire, and stuffed it into his long-stemmed, cherrywood pipe.

"You see," he continued after a moment, "one must always think ahead. I have offered Mr. Morley something which I do not possess. What do you suppose would happen, then, were we to come to the point of exchanging our wares?"

I did not reply, and he continued:

"Precisely, Watson! You perceive the difficulty! It is necessary, then, for us to amend the course of events. I have interested him in the crown jewels; now I must interest him in something even better."

"I cannot think what could be better," I remarked; "nor, in that case, why you should have mentioned the jewels in the first place."

"You are an honest man, Watson, but Morley is not. He has a devious, scheming brain, and our plan must therefore be equally devious if it is to succeed. Of just one thing can we be certain: whether Morley believes the story of the crown jewels or not, he will suspect Theokritoff of duplicity."

"Why should he?"

"Chiefly because he is a dishonest man himself, and tends to regard everyone else in the same light. We must therefore turn this fact to our advantage. I have left with him – ostensibly as a token of my good intentions – a few quite worthless imitation diamonds which I picked up this morning at Silverstone's in Oxford Street – you know the sort of thing: 'a twenty-guinea stone for only one and fourpence.' He will also be aware that there was an agent following me in the street this afternoon. This was your role, Watson, to make my activities appear as suspect as possible."

"He may not have noticed me," I remarked.

"On the contrary, I made certain that he did. I stared at you from the window of his study; he naturally enough followed my gaze, and could not have failed to see you, standing alone beside the lamp post."

"But why, then, the later charade in the street? Morley could have seen nothing of that."

"No, but his agent certainly did. Did you observe an odd little fellow, wearing a coat a size too large for him?"

"We nearly knocked each other over at the corner of Vigo Street," I replied. "He left Morley's house just a few moments after you did."

"That was Leveritt, Morley's right-hand man; he was following me, too, as I had expected he would. Here your presence served a second purpose, for it made it necessary for this man – who would perceive that you were following me – to hang back somewhat further than he might otherwise have done. This made it significantly easier for me to effect my escape – which I achieved, incidentally, by simply jumping into the first empty cab I chanced to come across."

"But why, then, could you not inform me of your plans beforehand?" I protested. "Had I known what you had in mind, surely I could have played my part all the better?"

Holmes shook his head. "I am sorry to have had to play this trick upon you, my dear fellow, and I very nearly did tell you all, but I judged in the end that your actions would appear most convincing if you were performing them in earnest."

"Should you ever require such assistance again," I responded, somewhat tartly, "I should prefer that you made me privy to your plans. I cannot promise, however, that I shall understand them any more than I understand the present ones, which appear, so far as I can see, to achieve precisely nothing. What do you intend to do next?"

"An agent of mine will call upon Morley tomorrow. He will present himself as having been upon Theokritoff s trail for many months, and will inform Morley that a considerable reward is offered for that villain, who is wanted on numerous charges of theft and fraud, from Constantinople to Amsterdam. He will tell Morley that Theokritoff was seen entering his house yesterday, and will ask him if he was offered any 'Arabian crown jewels,' giving the impression that this is one of Theokritoff s most tried and trusted lines of chicanery. As Morley will already have his own suspicions and doubts, this speech will, I hope, have a convincing ring of truth about it. It is always shrewd to play to a man's own prejudices if you wish to impress him – indeed, most society conversation consists of little else."

"Who is your agent?"

"Tilham Fox, the actor. I helped him once, and he is quite agreeable to returning the favour. If Morley has not by tomorrow discovered for himself that the gems I left him are bogus, then Fox will apprise him of this fact, also, which will of course add one further turn of the screw to the establishment of his own *bona fides*. He will then tell Morley that the only impediment to Theokritoff's immediate apprehension is that he has so far committed no crime in England. If he could be caught in some criminal act, and charged by an English court, then the foreign authorities would be able to get their hands upon him, and they would at once pay up the reward. Morley is therefore to let him have whatever it is he is after – which is of course the Harford Joyce Plate – when next he calls, and to let him carry it to the door, as if believing his story of the crown jewels.

Immediately he is past the front door, he will be arrested and charged with the theft of the Plate."

"When is Theokritoff s next appointment with Morley?"

"On Monday, at ten o'clock. When I pay my call, you and Fox will be positioned in the street below – if, that is, you have forgiven me for this afternoon. Good fellow! I knew you would! Your presence, which Morley will be watching for, should reassure him that all is going as planned, and that Theokritoff will get no further than his front doorstep with the Plate. I shall hand over a few more of my bogus gems, and inform Morley that I wish to have the Plate examined by an acquaintance of mine who is an expert on such things. I shall then slip the Plate into a cardboard box which I have purchased specially for the purpose, seal up the box and descend with it to the front door. When you see me there, you will rush across and arrest me, after which Fox will return the box to Morley, who will sign a prepared statement, accusing me of attempting to swindle him. I shall then climb with my captors into a cab, and we shall depart, apparently for the nearest police station. After that, Morley will never again clap eyes on any of us as long as he lives."

"What in Heaven's name will be the point of all that?" I cried. "For Morley will still have the Plate!"

Holmes threw back his head and laughed aloud. "He will have a china plate," he replied at length. "For the one thing he will not know is that there are two cardboard boxes, identical in every respect, one of which will be snugly concealed inside my large green coat. As I descend his stairs – which are poorly illuminated, as I discovered today – I shall exchange the box in my hand with that inside my coat. It is of the utmost importance, you see, that Morley's suspicions are never for an instant directed at you or Fox, and if it seems to him that the Plate – or its container – has hardly left his sight for an instant, then that should be sufficient to allay his fears. Besides, if I know my man, he will be so pleased with himself for over-trumping

Theokritoff's deceit with his own that he will never suspect that there is yet a higher card remaining to be played."

"It seems a somewhat over-complex plot," I remarked after a moment.

"But it must be, Watson, if it is to succeed," replied my friend in an earnest tone. "Without the story of the crown jewels, I should stand very little chance of gaining entry to Morley's inner sanctum – for he is, as we already know, rather selective in the visitors he receives. Even then, it is unlikely that he could be persuaded to remove the Plate from his safe until I produced my own treasure. After Fox's story, however, which will seem to promise a financial gain quite free of the risk and criminality of Theokritoff's scheme, he should feel far less anxiety upon the point, especially as he will feel assured that the Plate will scarcely pass beyond his front door. This last point is crucial: without some such contrivance, the possibility of the Plate's passing beyond even his study doorway must be considered remote. He is a man who keeps arms about the house, and who is quite prepared to use them. But, come! This game is in the future. Let us banish for a while the complexities and deceits of this mundane sphere, and turn our thoughts to the pure sweetness of a higher existence!"

He took his violin from its case and adjusted the strings. "It is a little thing by de Beriot," he murmured, as he began to play a perfectly exquisite and melancholy air. I had closed my eyes and allowed the music to surround me in the soft, dream-like folds of its beauty, when I was abruptly roused from peace by the voice of the maid. Holmes stopped playing, and put down his bow with a sigh.

"This was pushed through the letter-box for you, sir," said the girl, handing him a cream-coloured envelope. He took it from her, tore it open and scanned the contents. As his eyes reached the foot of the page they returned once more to the top, and he read it through a second time, a look of amazement upon his face. With a whistle of disbelief, he tossed the sheet over to me and threw himself back in his chair, his eyes upon the ceiling, his brow creased with thought. It was a plain cream sheet, with neither monogram nor address. The message, in black ink, was terse and to the point:

"MR. HOLMES," I read. "Further to our meeting today, I have decided after all to agree to the terms you offer on behalf of the Harford Joyce trustees. If you will bring the amount outstanding (one thousand and five hundred pounds) we can conclude the business this evening. Please be at the lamppost by the south-western corner of Primrose Hill, at eight o'clock sharp, where my agent will meet you. I shall bring the Plate. O. M."

"You observed when it was written, no doubt?" said Holmes, as I finished reading.

I glanced again at the top of the sheet.

"It is dated the twenty-third, at six-thirty p.m.," I replied. "Half an hour ago!"

"Precisely. Now, what on earth can it mean, Watson? What has wrought this sudden change in friend Morley's disposition? Why should he be now so desirous of obliging those he earlier treated with such disdain?"

"He refers to your meeting," I remarked, "but I understood you to say that he did not deign to see you."

"That is so; it is a curious slip, but perhaps it signifies nothing. He may simply be referring to the conversation I had with his servant."

"Perhaps Morley himself was eavesdropping upon that conversation in some way," I suggested.

"That is possible. There is something else which is odd about this message: he is claiming no interest upon the money he advanced to young Harford Joyce. For a man of Morley's persuasions, that is certainly the most unlikely omission he could possibly make. What can have happened, to shake his customary composure to this degree? Why is his summons so abrupt, and the rendezvous he suggests so singular? He has not used headed note-paper, he has not signed his name, and he has arranged to meet us neither at our house nor his own."

"It is almost as if he wishes to be able to deny in the future that the meeting ever took place at all," I suggested. Holmes nodded his head slowly. "Do you suppose," I added, "that it can have anything to do with your visit as Theokritoff?"

Holmes shook his head in silence, an expression of puzzlement upon his face. "I can suggest nothing," he said at length, "to account for this latest development. I do not believe that I have ever been so surprised at anything in my life." He glanced at the clock, and sprang from his chair. "Come, Watson; let us fortify ourselves with a little bread and cheese; the hour of our assignation draws near."

At half past seven we donned our coats. Holmes took his pistol from his desk and carefully loaded the chambers, glancing at me as he did so.

"I sincerely advise you to do the same," said he, in answer to my querying look. "There is no telling what adventures may await us in the darkness of the night. Many a man has answered a summons to a secret appointment and been heard of never again."

A few minutes later we left the warmth of our chambers, and stepped into a raw and foggy night. An empty hansom was trundling past, and I stepped forward to stop it, but Sherlock Holmes put his hand upon my arm and drew me back.

"One cannot be too careful," said he in a tense whisper. "We are responding to Mr. Morley's summons quite upon his terms, both as to time and as to place. Let us at least be sure that our carriage is of our own choosing."

Up Baker Street we walked, our footsteps sounding dully upon the pavement, and as we did so the greasy, swirling mist seemed to thicken around us and enclose us in its dark and unhealthy reek. A second empty cab passed us with a clatter of hooves and a jingle of harness, its lamps a momentary glimmer in the darkness, but Holmes ignored it. At the Metropolitan Station he selected a hansom which had just deposited a fare, and we were soon rattling up Park Road towards St. John's Wood, and, from there, along the north side of Regent's Park, beside the canal. Presently the driver reined in his horse, and we stepped down into the silent sea of mist. Holmes passed the driver a half-sovereign with the instruction that he should follow us at a distance of twenty-five yards wherever we should go, and come at once upon our whistle.

It wanted two minutes to eight o'clock when, as we stamped our feet and clapped our hands together in the freezing air, a dark figure stepped forward from the bank of mist which hid the other side of the road from our view. As he approached us, I saw that he was dressed in the livery of a coachman, a large cloak about his shoulders with the collar turned up high, and a top hat upon his head.

"Mr. Holmes?" said he, his voice harsh and sudden in the enveloping silence.

My friend nodded. "This is my colleague, Dr. Watson," said he, "who has an interest in this matter."

"That is all right," said the other shortly. "Please follow me." With that he turned upon his heel briskly and began almost at once to disappear into the fog. Holmes gave a last instruction to our cabbie and we set off after the muffled footsteps ahead of us.

"There is something decidedly odd afoot here," said my friend in a low voice, as we hurried after the dark retreating figure. "Be upon your guard at all times, Watson!"

My fingers closed around the pistol in my pocket, and I was glad to feel its reassuring shape and solidity. A loaded revolver was a good friend to have on one's side in doubtful and threatening circumstances.

Presently our guide turned in through a gateway by the zoo, we crossed the canal on a narrow footbridge, and found ourselves upon the Outer Circle of the Park. Still he did not pause, but pressed on through the blanket of darkness, around the long curve towards Gloucester Terrace.

"He has cut us off from our cab," said Holmes in a sibilant whisper. Even as he spoke, the figure ahead of us stopped abruptly and turned to face us, his arm upraised.

"We are almost there," said he in a gloomy and sepulchral voice. "Have you the money? Very good. If you will give it to me, I will fetch you that which you have come for."

"I am to deal only with principals," returned Holmes, making no move to withdraw the money from within his coat.

For a moment we all three stood in silence, then, with a shrug of his shoulders, our guide turned on his heel once more. Motioning us to follow him, he resumed his brisk pace. We had gone but a little further, however, when a sudden slight gust dissipated the fog and revealed to us the twin spires of St Katherine's upon our left hand, and, ahead of us, a four-wheeled carriage, the feeble glimmer of its lamps encircled by haloes of mist. The side-window of the carriage was lowered, but no lamp was lit within, and a heavy curtain veiled the interior from our view.

"They have brought the money," said our guide into the darkness.

In answer a gloved hand emerged from behind the curtain.

"The Plate," said Holmes, without moving.

The hand withdrew without a sound, and re-appeared after a moment bearing a large oblong object, which gleamed dully in the faltering light of the carriage-lamp. That it was heavy was evident, for it slipped a little in the fingers which held it. The dark man who stood beside us quickly took the weight and passed it over to us. Holmes examined it carefully, his eyes running rapidly over the details of its design; but there could be little chance of mistaking so unusual an object. At length, evidently satisfied that it conformed to the photograph he had seen, he glanced at me and raised his eyebrows questioningly. I nodded my head, and he reached deep within his coat and drew out Dr. Saunders's leather satchel. The coachman took it from him, and spoke once more to the silent figure within the carriage.

"Do you wish me to count it?" said he.

The disembodied hand waved from side to side in a dismissive gesture, and as it did so the sleeve fell back an inch or two, revealing a bare wrist which was so excessively thin and fleshless that I almost cried aloud in surprise. The skin was wrinkled and blotched, and seemed to hang loose upon the bones. It was only for a moment that I saw it, for as soon as the coachman had handed over the leather bag the hand vanished from sight once more behind the curtain; but so startling was the sight that I was as sure of what I had seen as I had ever been sure of anything in my life. As the coachman leapt aboard his seat and lashed the horse into a gallop, I looked across at my friend. It was plain from the expression upon his face that he was as surprised and perplexed as I was.

In a moment the carriage had disappeared into the darkness, south towards Park Square, and seconds later the clatter and rattle which indicated its direction had ceased to be audible, and we stood alone in the thick fog. Holmes put his hand upon my arm; "Come," said he; and we began to retrace our steps.

"Do you understand the purpose of this strange manner of meeting?" I asked, after we had gone a little way.

"Not I," said he. "It appears quite pointless, so far as I can see. "You recognised the coachman, I take it?"

"I don't believe I have ever seen him before," I replied in surprise.

"It is the Harford Joyce groom. He was just leaving with young Harford Joyce last night, as we arrived at Campden Hill Crescent."

"The Harford Joyce groom?" I repeated incredulously. "Surely you are mistaken?"

"There could be no mistaking the fellow."

"What on earth can it mean, then?" I cried. "Is the man in Morley's pay, or what?"

"There would be little point to such deceit," replied Holmes, shaking his head; "Morley needs no spies in the house to persuade young Harford Joyce to sink further into his debt. Besides, it was not Morley with whom we were dealing tonight."

He was about to say more, when a bulky figure materialized abruptly out of the gloom ahead of us. For a moment I tensed, and put my hand to the pocket which held my revolver, but when he spoke I recognized the voice of our own cabbie.

"There you are!" said he in evident relief. "I was wondering where you two gentlemen had got to. The cab is this way."

"Good man!" cried Holmes, clapping the cabbie upon the shoulder. "I feared that this fog would part us for ever! Back to Baker Street, then, and a hot toddy all round!"

As our cab was crossing the Marylebone Road, however, Holmes abruptly flung up the trap and directed the driver to take us to Campden Hill. Then he settled once more into the deep and frowning silence in which he had passed the journey back from Primrose Hill.

What was passing in his mind then, I could not begin to guess. To me, the events of the evening were incomprehensible. I had supposed that the meeting would shed some light upon Morley's sudden and surprising change of heart in accepting our money in settlement of young Harford Joyce's debts; in the event, however, our strange, fog-shrouded meeting by St. Katherine's had explained nothing, but had instead added further mysteries of its own. Why had the carriage been driven by the Harford Joyce coachman, and who was its unseen occupant?

"What can you hope to learn at Campden Hill?" I asked my friend, as our cab rattled along Sussex Gardens. "Do you intend to interview the groom?"

Holmes shook his head. "The coachman was simply carrying out his orders. I think it unlikely that he could tell us anything of interest. The one I wish to speak to is the one who gave him his orders, took our money, and handed over the Plate: the one with the weak, thin wrist, which startled you so much, Watson."

"You have some notion, then, who it was?"

"It was Lady Harford Joyce," said he simply.

"But that is absurd, Holmes! In the first place, she is not only ill, but virtually bed-ridden; in the second place, she was not even in possession of the Plate, which was in the hands of that odious fellow, Morley – a fact of which she was totally unaware; and in the third place, if, by some miracle, Lady Harford Joyce *had* regained possession of the Plate – the family's most prized heirloom, and the possession which we are told she values above all others – what conceivable reason could she have for handing it over to you for a mere fifteen hundred pounds? The idea is utterly fantastic!"

Holmes had nodded his head in silence as I spoke, and when he replied it was in a tone of some perplexity.

"You state the case fairly and accurately," he remarked, his chin resting heavily upon his hand; "and yet it *was* Lady Harford Joyce – the markings upon her wrist, which I had observed yesterday evening at Campden Hill, were quite unmistakable. Indeed, your own reaction upon seeing her wrist in the Park this evening led me to suppose that you, too, had recognised it." With a deep sigh he leaned back in his seat, and lapsed once more into silence. When he at length spoke again, it was in an altogether different, almost careless tone of voice.

"But perhaps we should simply make an end of the matter, and return to Baker Street, Watson. We have, after all, recovered the Plate, which is all that we were required to do – and that without recourse to the good Dr. Saunders's blank cheque, for which he will no doubt thank us effusively. All in all, it seems to me a job well done: what concern is it of ours to know how many strange and varied hands the Plate has passed through before coming into our own safe-keeping? It is scarcely knowledge which will add appreciably to the sum of human happiness – and certainly not to that of our client. *'Cui bono?'*, eh, Watson?"

For a moment I was quite dumbfounded. Never before had I known Sherlock Holmes elect to close a case which held still an unresolved riddle at its centre. Had one of the famous Nile explorers declared his total lack of interest in the whereabouts of that river's sources, it could scarcely have been more astounding to me.

"Holmes!" I cried at length. "You amaze me! You have the Plate, it is true, and so, to that extent, your commission is complete; but surely your mind cannot rest at ease in the midst of such puzzlement, while ever you possess the power to end it? If you tell me that it can, then I must confess that every conclusion I have reached regarding your character has been wrong. Surely there are some further enquiries you can make to throw some light upon this mystery?"

"It will not help Dr. Saunders," replied my friend laconically, with a shrug of the shoulders.

"But, Holmes! Consider, then, your own professional records! An unfinished case can be nothing but a blemish upon them!"

"Admit it, Watson," rejoined Holmes in a soft voice, a sly smile spreading across his features; "it is as much for your own mental satisfaction as for mine that you require this mystery to be uncovered. If you deny it, I shall not believe you."

"Very well, then," said I somewhat heatedly, for I was nettled by his tone of superiority. "I admit I would wish to get to the bottom of this riddle, if it were at all possible."

"Even if it benefited our client not one whit?"

I nodded my head.

"And if our investigation were therefore merely to satisfy your own curiosity?"

"I fail to see what you are driving at, but, if you insist on putting it in that way, then, yes, I admit it."

"Aha! I take it you therefore concede the point to me that man has an unslakable thirst for knowledge, irrespective of whether it will be of any use to him? It was, if you recall, a point upon which we differed in our discussion the other evening."

I saw then that his whole careless manner had been assumed simply for the purpose of forcing me to yield this abstract point to him. In any other man such a pretence would have irritated me beyond words, but I had become so inured to

Holmes's odd character over the years of our friendship that I simply shook my head and sighed.

"You never had any intention, then, of dropping the case?"

"Certainly not," said he in a more vigorous tone. "Besides, one can always find some justification or other for one's innate curiosity. It could be argued with some plausibility, for instance, that unless we understand the meaning of this night's events, we cannot in all honesty return the Plate to Dr. Saunders with the assurance that his troubles are now at an end."

"Indeed, that argument has perhaps a greater validity than you allow," I remarked after a moment's thought. "For, on reflection, it strikes me that we have a genuine duty not simply to recover the Plate, but also to apprise your client of any other danger with which it may be threatened; and unless we understand all that has taken place, we cannot swear that no such danger exists. To take your own metaphor, Holmes: the poison which entered the life of Dr. Saunders with such strange and unforeseeable consequences has not yet been extirpated. The consultant cannot yet claim his fee."

"Well said, my dear fellow!" cried Holmes merrily. "You would make a fine advocate, Watson. The issue is settled, then, and we confront Lady Harford Joyce tonight."

We left the cab at the foot of Campden Hill Crescent with the instruction that he should await our return, and walked slowly up the hill in the oily murk.

"There is one thing that troubles me still," I confessed. "You say you recognized the coachman, you say you recognized the mottled wrist; but if by any chance you are wrong, and Lady Harford Joyce is not involved in the matter in any way, then our visit will set at nought the whole purpose of our original mission, which was to keep her in ignorance of her son's shameful conduct."

"Perhaps a third piece of evidence, pointing in precisely the same direction as the other two, will convince you, then," replied Holmes, a trace of irritability in his voice. "I took the opportunity outside St. Katherine's of remarking any distinctive feature of the carriage that I could later use to identify it. Upon the panel to the right of the door there was a deep scratch, with a smaller scratch crossing it at right angles, close to one end, forming the shape of an elongated letter 't'. If that scratch is present on the Harford Joyce carriage, even you can scarcely argue against our proceeding, Watson!"

In silence we entered the gateway and made our way along the side of the house and to the stables, which lay in darkness, some distance to the rear. The door was not locked, and we slipped inside quietly. Holmes struck a match. In a stall at one end stood a glossy black horse, which shifted its feet uneasily and whinnied slightly at the sudden light. Holmes put his hand upon the animal's neck.

"He, at least, has had a busy evening," said my friend, wiping the moisture from his hand. "So far, so good." He struck another match and bent to the panelling on the side of the coach. In a moment he was pointing in triumph to a ragged scratch which ran for a foot or more across the centre of the panel. It formed the clear shape of a recumbent letter 't'.

The front door was opened to us by the butler, Milner. It was evident from the look of surprise upon his face that he recognized us at once, and equally evident that we were the very last two he had expected to find upon the doorstep that evening. Clearly nonplussed, he hesitated, then informed us flatly that his mistress had retired for the night after a particularly tiring day, and could not possibly be disturbed. We had come too far, however, to be turned away at the last, and Holmes, after a moment's thought, wrote a brief note upon the back of a visiting-card and instructed the butler to convey it to his mistress at once or bear full responsibility for whatever might otherwise occur. Still the man hesitated, and seemed inclined to refuse us, when a sudden and unexpected intervention resolved the situation in a moment. A door upon the right of the hall opened abruptly, and there, framed in the bright oblong of light, stood Lady Harford Joyce, supporting herself unsteadily on a pair of walking-sticks.

"Show the gentlemen in, Milner," said she, in a feeble, cracked voice. She turned round with some difficulty and we followed her into what I judged, from the crowded bookshelves around the walls, to have been Sir Douglas's library.

"Mr. Holmes, Dr. Watson," said she in a weak voice, when the three of us were seated at a large mahogany table in the centre of the room. "I trust it is something of importance which necessitates your disturbing me at this hour." She looked at us with an expression of great weariness in her eyes, and it seemed to me that she had a yet greater air of old age and infirmity about her than upon the previous evening. Involuntarily, my eye went to her wrist, thin and fleshless, and wrinkled with age.

"It concerns the Harford Joyce Plate," returned Holmes in a quiet voice. The old lady's eyes narrowed perceptibly, but she did not reply. "Someone gave it to me in the street earlier this evening," Holmes continued. He unbuttoned his coat and drew forth the object in question. Her hands started up from where they rested upon the table edge and her eyes opened wide with astonishment, as she stammered out a series of half-formed and scarcely intelligible questions, in a voice which trembled with fear and agitation.

"Come, come, Lady Harford Joyce," said Holmes at length, holding up his hand in protest at this uncontrolled outburst. "You and I both know that it was you that put the Plate in my hands, not an hour ago. Why you should take this strange action with an object you revere so greatly?"

He broke off as she waved her hand feebly. The colour had drained from her face as he spoke, and a dry, choking noise came from her throat. I stood up quickly, to render what assistance I could, but she waved me back to my seat with a gesture of impatience. Several minutes passed in silence as she sought to recover herself, and I feared that she would be too weak to speak further that evening. But she rallied remarkably, and when she spoke there was a note both of strength and decision in her voice.

"Gentlemen," said she firmly; "what you say is nonsense. You tell me that I revere that object; I tell you that I revile it. To me it is that most hateful of things—a permanent reminder of the one black cloud which cast its shadow upon my life. You speak to me of the Harford Joyce Plate as if you know something of it, but I, who know far more than you, readily confess that I have no knowledge of where on God's earth it might be."

I glanced across at my friend. The expression upon his face must have mirrored my own, for it was one of astonishment and stupefaction.

"Do not fear that I am raving," continued Lady Harford Joyce quickly, as if reading only too well the thoughts which were passing through my mind. She nodded her head towards the heavy silver object which Holmes still held in his hands: "That is not the Harford Joyce Plate."

Now it was our turn to protest our disbelief and plead our lack of comprehension; but she cut us short.

"It is a simple enough tale to tell," said she, in a tone of bitter resignation. "You are correct in one thing at least, Mr. Holmes: it was I that handed you that plate this evening. I should have known from your reputation that my own attempt at trickery was unlikely to succeed. However, you will understand why I was driven to such lengths when you hear the miserable history of the object you hold in your hand. I trust you on your honour as gentlemen to repeat nothing of what I tell you.

"The Harford Joyce Plate came into the family in the last century, when one of my late husband's ancestors performed some trifling service for an over-grateful Russian Empress, at the time of the Pugachoff Rebellion. The family has always been as intensely proud of its heirloom as of its own name, and my husband was no different from his kin in this respect.

"About a dozen years ago, my husband happened, in the course of his diplomatic career, to spend several years in the eastern lands of Europe. There, he became involved in certain matters which, let us say, fell somewhat short of his family's code of honour, and was led to commit certain indiscretions which he later came to regret most bitterly. Although I am not prepared to enter into the details of these matters, which cannot possibly be of interest to you, I can – and will – assure you that my husband's indiscretions involved neither loss of life nor injury to anyone, no threat to his nation's security or well-being, and absolutely no financial gain to himself.

"The matter passed into history, my husband retired, and we returned to England, to live in this house. He thought then that his past was dead and buried, and could not harm him, especially since certain documents and records had been lost in a fire. But some years later, in the autumn of '81, a certain man – no, a vile, unspeakable reptile! – paid him a visit and made it clear that he was in possession of documents, which, were they to be published, would bring back to life this ancient scandal, and would incriminate my husband quite unequivocally. He also made it clear that unless my husband were to do precisely as he requested, he would proceed with their publication forthwith."

Lady Harford Joyce paused, as a dry cough shook her body. I rose and poured her a tumbler of water from a carafe which stood upon a sideboard. Her voice had begun to tremble again as she was speaking, but when she continued, after taking a sip of the water, the firmness and strength were back once more.

"What was he to do?" said she, looking from Holmes to me, and back again, as if imploring our understanding. "It was not for himself he feared, but his family – or families, rather, for he had not only his own to consider, but also the one into which he had married. If you had known my husband, gentlemen, then you would know that what I say is the truth."

"The price of the blackmailer's silence was the Zodiac Plate?" interrupted Holmes, with a quizzical raise of the eyebrow.

Lady Harford Joyce nodded her head. "He would take nothing else. No amount of money could dissuade him from his wicked desire. At length, Douglas agreed to his terms, but on condition that the transaction be delayed a short while, in order that he might commission a craftsman to make a copy of the Plate. In this way he hoped to conceal its loss from the world. The copy was duly made, in conditions of the utmost secrecy, and the original handed over to this vile man in exchange for the documents he possessed. It is the copy you now hold in your hand, and a poor shadow of the genuine Plate it is, too. It was cast at a foundry in Birmingham, in a mould taken from the original, and afterwards plated. As a result of this process, much of the clarity and definition of the original design was inevitably lost, and the lustre of the duplicate is, of course, quite inferior. The gems, too, are the very cheapest of stones, and do not possess one tenth the fire of those in the true plate."

I saw Holmes look with surprise at the Plate, and shake his head, as Lady Harford Joyce raised the glass to her lips once more before she continued.

"From that day to this," she said at last, "no one has known of this deception save only my husband, our old butler and myself. I have endeavoured to keep that object locked away, out of sight of the public gaze. When you came here with James last night, I could tell by his manner that he was not speaking the truth to me. In my eyes he is still the small boy he was forty years ago, and he can never hope to deceive me. When you had gone it took me only a few minutes to learn the truth from the servants, and I at once saw the great danger into which Robert's foolish action had thrust us – a danger which none but myself could fully appreciate. For if this man Morley were to show the Plate to anyone who knew about such things, or attempt to have it valued, then my husband's secret disgrace would inevitably become public knowledge. It was imperative that the Plate be recovered at once, to save the family name. How that could be accomplished, I could not at first see, but decided in the end that there was no other recourse but to tell Robert the whole story, and make him realise the urgency of the situation. In making this decision, I consoled myself with the thought that he must, at any event, know his father's secret one day.

"To my great pleasure he reacted to the news as I had hoped he would, and was riven with horror at the thought of what he had done. This afternoon I supplied him with sufficient funds to cover his debt, and he called on the moneylender to reclaim the Plate. Apparently, Morley was none too keen to part with it. It seems he had some profitable plan afoot, in which he attempted to interest Robert, involving someone's crown jewels. To cut a long story short, the interview ended with Robert's punching him on the nose. I suppose that that puts an end to all further financial transactions between them, but I cannot say that that is a prospect I view with any great regret. I am glad to see that you are amused, Mr. Holmes."

"Would you tell me," said Holmes, his whole body shaking with silent laughter, "why it was that you felt it necessary to put on that strange performance in Regent's Park this evening?"

"I did not wish my brother to learn anything of my own involvement in the Plate's recovery, and perhaps suspect my motive. He had always had a most high regard and respect for Douglas, and I could not bear my husband's memory to be tarnished in his eyes. I decided, therefore, to let the Plate be returned to the house through his efforts, as he had planned, and when Robert told me of Morley's mentioning your visit to him this morning, it seemed the best idea to send you a note pretending that Morley had changed his mind. I thought it unlikely that you would ever learn the truth. What do you intend to tell James when you see him again?"

Holmes sat a while in silent thought. "I shall tell your brother," said he at last, "that after some initial difficulty, Morley evidently saw the pointlessness of his obduracy, and agreed to our terms."

"That is all?"

"That is all. You need not fear for the safety of your secret, Lady Harford Joyce. It is yours to keep or to reveal as you will."

We had stood up and were preparing to take our leave, when my friend paused.

"One final thing," said he: "I wonder if you would satisfy my curiosity on one point, Lady Harford Joyce: the name of the man who blackmailed your husband, the man with the documents—"

"I cannot bring myself to speak it, Mr. Holmes," replied the other firmly. "It would be an affront to my ears."

Holmes took a card from his pocket and scribbled a word upon it.

"Was it by any chance this man?" said he, handing the card to Lady Harford Joyce.

She glanced at the card for but a moment before crushing it in her hand; then she stared hard at my friend, an expression of amazement upon her face.

"Can it be true, then, what they say of you," said she, incredulously, "that there is nothing you do not know?"

"Not at all," replied Holmes, with a smile and a shake of the head. "But in this field I am a specialist, and make it my business to know all there is to know of those whose prosperity is wrung from the misfortune of others. On silver plate, however, my knowledge is somewhat less profound!"

THE WATCHER IN THE WOODS

DURING THE YEARS I shared chambers with Mr. Sherlock Holmes before my marriage, I was able to experience at first hand the immense variety of cases upon which he was consulted; most of which he succeeded in bringing to a successful conclusion. Among these cases were a great number that were odd or unusual, and not a few that were so strange as to seem at first unfathomable. Among these latter cases I would include that which concerned the singular experiences of Mr. Cuthbert Lidington in the Isle of Apstone and the surprising sequel, and it is this case I now propose to recount.

It was a chilly, foggy morning towards the end of October. The preceding weeks had been moderately sunny, but there had been little warmth in the sunshine, and with each day that passed, the air had seemed to become a degree colder.

Sherlock Holmes had been working his way through the morning papers for some time, alternately groaning and sighing at what he read there.

"It sometimes seems to me," said he at length, tossing aside the last of the papers, "that the daily press has come into existence merely to record all that is banal, ignorant and stupid in our modern world."

"You can scarcely expect profound philosophical reflections on life to appear every day in the morning papers," I remarked without looking up from my own reading.

"Perhaps not, but there must surely be something more intellectually stimulating for them to report than that one group of men kicked a leather ball more efficiently up a muddy field than another group of men, or that the Duchess of Deptford wore a striped hat to the theatre last night!"

I laughed. "Perhaps you will be presented with an interesting case soon," I said, "and then you can bid *au revoir* for a time to the commonplaces of existence."

"I hope so," said he. "I am in need of a case, Watson. I feel like a man who has become accustomed to having a tumbler of rum every morning with his breakfast. The bottle has been empty now for some time, and the absence of my stimulant is making me irritable!"

"So I had noticed," I remarked. As I spoke there came a sharp peal at the front doorbell. "Here is someone," I said. "Perhaps it is a caller for you."

"Yes," returned my friend in a pessimistic tone; "no doubt someone wishing to sell me half a dozen 'lucky' clothes-pegs, or someone come to inform me that if I contribute a shilling to whatever worthy cause he represents I can have my name engraved on a brick!"

A moment later, a slight, nervous-looking young man was shown into our sitting-room, and announced as Cuthbert Lidington.

"Good morning," said Holmes, waving the visitor to a chair. "What can we do for you?"

"I understand you are accomplished at unravelling life's mysteries," the young man began in a hesitant tone.

"I have had some experience of it, at least," returned Holmes. "Do you have a mystery for us?"

Lidington nodded. "If I can't get to the bottom of it, I feel I shall go mad. That may sound a somewhat dramatic, exaggerated thing to say," he added quickly, "but that is the state I have been driven to."

"Pray, give us the details."

"First of all, you should know that I am not one given to fancies or whimsical notions. I studied scientific subjects for some years at London University. I then held a senior position with the South Eastern Railway at Ashford, in Kent. However, my own private reading was leading me in a very different direction. My study of early scientific works had introduced me to the subject of alchemy, in which I developed a very great interest."

"Alchemy?" I cried in surprise. "Is that not the mediaeval pseudo-science that claimed that with the right formula base metals could be turned into gold, and, with some other formula, men could be made immortal?"

Lidington shook his head. "I would not dispute that you enunciate the popular view of the subject accurately," said he, "but there is much more to alchemy than that. It is an all-embracing doctrine of a mystical, spiritual kind. Anyway, to continue: I had been looking for some new lodgings for a while, as the place at which I was staying in Ashford was very cramped, and some of the other people staying there were not to my taste. Then, one day when I was in the house-agent's office, I saw that a house in the village of Apstone was available to rent. When I saw the name of the house, I could hardly believe it!"

"Why was that?" asked Holmes.

"Well, you see, it was Naxon House, and I recognized the name as being that of the residence for many years of Serenus Charling, one of the leading writers on alchemy of the last hundred years. I felt that fate must have placed this opportunity in my hands, to live and work in the very house that had been occupied for so many years by one of the writers I admired the most. Within twenty-four hours, I had taken a two-year lease on the house, and within a week I had handed in my notice to the South Eastern Railway, so that I could devote myself entirely to my alchemical studies. That was just under two years ago.

"The village of Apstone is a very small place, little more than a hamlet, really. It stands on a slight eminence, known as the Isle of Apstone, which overlooks the flat expanse of the Romney Marsh to the east, from which dense, cold mists frequently roll in, shrouding everything in a grey veil. To the west, the countryside is quite different, being hilly and thickly wooded. The village is always very quiet, and becomes even quieter when the mist sits upon it, but that suits my requirements exactly. It used to be a little more important than it is now, and had its own church, but that collapsed during a great storm in the middle of the last century and was never rebuilt. Local legend has it that the church tower was struck by a bolt of lightning and that the rector – who was in the church at the time, and who was killed when it collapsed – was some kind of sinner or heretic, and that it was his misdemeanours that brought this retribution upon his church. The story of the lightning strike may be true, but I think the collapse of the church was almost certainly the result of subsidence, caused by the terrible floods in the area at the time, when the marsh became so completely flooded that the water overflowed onto the surrounding land, washing much of it away. I am telling you these things so you will appreciate what a very quiet place it is in which I live, but one with its own curious history. It is largely untouched by the modern world, but not entirely cut off. It is, for instance, only a ten-minute walk to the larger village of Ham Street, where there are shops and the local railway station.

"To come now to recent events," Lidington continued after a moment: "I receive little correspondence at Naxon House, but two weeks ago I received this puzzling letter." He drew a small envelope from his inside pocket, which he passed to us. I saw that it was addressed to "The Occupier, Naxon House, Apstone." The postmark was that of Ashford, which indicated that the letter had been posted locally. Holmes took out the letter from within, and held it so I could see it. There was no address at the head of the sheet, nor any salutation, and the brief message ran as follows:

Will come soon, as arranged.
"Those who have done no wrong have nothing to fear."
C.

"The date is a very singular one," said Holmes.

I had not noticed the date at the top of the letter. Now I looked again and saw that it read "April 25th 1869".

"How very strange," I said. "What on earth can that mean?"

Holmes shook his head in puzzlement. "According to the postmark, the letter was posted on October 13th," he said.

"That would be right," said Lidington. "I received it on the fourteenth."

"Does the letter mean anything to you?" asked Holmes.

"Nothing whatever. I have not arranged anything with anybody, and know no one with the initial 'C'."

"Very well. Pray continue."

"I leave the house very little – the local carter who calls twice a week supplies most of my needs – but except when it is raining heavily, I go for a walk every morning at ten o'clock, to take a little exercise and think about what I will be studying later. I generally go the same way every day. I was out one morning, about two weeks ago, and was passing along the edge of a large field. All along the other side of that particular field is a dark and dense wood. As I passed along, I chanced to glance across the field, and was surprised to see a man standing there, at the edge of the wood, apparently watching me."

"Was it anyone you knew?" asked Holmes.

Lidington shook his head. "I don't think so. He appeared to be wearing a long black coat or cloak, which reached down to his feet, a low-crowned black hat with a wide brim and – as far as I could make out – dark-tinted glasses. I had never before seen anyone in the district who looked even remotely like that."

"What made you think he was watching you?" queried Holmes. "It sounds from your description as if he would be too far away for you to be certain about that, especially if he was wearing dark spectacles."

Lidington nodded. "Yes, you are right. I suppose it was because he remained so still, and because each time I glanced across at him – which I did several times – his face seemed to be turned my way. When I reached home, I threw myself into my work, and gave no more thought to this strange figure. Two days later, however, I was out for a walk in the same place, at the same time, and there was the man again, standing perfectly still at the edge of the woods on the other side of the field, staring across at me. I considered crossing the field to where he stood – although I admit I felt strangely nervous and disturbed by his appearance – but the field had been recently ploughed and was nothing but a sea of rutted mud. I was not wearing suitable footwear, and judged that if I left the path I should become caked in mud, so I abandoned the idea.

"The field is slightly higher in the middle than at the edges, and as the side I was on dipped down a little, I lost sight of the other side, and of that strange, still figure. As my way rose up again a little, I looked again across the field, but there was no sign of him.

"A few days later, I set off for my morning walk as usual, wondering as I did so if I should again see the sinister dark figure. As I made my way along the lane near my house, I happened to run across one of my neighbours, Colonel Strother, a retired military man who lives by himself about half a mile away. He said he was out to get some fresh air and stretch his legs, as he put it, so we walked along together. I was tempted to ask him if he had seen the dark figure loitering at the edge of the woods on his recent walks, but I resisted the urge. I was aware from remarks my cleaning-woman had made that I was already regarded as something of a reclusive figure, an oddity, in the district, and I did not want to give Colonel Strother or anyone else any reason to regard me yet more oddly. It had occurred to me that I had been putting a strain on myself, working very hard recently, and although I could not really believe that the dark figure I had seen was simply the figment of an overheated brain, I knew that that is what others might think. I thus said nothing to the colonel.

"As our way brought us to the field across which I had seen the figure, I glanced nervously over to the dark woods on the other side. It was at first difficult to make anything out there, as it was a dull and gloomy morning. The woods appeared dense and dark, and a thin mist was drifting about the field in front of the trees. After a moment, however, I saw that the dark figure was standing where I had seen him before, at the edge of the wood, against the trees.

"'Colonel,' I said, interrupting his flow, for he was at the time discoursing at length on the different owls he had seen in the district, 'do you see that man over there?'

"'What man?' he responded, turning and squinting in the direction I had indicated.

"'The man in the black coat and hat, with the dark glasses on,' I said, 'standing just between those two tall trees.'

"'No,' said he at length, shaking his head. 'I can't say that I do. It's probably just a trick of the light, Lidington. Of course, no one likes to think they're imagining things, but sometimes your eyes or brain, or whatever it is that arranges these things, makes you think there's something there when there isn't. I remember one morning when I was in India. I'd had to rise very early – before the sun was up – and had had less than three hours sleep. As I walked down a rural lane in the dark, I saw a man about thirty yards away, coming straight towards me. He was a big, strong-looking fellow, and there seemed something determined and a little menacing in his manner, so I braced myself for a possible attack. Next moment, I looked again, and there was no one there at all. I could hardly believe it. I'd seen him as clearly as I see you now – or thought I had, anyway.'

"'But,' I interrupted him again, 'we've moved on some distance now, and I can still see him. Are you sure you can't see anybody there?'

"He stopped and looked again across the field. 'No,' said he at length. 'I don't think there's anybody there, Lidington. I can see a bit of shadow between two trees. That's probably what you're seeing. Funny things, eyes, the way they play tricks on you. You can't trust them for a minute.'

"I didn't pursue the matter. I don't think Colonel Strother's eyes are very good now, so his testimony was not really of any value, and I could not say for certain whether the man by the woods had really been there or not.

"Mercifully, I did not see him again for several days, and I was able to pursue my studies without the man in the black coat and hat constantly intruding into my thoughts. I did learn something, however, which I found more than a little disturbing. Another of my neighbours, Mr. Meade Taylor, invited me round to take tea with him on Sunday afternoon. He also invited Colonel Strother. Over our tea, we chatted about matters of local interest, and the other two, who had both lived in Apstone much longer than I had, told me some interesting facts about the district.

"'Your residence, Naxon House, has a somewhat odd reputation,' remarked Colonel Strother. 'I wouldn't have mentioned this to you when you were first here, in case it bothered you. But now you've been here a couple of years and got to know the district, I may as well tell you. I have heard it said that the house is built on the site of an ancient temple that predates the Roman occupation by several hundred years, and that the influence of this persists to this day. Of course, that sounds a lot of nonsense, but it can't be denied that odd things have happened there over the years, some of them before my time, but some even since I've lived in Apstone, which is thirteen years last July.'

"'What do you mean?' I asked. 'What sort of things have happened?'

"'At least two occupants of Naxon House have gone mad, for a start,' Strother replied. 'It was lived in for many years by a writer of mystical stuff, Serenus Charling.'

"'Yes,' I said; 'I'm aware of that.'

"'But do you know what happened to him in the end? No? Well, I'll tell you: they found his body one morning, floating in the old Military Canal. It seems he'd gone out in the middle of the night and flung himself in there. No one could explain why, and the general belief was that he'd lost his mind. People said he'd been acting strangely for a while, so in a way it wasn't such a surprise as it might have been. That was about two years before I moved into the district. Then, two years after that, the man who was living at Naxon House when I first came to Apstone was by all accounts a very mysterious, reclusive sort of fellow. I was told that he hid himself away all day, and only ever went out after dark. He had been a friend of Charling's, so I understand, so perhaps he was a bit unbalanced as well. Anyway, they came and took him away early one morning, and that's the last anyone ever saw of him. That was just a month or two after I'd moved here.'

"I can't tell you," said Lidington, "how appalling it was to hear Colonel Strother speaking of these dreadful matters in so off-hand and careless a tone, just as if he were relating the latest racing results from Epsom."

"Did you know already that Charling had lost his life in the canal?" asked Holmes.

Lidington shook his head. "No," said he. "Although I had read several of his books, I didn't really know anything much about the man himself. I did know that he had lived somewhere in Kent, at a place called Naxon House, but I'd never known where that was until the day I had chanced to see the name at the house-agent's in Ashford. Anyway, you will imagine that I returned home in a somewhat disturbed state of mind after the conversation with Colonel Strother and Mr. Taylor.

"That evening I felt horribly nervous, to be all alone in what now struck me as an over-large and gloomy house. I went all round the house twice, ensuring that the doors and windows were all securely fastened. The utter silence, other than the slight noise I myself made as I passed from room to room, I now found stifling and oppressive, and I longed for the sound of another human voice. About eight o'clock, a good three hours after it had gone dark, this silence was suddenly broken in the most dramatic and alarming fashion. I was sitting at my desk, writing, when there came a sudden thunderous hammering on the door-knocker. I picked up the lamp from the desk and carried it to the front door. There is a frosted glass panel in the door, but as it was pitch black outside I could see nothing through it.

"'Hello,' I cried. 'Who is there?', but no answer came, only a complete, deathly silence. 'Who is it?' I tried again, but was met again only with silence. My hands were shaking, I remember, as I made sure yet again that the front door was locked, and returned, consumed by fear and trepidation, to my study. I lay long awake in bed that night, every slight noise from the garden outside setting my senses alert and my nerves jangling. Then, just as I was drifting off to sleep, I heard a creak on the stairs outside my room. I sat bolt upright and listened for a minute, but heard nothing more. Taking the lamp from beside my bed, which I had left burning, I opened the bedroom door. There was nothing to be seen there but the dark, shadowed staircase descending to the blackness of the hall below. I returned to my bed, locking my bedroom door as I did so, but I could not sleep. Sometime later, there came a slight tap-tapping noise, as of a small branch of a climbing plant knocking against my bedroom window in the wind. I left my bed again, drew back the curtain and looked out. It was dark, but I could see that the wisteria on the house-wall was nowhere near my window, and could not have caused the tapping noise. However, the noise had ceased as I opened the curtain, so after a moment I returned to my bed and at length fell asleep.

"The following day I did not leave the house at all. As the afternoon was turning into evening and the light was fading, I was working in my study, which overlooks the back garden, and the curtains were still open. It had been my habit to have them so throughout the summer and early autumn. I dislike closing the curtains before it is absolutely necessary to do so; I like to enjoy the evening light for as long as possible. As I worked away at my desk, making notes from one of Serenus Charling's books, a difficult volume which seemed to lie somewhere on the vague and meandering border between mysticism and magic, I heard a slight noise in the garden.

"I looked up. The light was fading rapidly now, and had almost gone completely. Thin wraiths of mist were drifting across the garden, and at the far end, where a hedge separates the garden from the field beyond, it was difficult to make anything out through a dense grey curtain of mist. Then, as a little eddy of wind stirred the mist a little, I saw, with a sickening shock of horror, that there was someone standing there, perfectly motionless, and staring into the study.

"I sprang to my feet, but could move no more than that, so transfixed was I with terror. It was the man I had seen at the edge of the woods, clad in a long black coat, broad-brimmed black hat, and, on his strange round, pale face, a pair of dark spectacles. At the end of the garden is a large ornamental stone urn on a pedestal, and it was by this urn that the dark figure was standing, staring straight at me. Then, as I remained frozen with fear, the urn began to rock a little on its base, as if by some power of its own, and slowly, very slowly, it toppled over, onto the man beside it. It is a heavy urn, and as it fell it crushed the man beneath it in the most dreadfully gruesome way imaginable. I have never been struck with such horror in all my life. I dashed forward and pulled the curtains closed. Then I think I must have fainted, for I can remember no more.

"When I came to my senses, I was lying on the floor in the study. I had clearly caught my head on the corner of a chair as I fell, for it was bleeding and throbbed with pain. I rekindled the study fire, the only fire in the house still alight, and poured myself a glass of brandy to steady my nerves. Then, taking the poker from the hearth, I made a slow and cautious survey of the whole house, but found nothing amiss, and no sign that anyone had been in there.

"I spent the night sitting in a chair by the fire, with the poker on my knee. I suppose I did drop off to sleep once or twice, but awoke instantly at the slightest sound. I did not open the curtains again until it was broad daylight – about eight o'clock. To my astonishment, the garden outside looked as it had always done. The urn was still on its plinth, and there was no sign that anyone had been in the garden. I was stunned by this. Had any of what I thought I had seen the previous evening really taken place? Or had I perhaps fallen asleep at my desk and imagined the whole thing? No, that could not be, I told myself. I had been so frightened that I had fainted, and the cut on my head, where it had struck the chair, was real enough. Anyway, you will perhaps appreciate why I thought I might be going mad.

"That was yesterday. I eventually fell asleep and slept away much of the day. Then, last night, either because I had slept too long during the day, or because of anxiety at what might happen in the night, I scarcely slept a minute. This morning I was up early, and caught the first train I could from Ham Street, in the hope that you could advise me, and perhaps shed some light on the horrible predicament I find myself in."

Sherlock Holmes sat for some time in silence. "I take it from your account, Mr. Lidington, that you do not keep any resident domestic staff," he said at length.

"That is correct," replied Lidington. "I could not afford to do so even if it were necessary, which it isn't. A local woman comes in twice a week to clean round a little, and comes in other days to prepare a meal for me, which I find sufficient for my requirements. I dislike having people bustling about when I am trying to study."

"Am I also correct in inferring that your two-year lease is shortly up for renewal?"

"Yes, next month."

Holmes nodded. "Have you, or anyone else, seen any strangers in the district recently?"

"I don't think so. No, wait," added Lidington, correcting himself. "There has been a commercial traveller about recently, an elderly, grey-haired man. I have seen him a few times, lugging a suitcase about, and one day we exchanged a few words when I bumped into him on the road to Ham Street."

"A commercial traveller?" queried Holmes. "It did not appear, from your description of Apstone, that there would be any shops there for him to visit."

"That is true. I think he must be one of those fellows that go from door to door with a case full of samples."

"Do you know what he is selling?"

"No. He's not called on me, nor any of my neighbours, so far as I am aware."

"Is there anywhere in Apstone where he might stay?"

"No. But in Ham Street there are several inns, at least two of which cater especially to commercial travellers."

"Look up the trains to Ham Street in Bradshaw, would you, Watson?" said Holmes to me.

"You intend to come down to Kent with me?" said Lidington in a tone of relief.

Holmes nodded. "There are one or two things I wish to see for myself."

"I cannot quite see the drift of your questions, Mr. Holmes – my lease, whether I keep servants or not and your interest in the commercial traveller."

"It is simply a question of ascertaining all the facts," returned Holmes. "The more facts we have, the more likely it is that we shall solve the problem."

"There is a train leaving shortly from Charing Cross," I said, my eye running down the columns of figures. "I think we could catch it if we leave within the next five minutes and secure a cab straight away. There isn't another one for a couple of hours."

"Then we must catch this one," said Holmes, springing to his feet. "Throw your razor and a spare collar into a bag, Watson, and be ready to leave in two minutes!"

The next twenty minutes were a frantic dash through the crowded streets. It was not until we were ensconced in a first-class smoking compartment in the Dover express, *en route* for Ashford, where we would change for Ham Street, that we were able to relax and discuss further Mr. Lidington's alarming mystery.

"Do you see any possible meaning to these recent events, Mr. Holmes?" he asked.

"It is too early to speak with any confidence on the matter," returned Holmes, "although I think the evidence so far permits us to make one or two conjectures. The first sightings you had of your mysterious persecutor were somewhat ambiguous in nature. He appeared to be watching you from the edge of the woods, but that might not have been the case. He might, for instance, have been watching and waiting for someone else. However, the more recent events at your house, especially the performance he put on in your garden the night before last, which you found so disconcerting, can surely mean only one thing."

"What is that?"

"If we set aside any supernatural explanation, we must conclude that someone has been deliberately trying to frighten you."

"He certainly succeeded in that," said Lidington with feeling. "But why should he? What have I ever done to harm anyone?"

"It may not be because of who you are, but because of where you are. You mentioned that your two-year lease on Naxon House is coming to an end. Perhaps someone does not wish you to renew it, because he wishes to rent the house himself."

"It would seem a somewhat elaborate scheme if that is his only aim."

"I agree, but it is possible. However, there is another possibility, which is that someone wishes to frighten you away from the house for just a day or two."

"Whatever for?"

"So that he can break into the house for some reason. If that is his aim, then it is possible that your visit to London today may have provided him with just the chance he has been waiting for. The fact that you have no domestic staff in the house would of course make his task easier."

"Good Lord!"

"Do you have anything of significant value in the house?"

Lidington shook his head. "No, nothing at all that I can think of. But," he added, "I saw the sinister-looking figure crushed flat by that heavy garden urn the night before last. I am sure if you had seen it, you would have been as horrified as I was. Yet in the morning there was no one there, and no sign that there ever had been. How can you explain that?"

"It is not so very difficult," said Holmes, filling his pipe with tobacco and putting a match to it. "The dark suit of clothes – the long coat, hat and spectacles – that you had previously seen worn by the figure in the woods, were in this case, I suggest, hung upon a wooden frame of some sort. An upturned rake or broom would serve the purpose adequately, I should think. Perhaps they had always been on such a frame – you were never close enough to see before."

"But the person in the garden had a head. I could see that clearly enough."

"Yes, but your gaze would inevitably have been drawn to the most prominent feature, the dark spectacles. I doubt you would have scrutinized the rest of it very closely."

"What are you suggesting?"

"That what you thought was a head was in fact some kind of inflatable ball, with the hat perched on top of it and the spectacles secured at the sides."

"I suppose it is possible," conceded Lidington. "The face – what I saw of it – did seem strangely pale and rounded. But the urn seemed to tip over of its own volition, as if by magic."

"I fancy I could achieve the same effect, given the circumstances," returned Holmes, much to Lidington's surprise. "It was, I suspect, an ancient and time-honoured conjuring trick, which is simple but always effective. All the villain would have needed was a large piece of black cloth to hide behind as he pushed the urn over. You were very unlikely to see what was really happening in the late twilight, when, as you described, the light had almost completely gone. The fact that he had all the equipment necessary for the performance suggests that that was his ultimate aim, and that the sightings you had had of the figure by the woods formed a sort of deliberately disturbing prologue."

"You may be right," said Lidington, "but that still leaves unanswered the question of why I am being persecuted in this way."

"There are, as I mentioned, several possibilities," said Holmes. "If I knew which was the correct one, I should not be travelling down to Kent with you, but should be sitting at home with my feet up, having already solved all your problems for you. Let us therefore leave the matter there for the moment and see what we turn up in and around Apstone."

In two hours we had reached Ashford. The branch train stood waiting in the bay platform, but Holmes went to consult a time-table on the wall by the exit.

"This train leaves in eight minutes," he said, "but there is another later this afternoon that we can take. I want first to have a word with the house agent who deals with the rental of Naxon House."

Lidington took us through the streets of the busy town to an office bearing the sign "Sandhurst and Martin, House Agents". Inside, a young man whom Lidington introduced to us as Mr. Carter was seated behind a large desk. He greeted us cordially, but when Holmes asked if anyone had recently expressed an interest in Naxon House, he shook his head.

"No, not at all," said he. "We were rather hoping that Mr. Lidington would renew his lease next month. That would keep things simple from our point of view," he added with a chuckle. "I hope there is no problem – loose tiles, leaks, or anything of the sort?"

"No," said Holmes with a glance at his client. "We are interested in the past history of the property, though. Could you tell us who was in the house before Mr. Lidington?"

"One moment," said the young man. He leaned over, pulled open a large drawer in a cabinet behind him, and, after a moment, took out a large manila envelope. "As far as I recall," he said as he tipped the contents of the envelope onto his desk, "the house had been unoccupied for six months before Mr. Lidington took it, and prior to that the owner himself had lived in it for some years. Yes," he continued after a moment, "the owner of the property is a Mr. Westerton – he lives at Hythe now – Cliff Road, which always sounds a bit dangerous to me," he added, laughing at his own joke. "He lived at Naxon House from '81 to early '84. Before that, it was rented out for about eight years, from '73 to '81, to an officer of the South Eastern Railway, a Mr. Stroulger. Before Mr. Stroulger it was rented to a Mr. Smith for about two years. That takes us back to 1871, which was the first year we had anything to do with the property. I believe it had previously been occupied by the owner, who died in that year. He was probably some relation of the present owner, I should think."

"If I remember correctly," said Holmes to Lidington, "Colonel Strother told you he had lived in Apstone for thirteen years, which means he came in '73. He also said that the incident of the man who had gone mad and been taken away early one morning occurred just a couple of months after he moved there, so that must also have been in '73, and the man in question must be the Mr. Smith that Mr. Carter referred to. Do you know any more details of the matter, Mr. Carter?" he continued, turning to the house agent.

"I'm afraid not," replied Carter. "That was long before my time. My superior, Mr. Martin, might possibly remember. He's been here a long time."

The young man disappeared through a doorway at the back of the office, but reappeared a few moments later. "If you come this way," he said, "Mr. Martin will see you now."

We were shown into a warm office at the rear of the building, where a fire burned merrily in the grate. An elderly, grey-haired man stood up from behind a desk and waved us to the chairs in front of it. "I understand you are interested in our mysterious Mr. Smith, who got taken away from Naxon House one bright morning," said he in a dry tone.

"Among other things," returned Holmes. "Why do you refer to him as 'mysterious'?"

"Well, his name wasn't Smith, for a start," said Martin, "as we discovered after he'd gone. It was Farley."

"Had you not taken up his references?" asked Holmes in surprise.

Martin shook his head. "The whole business was quite irregular, which is why I recall it so clearly. The first time we ever had anything to do with Naxon House was when the owner, Serenus Charling, died. That was an odd business in itself. Of course, he was a fairly well-known local character, being a writer of some repute, but he was also a decided eccentric. He used to wander about the Romney Marsh at all hours of the day and night, wearing a large ankle-length black cape and wide-brimmed black hat, generally talking to himself and ignoring everyone else. Most people thought he was slightly mad, so when he was found one morning, drowned in the Royal Military Canal, no one was altogether surprised. Whether he slipped in or jumped in, no one could say, and the verdict at the inquest was death by misadventure.

"Shortly after his death, we were approached by a distant cousin of his, a Mr. Westerton, who had inherited Charling's property. He himself lived in Ashford at the time, and wanted us to deal with the letting of Naxon House. We had just agreed to this, when he called on us again a few days later to say that an acquaintance of Charling's had turned up at Naxon House while Westerton was there looking round the place. This acquaintance, who gave his name as Smith, said he had been staying with Charling for some time, although he hadn't been there at the time of his death. Now, he said, he was interested in renting the house for himself, and, as an old friend of the dead man, would prefer it if Charling's furniture and other belongings were left in place. This suited Mr. Westerton perfectly, as it meant he would not have the trouble of sorting out his late cousin's possessions, so he told us to go ahead and rent the house to this man, Smith. I was a bit dubious about this, as I didn't much care for the look of Smith, a deceitful-looking, rat-faced man, but it was Westerton's house, to do with as he wished, so I went ahead and wrote out the lease.

"Nothing much happened for the next two years, although I heard occasional reports from people I knew who lived down that way that this Smith fellow was every bit as eccentric as Charling had been, scarcely ever leaving the house until it had gone dark. Then, early in the autumn of '73 I had a visit one day from a police inspector, accompanied by a senior officer from Maidstone Prison. They informed me that they were on the track of a man called Farley, who had escaped from prison three years previously and who, they now had reason to believe, was one and the same person as the man called Smith, who was living at Naxon House. I was astounded at this, although it did confirm that the unfavourable impression I had formed of him in the first place had been correct. I told them what I knew of him – which wasn't much – and gave them my spare key, and the next morning at dawn they entered Naxon House and arrested him.

"I later heard that there was a rumour in the district that Smith had been insane and had been taken away for his own and others' safety. How this rumour began, I cannot say, but I never went out of my way to correct it. From the point of view of letting the house, it was bad enough that it had been occupied by a man who had gone mad. It would have been even worse, I thought, if it were known that the occupant had been a hardened and vicious escaped convict."

"Is there any particular reason why you refer to him as 'hardened and vicious'?" asked Holmes.

"He was a member of the gang that carried out the notorious bullion robbery here in Ashford in the late 'sixties, in the course of which several railway employees were badly beaten. I don't suppose any of you have heard of that."

"I have read something of it," said Holmes. "A quantity of gold bullion – both bars and coins – was being shipped in great secrecy from Dover to London by the South Eastern Railway. One of that company's employees got wind of what was being carried and hatched a plan with his confederates to rob the train just north of Ashford station. As I recall, there were some ingenious touches to the scheme, involving replacing the couplings either side of the wagon containing the bullion with loops of thick rope which could then be cut with a knife – first the back one and then the front one – thus isolating that wagon from the rest of the train. Unfortunately for the gang, the execution of the scheme was not so accomplished as the planning of it had been. They cut the ropes too soon, and too close together, so they didn't remain isolated for long enough to make off with much of the gold."

"Your account of it is very accurate," said Martin in surprise.

"The history of such crimes is a little hobby of mine," returned Holmes. "Could the date of the robbery have been April 25th, 1869?"

Martin frowned as he tried to remember. "Yes, that would be about right," he said at length. "I remember it was in the spring. Anyway, all five members of the gang were soon caught and convicted. Three of them, including Farley, were sentenced to ten years in Maidstone Prison. The other two, who were evidently judged less culpable, got seven years. As far as I remember, most of the stolen gold was recovered, but not quite all of it." Martin paused. "We seem to have drifted quite a long way from your question about previous tenants of Naxon House," he remarked, scratching his head.

"Nevertheless, it is all interesting, and we are very grateful to you for sparing us the time," said Holmes.

As we walked back to the railway station, Holmes was silent, with a look of intense concentration on his features. I knew better than to bother him with questions when he was so deep in thought, and knew he would share his thoughts on the matter when he felt he had reached a worthwhile conclusion, but Lidington asked him if the information we had received from the house agents had altered his views of the matter.

In answer, Holmes shook his head in a puzzled manner. "Sometimes," said he at length, "a little fresh information can clarify a case considerably. In this instance, however, the new information has served only to complicate the matter further. It now seems very likely that the bizarre and puzzling date on the mysterious letter you received a few weeks ago is in fact the date of this notorious bullion robbery, but what might be the significance of that, we cannot say. Let us therefore possess our souls in patience a little longer before attempting to reach any conclusions."

We caught the next branch train and a short time later alighted at Ham Street, the first stop on the line. A brisk walk of ten minutes brought us to the hamlet of Apstone, its scattered houses dotted about among the fields and woods. Away to the east, the vast flat and featureless expanse of the Romney Marsh stretched far away. After a moment, following Lidington's lead, we turned from the main road into a muddy lane. A short distance up this lane an equally muddy track went off to the left, and just beyond this track stood a substantial double-fronted house built of dark red brick, which Lidington informed us was Naxon House.

"If you will wait here in the lane," said Holmes, "I shall inspect the area around the house."

We watched as he made a slow and careful examination of the path from the garden gate to the front door of the house, then of the lane outside the garden, and lastly of the side-track. Something there seemed to particularly catch his attention, and he followed the track all the way along the outside of the garden hedge, and beyond the hedge, into the field behind the house.

"It is as I thought," said he as he rejoined us.

"You have discovered something?" queried Lidington.

Holmes nodded. "Fortunately, it rained here last night. As a result, all the footprints are fresh and clear, and I can be sure that they were all made today. The first thing that happened this morning, Mr. Lidington, is that you left the house, got half-way down the path to the gate and turned back. You then re-entered the house, came out again and made your way out of the garden and down the lane here."

"That is true. I realised that I had come out without any money, having left my purse on the kitchen table, so I went back to get it."

"The second thing that happened," Holmes continued, "is that a man with a nick in the outside edge of his right shoe came up the lane. In several places his footprints overlay your own, going in the opposite direction. Interestingly, he did not proceed to your garden gate, but turned off into the track at the side of your garden. He had not gone very far up the track, however, when he met someone with large feet coming down the track from the field behind your garden."

"That must have been Colonel Strother. He has large feet, I have noticed, and he often comes down that track when he has been for his morning walk over the fields."

"The two of them stood together for a few moments, then both of them came down the track, into the lane, and so down to the main road. In other words, large feet continued on the way he had been going when they met, while the other man, the one with the nick in the side of his shoe, turned round and accompanied large feet down to the road."

"Can you really see all that?" asked Lidington in an incredulous tone.

"Certainly. The footprints are very clear."

"Do you think the two men met by arrangement?" I asked.

Holmes shook his head. "It looks to me as if they met by chance," he replied. "After their brief conversation, which is indicated by the area on the track where their feet shuffle about a little, the man with the nicked shoe evidently changed what he was planning to do, as he turned round and accompanied the other man back down to the road. This suggests that large feet told him something that obliged him to change his plan."

"What could that have been?" I asked.

"Probably that Mr. Lidington was not at home."

"How could the man with the large feet have known that, if he had just walked down from the field behind the house?"

"Probably he had observed that there was no smoke rising from any of the chimneys, and had seen from over the back hedge that Mr. Lidington was not in his study. If large feet were indeed Colonel Strother, as Mr. Lidington suggests, then you must remember that he is an old military man, and would be used to making such observations as a matter of habit. Anyway, although he could not admit it, the other man was no doubt already aware, of course, that Mr. Lidington was not at home. He had probably watched him go for the train at Ham Street. That is why he had not called at the house in a normal sort of way, but was making his way up the little track at the side of the property when he encountered the colonel."

"What do you think he had intended to do?" asked Lidington.

"Probably to break a window round the back of the house and gain entry that way. Only the colonel's chance arrival prevented it."

"What a pity that we do not know who the other man was," said Lidington.

"Oh, there's no mystery about that," said Holmes. "It was undoubtedly the commercial traveller."

"How can you be so sure?" I asked in surprise.

"It is an elementary matter of observation, Watson. Come and see," he continued, leading us up the side-track a little way. "This is where the two men stood together for a few moments, as you can see from the scuffed footprints on the ground. Large shoes has come down the track, nicked sole has come up the track, and they have both stopped here. But what else do you see?"

I looked where he was pointing and saw that at the side of the footprints was a large, square-cornered oblong mark, about two and a half feet long by eight inches wide.

"It is his suitcase!" I cried, as I realised the meaning of the mark. "He has put it down while the two of them were speaking!"

"Precisely! Come, let us now make haste back to Ham Street and see if we can find where this bogus commercial traveller has been staying!"

"It is all very puzzling to me," said Lidington, as we walked along. "When he and I spoke the other day, he struck me as a quite exceptionally pleasant man."

"Perhaps he did," remarked Holmes, "but as a commercial traveller he is certainly something of an oddity. In the first place he appears, from your description of him, to be a little mature for that sort of work. In the second place, he seems to have spent at least a week, perhaps more, wandering about Apstone and the district when it is apparent that there are only enough houses here to occupy him for an hour or two at most. In the third place, considering how few households there are, it is strange that he does not appear to have actually called at any of them."

We were soon back in Ham Street, and Lidington took us first to an inn called the Plough, but the landlord there did not recognize the description he gave him. Lidington then led us down the village high street until we came to a large, imposing inn, painted in a black and white Tudor style. A sign hanging over the entrance identified this as the George. "This is the most popular place with commercial travellers, I believe," said Lidington as he pushed open the door. Inside was a large tap-room, with five or six men sitting in lively conversation and another couple leaning on the bar, talking to the landlord. Lidington described to him the man we were looking for, at which he nodded his head.

"That would be Mr. Beresford," said he in a jovial tone. "He's in the back parlour now."

We thanked him and pushed open the connecting door which led to the parlour. There, sitting by himself at a small table, was a grey-haired man in a tweed suit, nearer sixty than fifty, I judged. He had a pipe in his mouth and a tankard of ale before him, and on his face was a far-away, thoughtful expression. As the three of us approached his table, he turned. Upon his face was a look of surprise and also, I thought, of apprehension. He put down his pipe and began to rise to his feet.

"Don't trouble to get up," said Holmes in an affable tone. "Instead, we'll sit down. it's Mr. Beresford, isn't it?"

The man nodded his head. "What can I do for you, gentlemen?" he asked, as we drew up chairs to the table at which he was sitting.

"You could answer a few questions," returned Holmes.

"What sort of questions?"

"First and foremost, you could tell us why you have been persecuting Mr. Lidington here recently."

"I don't know what you are talking about. Why should I answer your questions, anyway? Who are you?"

"My name is Holmes. I am an investigator of mysteries."

"What, another one of those infernal crack-brained and fraudulent alchemists?"

"Not at all. The mysteries I investigate have no such pretensions to profundity, but nevertheless affect people's lives more directly. Such mysteries cause people to become puzzled or anxious, miserable or frightened. That is why I try to solve their problems for them."

"Best of luck with that," said the other in a sarcastic tone, picking up his pipe again from the table, "but I don't see what it's got to do with me."

"Why do you refer to alchemists as 'crack-brained' or 'fraudulent'?"

"I misunderstood you, that is all. It's not important."

"On the contrary, I think it is very important. My client, whom I believe you have met," Holmes continued, nodding his head in the direction of Lidington, "happens to live in Naxon House, which was once owned by Serenus Charling, a noted alchemist, and there you are, bringing up the subject of alchemy without any prompting from me. That seems something of a coincidence, would you not agree? Incidentally, we know that you were out at Naxon House today. Unfortunately for your plan to force an entry to the house, you ran across one of Mr. Lidington's neighbours in the lane beside the house and had to abandon the scheme."

Beresford seemed about to reply, but hesitated and remained silent.

"I might also mention," Holmes continued, "that we know all about the bungled railway robbery of 1869, of Farley's escape from Maidstone Prison the following year and his subsequent recapture at Charling's house."

Beresford remained silent a moment longer, then he turned to Lidington, a bitter expression on his face. "You are, I take it, a relative of that devil, Charling?"

"I?" returned Lidington in surprise. "No, I have no connection with him at all. I just happen to live in his old house."

"I don't believe you," said Beresford sharply. "I made enquiries some time ago, and learned that Naxon House was now owned by a relative of Charling's."

"I believe that that is true," said Lidington, "but I am not that man. I am a mere tenant. The owner of the house lives somewhere else, and I have never even met him. I know nothing whatever about him, nor, for that matter, about Serenus Charling himself. I have read one or two of Charling's books, that is all."

"I made other enquiries locally," persisted Beresford, "and was told that you have spent most of your time in the last two years studying alchemy."

"That is also true," said Lidington. "I had had an interest in the subject for some time, and when I was looking for somewhere to live, I happened to discover quite by chance that Charling's old house was vacant. I thought then that fate must have intended me to move in there, and took a two-year lease on the place. That is my only connection with it, or with Serenus Charling."

Beresford bowed his head, blew out his cheeks and ran his hand through his hair. "It seems I have made a mistake," said he at last, raising his head after a long silence. "I put two and two together and made five."

"More pertinently," said Holmes, "you also frightened the wits out of my client."

Beresford nodded his head slowly. "I wouldn't blame you if you never forgave me," said he to Lidington in a voice full of contrition, "but please believe me when I say I am sorry if I have caused you distress."

"You appear to have some grudge against Serenus Charling or his family," said Holmes. "Would you care to tell us about it?"

"You would not believe me if I told you," said the other after a moment.

"We might if what you told us was the truth," returned Holmes. "I think we are entitled to some sort of explanation."

"I agree," said Beresford. "Perhaps the first two things you should know, then," he continued after a moment in a dignified tone, "is that my true name is not Beresford but Walters, and I, like that man Farley that you mentioned, am an ex-convict."

"I find that difficult to believe," I said in surprise.

"Thank you, sir," said he; "but it is true. I was convicted, along with four other men, of that bullion robbery in '69 that your companion mentioned, although I had nothing whatever to do with it."

"Then how came you to be convicted?" asked Holmes.

"Purely on the lying testimony of others. I will explain, so you will understand the depths of bitterness that have poisoned my soul for nearly twenty years. As a boy I had little formal education, but I was a very keen reader, read every book I could lay my hands on, and thus educated myself in that way. I was born and raised in Ashford, and at the age of thirteen was apprenticed to a small engineering concern there, owned by a very kind and generous man by the name of Beresford. It had begun by making various items of ironwork for farm carts and the like, but the coming of the railway had increased the demand for all sorts of ironwork enormously, and we were very busy. As the years passed, it became clear to me that Mr. Beresford had come to rely heavily on me, but I was taken by surprise one day when he offered me a half-share in the business. He and his wife, who had died by then, had never had any children, and I think he had come to look on me as a son. More years passed, and when Mr. Beresford himself died, I discovered that in his will he had left me the other half of the business, saying that he wished above all for it to continue successfully. I was thus, at a relatively young age, the owner of a prosperous business, comfortably-off and well-respected in the area. Sadly, my wife had not lived to enjoy this prosperity, but she had borne me a child, our daughter, Florence, who was now my greatest source of happiness.

"There is in Ashford – or, at least, there was in those days – I know nothing of it now – a literary and scientific society, whose members would meet once a month to discuss various intellectual matters. Often someone – one of our members or a visitor – would read a paper on some subject or other and then we would discuss it. On one occasion, Serenus Charling, the well-known writer on alchemy, read a paper. In the discussion afterwards, I raised several objections to points he had made, as did some of the others, and a good discussion ensued. A couple of months later, I myself read a paper defending the conventional, scientific view of the world and, I suppose, dismissing alternative 'mystical' views. My criticisms of the latter were not particularly harsh, and I had certainly intended to make them in the friendly, open spirit which usually marked our discussions, but I felt afterwards, from Charling's manner towards me, that I had perhaps offended him and he had taken against me in a personal way. Still, on the surface at least, we remained on good terms, and he invited me to his house on a number of occasions to discuss our intellectual differences.

"I must now mention the one mistake I made in running the firm of Beresford and Walters, as it was still known. Generally speaking, when taking on new men, I prided myself on being able to judge the character of each prospective employee, but on one occasion I erred badly. I took on a man by the name of Seth Woodall, who soon proved to be nothing but trouble. From the very start, he showed a marked reluctance to put any effort into what he was supposed to be doing, and he had been with the firm scarcely two months when he began to complain about everything – the premises, the equipment, the work he was required to do and his fellow workers. None of these complaints was justified and they were generally made simply to explain away his own shortcomings and mistakes. Matters finally came to a head when there were a number of petty thefts, both from the firm and its employees, and after a thorough investigation it became clear that Woodall was responsible. I had no choice but to dismiss him, but it was an unpleasant situation, and he left the premises mouthing the foulest of oaths and vowing vengeance against me.

"I come now to the fateful evening of April 25th, 1869."

"The day of the bullion robbery."

"Exactly, Mr. Holmes. I had gone down to Apstone to see Charling. We had supper together and discussed our differing views on alchemy. Then, leaving with him an essay I had written on the subject, summarising my opinions, I drove myself home to Ashford. The following morning, news of the robbery had spread round Ashford like wildfire. Two of the four criminals had been captured at the scene of the robbery and the other two were being sought in Ashford. By the time the local evening newspaper appeared, all four men were in custody.

"Early that evening, I was sitting at home, having a cup of tea and reading the paper, when there came a ring at the bell. Next moment, three large policemen were shown in, one of whom produced a warrant for my arrest. I was utterly astounded at this, but even more astounded to learn that I had been incriminated in the robbery by one of the captured men. This man was Seth Woodall, the man I had had to dismiss from his job for dishonesty the previous year. That evil, lying rat had told the police that I was 'the clever one' they suspected had planned the robbery. He had evidently seized the chance to wreak vengeance upon me, as he had threatened. His confederates, evidently as foul and depraved as he was, said nothing to dispute his false claim.

"If I had been shocked and astounded by these base lies, I was soon to find that there was a yet greater shock awaiting me. I told the police that I knew no more about the robbery than any other member of the public, and that I had been visiting Serenus Charling on the evening it took place, but when they interviewed Charling he denied ever having seen me that day. I said I had taken him an essay I had just finished writing, as my housekeeper could attest, as she had seen me writing it, but Charling said he had no knowledge of any such essay. My mind was reeling at this, and I could not believe what I was hearing. Surely the man's mind could not be so poisoned with hatred for me just because I had argued against his opinions, so poisoned that he would condemn a perfectly innocent man to a brutal term of imprisonment? But that was how it was, and what was seen as my lie in stating that I had visited Charling on the evening of the robbery only added to my appearance of guilt in the eyes of the authorities. I was convicted and sentenced to seven years' hard labour in Maidstone Prison. For seven years I was locked away from the world, with only the most vicious and brutal of men for company. For seven years I was separated from my only daughter, Florence. She had gone to live with my sister in Canterbury upon my arrest, and it was there she grew from childhood to adulthood, and eventually married, from all of which I was completely cut off.

"I was released back into the world in '76, almost broken both in body and spirit by my time in prison. Florence and her husband invited me to join them in York, where they now lived, and where her husband had a small engineering business not so dissimilar from the business I had once had in Ashford. This I eventually did, and I like to think I have proved myself useful to the business, but first I returned to Ashford, to tidy up my affairs there. I spent some time reading old newspapers, and soon learned that Charling had died five years previously, in '71, and that after Farley's escape from prison in 1870, of which I was already aware, he had lived at Charling's house until he was recaptured in '73. What had become of Woodall and the other lying criminals, I neither knew nor cared. I do remember wondering if Farley had in fact murdered Charling. It did not seem that the authorities had ever considered that possibility, but as I was only too well aware, the authorities were capable of making dreadful errors. However, I did not wish to dwell on the past, so when I had finished my business in Ashford, I shook the dust of Kent from my feet and set off for the North, doubting that I should ever return.

"Several years passed. My son-in-law's business was flourishing, Florence had borne two children, so that I was now a grandfather and in constant demand from that quarter, and the events of the past had almost faded from my memory. Then, one afternoon, as I was walking home and crossing a bridge in the middle of York, I paused to look down at the river, and for no reason I have ever been able to determine, Charling, Naxon House and all the rest of it came flooding back into my mind. As I stood there a moment, almost overcome by the suddenness of these recollections, a fresh thought struck me like the blow from a sledgehammer, something I had never considered before, even in my wildest imaginings. Could it be that there really had been a 'clever one' behind the bullion robbery, as the police had always suspected? It was certainly not me, but could that 'clever one' have been Charling?

"The more I thought about it, the more possible did it seem. It would have given Charling a stronger motive for lying about me than simply his dislike of my intellectual arguments and criticisms. Woodall's initial lies about me would in fact have given Charling the opportunity to use me as a sort of scapegoat, to provide the police with the 'clever one' they were looking for, and take any attention away from Charling himself. Charling's involvement might also explain the whereabouts of the missing gold. Perhaps after I had left him, on the night of the robbery, the two men who remained at large for nearly twenty-four hours had arrived with the gold and it had been hidden for safekeeping at Naxon House.

"Charling's involvement in the robbery would also explain why Farley had ended up at his house after his escape from prison. For, if my speculations were true, one could readily imagine that Farley might have threatened to expose Charling's part in the robbery unless he hid him away at Naxon House. One could further imagine that Farley and Charling had subsequently fallen out – probably over the gold – and Farley had murdered Charling, as I had speculated before.

"But why should Charling have become involved in the robbery in the first place? As soon as I posed myself this question, two possible answers at once suggested themselves, both of which, I judged, could be true. In the first place, I had long suspected that Charling was not so well off as people supposed. Although he adopted the pose of 'the distinguished local author.' and made the most of it in the district, I had long suspected that his books were not, in fact, read very much, and brought him little if any income. If so, the prospect of acquiring a quantity of gold might have proved irresistible to him. In the second place, he had once told me that he had managed to produce a very small quantity of gold by one of his alchemical processes and was hoping to repeat the experiment on a larger scale. I did not believe him – I had come to feel he was both a liar and a fraud – but, out of politeness, I had not expressed my disbelief openly. It now seemed possible to me that he might have intended to melt down some of the stolen gold and pretend that he had produced it by alchemical means.

"Of course, the men who were imprisoned for their part in the robbery would presumably have expected to receive their share of the gold upon their release from prison. But by the time they got out of prison, Charling had been dead some years and his house was in the hands of another, so perhaps they simply abandoned the idea as futile and did not pursue the matter. Anyway, as I considered all these possibilities, I became consumed with the idea of gaining entry to Naxon House in the hope that I might find there something which would prove Charling's guilt, and my own innocence. Unfortunately, I soon learnt that the present occupant of Naxon House hardly ever went out for longer than an hour at a time, so I had to find some way of driving him from the house just long enough to allow me to get in there and look for evidence. The idea I came up with – forgive me – was to try to frighten him away by pretending to be Serenus Charling returned from the dead. The rest you appear to know."

"What made you think that you might be able to find any evidence after all this time?" asked Holmes. "Surely it was more likely that any evidence would be long gone, found by Charling's relative or one of his tenants."

Walters hesitated. "Do you believe all that I have told you?" he asked at length.

"Yes," replied Holmes, at which Lidington and I nodded our agreement. With such intensity and conviction had Walters told his tale that I could not doubt for a moment that it was the unvarnished truth.

"Can I trust that you will pursue the truth, no matter what the consequences?" he asked.

"Certainly you can," said Holmes. "It is in everyone's interest that the true facts be known."

"Very well, then," said Walters. "I will tell you. There is a secret room in Naxon House which I doubt anyone knows about but me. Charling himself had it constructed many years ago so he could have somewhere private in which to conduct his secret alchemical experiments. I only learned about it by chance: I had called round to see him in the early days of our acquaintance, and, finding the door open, assumed it had been left so for me. I walked straight in, calling a greeting to him as I did so, but either I was earlier than he expected, or he had forgotten I was coming, for just as I walked in, he emerged from the entrance of the secret room. He showed it to me then – he could hardly do otherwise – but asked me not to tell anyone else about it. I very much doubt he would have shown it to Farley or anyone else, and it is very unlikely to have been discovered by chance. It is just possible that there is something in there which will shed some light on what happened all those years ago."

Holmes rose to his feet. "Let us get down to Apstone, then, before the daylight goes," said he.

The sun was setting as we left the inn, and, by the time we reached Naxon House, twilight was well advanced. Cold air was drifting off the marsh, and on its surface small clouds of evening mist were forming. Lidington unlocked the front door of the house and we followed him inside.

"Where, precisely, is the secret room?" Holmes asked.

"It is in the attic," Walters returned, "but one cannot get into it up there. I believe there was originally a large trap-door between the attic and one of the bedrooms when Charling was first moving furniture up there, but that was later sealed up, and the only entrance now is in the study. I'll show you." He led the way towards the back of the house and we entered a room which overlooked the rear garden. As I looked out of the window, I saw the large urn on its pedestal at the end of the garden, as Lidington had described it to us. Wisps of mist were drifting about the foot of the pedestal and the hedge behind it.

"You see how peculiarly thick the walls are here," said Walters, standing beside the window. "That is because there is a steep and narrow staircase within the wall."

In the corner of the room, between the fireplace and the window, a large, tall cupboard had been constructed, as high as the picture-rail. Walters opened the doors of this, to reveal broad wooden shelves on which were piled numerous books and documents. "May I move these out of the way?" he asked Lidington, who nodded his head. I lent a hand, and soon all the books and papers were piled upon the floor by the desk. Then Walters lifted up the shelves in the cupboard, which were not fastened to the brackets upon which they rested, and stacked them all against the wall by the window. "This side panel inside the cupboard conceals the staircase," he said. "One of these little brackets is actually attached to a latch on the other side, and if we lift it, it should release the panel. Yes, there we are." He had lifted the bracket slightly and pulled it forward, whereupon the whole wooden side-wall of the cupboard hinged forward, revealing a steep and narrow staircase behind it.

Holmes had lit a lamp which stood on the desk. This he handed to Walters, who set off up the stairs holding the lamp in front of him, as we followed behind. It was so very cramped that one's shoulders brushed the side-walls as the staircase twisted round in a tight spiral, and so extremely steep that our ascent seemed almost as vertical as climbing a ladder. At the top of the stair we entered one of the strangest chambers I have ever seen. It was surprisingly large, and must have occupied half of the loft space. That we were immediately beneath the roof-tiles was apparent from the steeply-sloping ceiling. All about us were large, highly-coloured and mysterious-looking pictures, covered with strange figures and symbols, and in the centre of the room were various chests, cupboards and tables, on some of which stood items of chemical equipment and bottles of vividly-coloured chemicals. Over everything was a thick layer of dust, and uncountable numbers of old, dusty cobwebs.

"A little more light would be helpful," said Holmes as he lit two lamps which stood on one of the tables. "Now let us see what we can find," he continued, pulling open a drawer in a small bureau which stood by the wall. "There are a lot of papers in here," he said, "and a number of newspaper cuttings relating to the bullion robbery. Ah! Charling's vanity may have betrayed him! He has underlined those parts of the newspaper reports that say what an ingeniously planned robbery it was! And here is something in a different hand: 'A Critical Examination of the Claims of Alchemy'."

"That is my essay!" cried Walters in delight.

"I wonder why he kept it," I said.

"I cannot imagine," said Walters, "but perhaps it was because he recognized that the arguments it contained were valid, and he had never succeeded in countering them. Anyway, it's the essay I brought him on the evening I was supposed to have been involved with the robbery."

"May I have a look at it?" asked Lidington.

"By all means," returned Walters. "What is it, Mr. Holmes?" he asked, as Holmes let out a cry of surprise.

"There is a drawer full of gold coins here," replied Holmes.

"These look like gold, too," I said as I opened the lid of a small chest and lifted out two small bars, each stamped with an assay symbol.

Thus we continued searching this strange room until we were certain there was no hiding-place we had missed. Then Holmes stood for some time in silence, his chin in his hand.

"What are you thinking?" asked Walters.

"I am considering what to do about all this," replied Holmes. "I think you had best let me handle the matter, Mr. Walters. I may not yet have much of a reputation in Ashford, but I am well known to some of the senior officers at the headquarters of the Kent Constabulary, and am very well known in London. If I give an account of what you have told us and what we have found here, I am more likely to be believed straight away than you are. We don't want to run the risk of your being suspected of knowing about this gold all along and simply wanting to get your own hands on it."

"Good Lord!" cried Walters. "I had not thought of that! You do believe what I have told you, don't you?"

"Of course," said Holmes. "I believe every word you have spoken. I have never doubted you for an instant."

At this, much to my surprise, Walters abruptly put his hands up to his face and burst into tears. "Do excuse me, gentlemen," he said, taking a handkerchief from his pocket. "Do forgive my weakness."

It is always a surprising and striking thing to see a grown man weep, and is nearly always of some special significance. In this case, it was evident that Holmes's prompt and unreserved declaration of belief in Mr. Walters had completely undermined the hardened natural defences of one who had been disbelieved, abused and vilified for so long.

"No apology is necessary," said Holmes, ushering the other to a chair. "Sit down here and compose yourself for a moment. Courage, Mr. Walters! Fate certainly dealt you a bad hand, but it may be that some of the cards in it are not quite so weak as they appeared. Tomorrow we shall go to the best solicitor in Ashford and swear an affidavit of all that we have learnt, and then present the facts to the authorities."

Once we had completed all the formalities, and the police had examined and searched Naxon House to their satisfaction, Holmes and I returned to London. As our train sped along through the Vale of Kent, Holmes was in a thoughtful, reflective mood, and when I remarked how deeply moved Walters had been by Holmes's generous expression of confidence in him, he turned to me in surprise.

"I had no intention of being 'generous', as you put it," returned my friend; "I was simply stating a fact."

I asked him then why he had been so confident in Mr. Walters's veracity.

"It is an instinctive thing," said he at length, "and not easy to put one's finger on. You may as well ask me how I know that two and two make four. That they do is instantly clear, but explaining precisely why they do takes a little longer. I suppose his eyes played a part in it."

"His eyes?"

"Well, the look in them, at least. One can generally tell an honest man by the look in his eyes."

"I seem to remember your saying that one should never trust to generalized impressions, as they can be misleading."

"There is no contradiction, Watson. I had already moved beyond my first general impression of Walters when I looked into his eyes and knew at once he was an honest man. It has been said, as you are no doubt aware, that the eyes are the windows of the soul, and when you have scrutinized as many faces as I have, you know that to be true."

The wheels of justice are sometimes very slow to turn, and it was many months before Mr. Walters's attempt to clear his name received a proper hearing. Even then the result was indecisive, and the matter was passed on to a higher court. Eventually the case reached the House of Lords. There, the judicial committee declared at length that although his original conviction had not been unreasonable on the evidence available at the time, it was now clear that it was mistaken, and should be struck from the record. Mr. Walters was at last, therefore, granted a complete and unconditional pardon.

As for Mr. Lidington, whose mystery had brought us into the case in the first place, he did not renew his lease upon Naxon House. He also gave up the study of alchemy, which he said he had quite lost the taste for, and, the last I heard, he had applied for and succeeded in regaining his former post with the South Eastern Railway.

THE YELLOW GLOVE

"IF ONLY CRIMINALS would occasionally display a little imagination," remarked Sherlock Holmes, as we sat in conversation after breakfast, one morning towards the end of the summer, "it would surely make life so much more interesting for everyone, and – who can say? – the criminals themselves might find that they derived an increased satisfaction from their work."

"The general opinion, I fancy, would be that criminals show quite enough imagination as it is," I responded with a chuckle. "They imagine that what is in someone else's pocket might be in their own, and then take steps to bring their imagined vision to reality!"

"Tush!" cried my companion, waving his pipe in the air in a gesture of dismissal. "You must not confuse simple activity, however energetically it is pursued, with the creative application of the imaginative faculties. Of course, oafs will continue to hit their victims over the head with lumps of wood, and hurl bricks through windows in pursuit of their aims. Every day brings fresh accounts of such crude and uninspired villainy. But where today is the carefully conceived plan, the enterprise so daring and subtle that it leaves the authorities baffled, and the victims themselves half admiring of the crime?"

"You have an unusual point of view," I ventured. "Indeed, some might describe it as beyond the bounds of eccentricity."

"Perhaps so," my companion conceded. "I'll own my view is coloured somewhat by professional considerations. I long for that spark of originality in the criminal which might kindle a little interest in my own slumbering intellect. As it is, I fear that my brain is in danger of suffering atrophy from lack of use."

"Might I enquire if anything in particular has prompted these reflections?" I asked after a moment.

For answer he picked up a sheet of note-paper which lay on the floor beside his chair, and passed it to me. "I received this note by the first post," said he.

I took the sheet from him and read the following:

MY DEAR MR. HOLMES – I wish most urgently to consult you. I have had the most bizarre and inexplicable experience of my life. What it means, I simply cannot imagine, but I fear that it may have some sinister implication for my employers, for whom I am at present acting in a senior capacity until our principal returns from abroad. I shall call at ten-thirty in the morning, and hope that that is not inconvenient for you. – MICHAEL ELDER

"I do not understand," I remarked in some puzzlement, as I finished reading the letter. "For one who laments the lack of intellectual stimulation, this letter is surely a cause of hope rather than the opposite!"

"Ah!" said my companion. "There, my dear fellow, you put your finger on the very nub of the matter! It does, I agree, appear to afford some justification for hope, and for a moment, as I read it, my spirits rose accordingly. But next moment I recalled how frequently my hopes have been dashed, how many times that which a correspondent describes as 'bizarre' or 'inexplicable' is revealed upon inspection to be so commonplace that the most egregious imbecile at Scotland Yard might be expected to fathom it. Thus, I fear that what appears to promise hope, presages instead only disappointment!"

"You are a pessimist!" said I, smiling at my companion's forlorn countenance.

"Not at all," returned he quickly. "On the contrary, Watson, I am by temperament a perennial optimist. But experience has taught me – alas! – that my optimism is very often unwarranted. However, we shall soon learn what it is that Mr. Elder finds bizarre and inexplicable, for that is probably his hand on the bell now!"

The front doorbell had jangled as he had been speaking, and a moment later our landlady showed a neatly dressed young man into the room, whom she announced as Mr. Michael Elder. He was youthful in appearance, scarcely more than twenty years of age, I judged, and was of slight build, with a pale, clean-shaven face.

"Pray take a seat, and let us know how we can help you!" said Holmes, vacating his own chair by the hearth and ushering the young man into it.

"Thank you," returned the other in a pleasant tone. "I'll come straight to the point," he continued after a moment, but then paused, and stroked his chin in silence. "The facts of the matter are these," he resumed eventually: "I am in the employment of a highly respected firm, somewhere in London. Our principal, who also happens to be my cousin, is away at present, in consequence of which I have had to assume a little more responsibility than I had before. I am confident that I have done nothing wrong, but am concerned, nevertheless, that something which has occurred, for which I must accept some responsibility, may have compromised the confidentiality of our business. I therefore wish to discover – simply for my own peace of mind, you understand – whether or not this is so. There," he concluded, breathing heavily; "that is the matter in a nutshell."

Sherlock Holmes raised his eyebrow, and regarded the young man for a moment.

"Really, Mr. Elder," said he at length; "you can hardly suppose that I shall be able to offer you any sensible advice, if the details of the matter, on which, perforce, my advice must be founded, are kept from me!"

"I beg your pardon," returned Elder. "I am a little afraid lest I endanger the commercial confidentiality of the company yet further. It is difficult to know what to do," he added, scratching his head.

"Then let me make it a little easier for you," said Holmes. "Your employers, I believe, are Elder and Kemp, the well-known engineering firm, of Southwark. The principal of the firm is your relative, Sir George Elder, who was knighted two years ago for his contribution to the engineering feats of the century. He has been in Russia for some time, where he has been supervising the construction of a new railway bridge across the river Volga, but is presently on his way back to England. His ship docks in London on Saturday afternoon. You therefore have three days in which to resolve whatever it is that is troubling you."

The young man's mouth fell open in astonishment. "How do you know all this?" he asked.

"I observed as you sat down that you had a small slide-rule in your pocket. Who but an engineer would carry a slide-rule about with him? From that observation, and knowledge of your surname, it is scarcely a super-human feat of intellect to associate you with the engineering firm of which Sir George Elder is the head. As to his activities in Russia, and his imminent return, there was an interesting report on the matter in this morning's *Times*."

"Well, I'll be blowed!" exclaimed the young man. He scratched his head for a moment before continuing. "You appear to know so much of my business already, that any further attempts at discretion on my part would seem pointless."

"That is something upon which we are agreed, then," said Holmes in a dry tone. "Pray, proceed!"

"Very well. You should first know a little of my own personal situation, for it has some bearing on the matter. I may carry a slide-rule in my pocket, as you observed; but I am not yet, I regret, very advanced in engineering expertise. I am still in the early stages of a training that will continue for some years before I am able to put any letters after my name.

"My father is a solicitor in Guildford, and the original idea was that I should follow him into that game. I did my best to stick it out for a couple of years, but it was all torts and contracts, parties of the first part, and that sort of nonsense, and I didn't really seem to be getting anywhere with it. Of course, I didn't want to disappoint the old man. He seemed so keen to see me in his dusty old chambers, and you know how touchy parents can be when you tell them you don't really care for something they've spent thirty-odd years at. I did my best to humour him, but it was no go in the end. He saw it as well as I. So, to cut a long story short, he offered me to his cousin, old George Elder, to train as an engineer. To be frank, I don't think my cousin was quite so enthusiastic to receive me as my father was to give me away, but he was civil enough about it, and took me under his engineering wing, as it were. When I came to London, I lodged for a while at Sir George's house, out Holland Park way, but we didn't always see eye to eye about what time I should come in of an evening, and other things, so eventually it was agreed that it might be better if I had diggings of my own, so that we could each keep the hours we wished without either of us putting the other out. I therefore took up lodgings in Notting Hill, an arrangement which seems to suit us both. Sir George's carriage passes the end of my road every morning, I wait there and get into it when it comes, then travel with him to Southwark. Once or twice, perhaps, he has had to send his coachman to look for me, when I didn't appear to be waiting there in the morning as he expected, but on the whole the arrangement has proved satisfactory.

"However," our visitor continued after a pause, "–and this will bring me to the point of the matter – I have reason to know that my cousin is an irascible man, and should he feel that I have fallen significantly below some standard of conduct that he keeps in his head, along with all his engineering standards, I might find myself obliged to seek other employment." Elder paused again and scratched his head. "Have I explained myself clearly, gentlemen?"

"I believe we understand the situation," responded Holmes. "What is it that has occurred, to cause you to fear your cousin's disapproval?"

"I'm not sure that 'disapproval' quite does the matter justice," returned Elder in a wry tone. "'Unappeasable wrath' might, perhaps, be nearer the mark. Anyhow, I'll tell you what's happened and see if you can offer any suggestions.

"The construction of the Volga bridge is a very big job, as you will imagine, and has been going on for a couple of years. Although Sir George has had to hop over to Russia every now and then, he has, for the most part, been content to leave the matter in the hands of subordinates. However, the completion was planned for this summer, so it was necessary for him to be there to supervise the final stages, to officially hand the bridge over to the authorities, and to collect the payment for the job. Just before he left, he took me aside. 'Michael,' said he to me in his gravest tone; 'I shall, as you know, be away from England for several months, and I am looking to you to uphold the good name of the firm in my absence.'

"'Yes, sir; of course,' I returned promptly, wondering why he should have selected me to receive his thoughts on the firm's good name, when there are many in his employ who are far senior to me, and, I dare say, much more important to the business.

"'I am addressing these remarks to you,' he continued, as if reading my mind, 'because you, Michael, are the only man here that bears the name of Elder, and that is a not insignificant matter.'

"'No, sir,' I responded, wondering where the conversation was leading.

"'I do not, as you know, have a son of my own, Michael. That being so, I have come to look upon you in that capacity. Although we have had our little disagreements, I entertain hopes – keen hopes, I might say – that you will one day make your own mark in the world of engineering, and perhaps succeed me as head of this firm. I have recently requested a report on your progress from Mr. Troughton, and he informs me that your work has been satisfactory. This encourages me to hope that my confidence in you will not be disappointed. Do I make myself clear?'

"'Certainly, sir,' said I, in as reassuring a tone as I could muster. But I don't mind admitting I felt a little oppressed by my cousin's weighty manner. It seemed to bear a remarkable family resemblance to that of my father. It is no uncommon thing for a father to have two sons; it is somewhat less common, I should imagine, for a son to have two fathers, and the responsibility of it weighs a bit heavy, I can tell you. I was pleased, anyway, that old Troughton had given me an acceptable report, even if it was not exactly glowing in its praise. He's the senior draughtsman at Elder and Kemp, and a grim, humourless fellow if ever there was one. He always gives me the impression of looking down upon me from a great height, which is no doubt how he sees the relations between us.

"Anyhow, things have been fairly quiet over the last couple of months, so the good name of the firm has been in no danger. Sir George very thoughtfully instructed his coachman to call for me every morning and evening as usual, so I've been on time every day, and given no cause for complaint. Recently, however – just this week – a very strange thing has occurred. I don't know how to explain it, and I am anxious in case I have inadvertently done something wrong."

"The details, please!"

"Two days ago, that is, on the thirtieth, Mr. Wade, the company secretary, called me into his private office. He had received a letter that morning, he informed me, from a Señor Fernando Rodriguez, a Chilean gentleman resident in London, who proposed to call that afternoon at three-thirty. He wished, he said, to consult Mr. Elder upon a civil engineering project in South America, which he described as of the very first importance.

"'I expect by "Mr. Elder" he means Sir George,' I remarked.

"'No doubt that is so,' returned Mr. Wade; 'but he makes it clear that his business is so important he will speak to no one but 'Mr. Elder.' He is evidently one of those people who sets great value upon seeing the principal. As Sir George is absent, it might be best if you stood in for him, Elder. You at least bear the same name, and that may suffice to satisfy Señor Rodriguez. You will probably only need to take preliminary details of the matter. Sir George can deal with it in greater depth upon his return. Of course, this Señor Rodriguez may be a puffed-up, self-important fool, and his business of no interest to us. On the other hand, however, the project he mentions may be every bit as important as he implies, and, if so, we should not wish to lose what might prove a lucrative commission, simply because Sir George is not here. Do you think you could cope with the matter?'

"'Certainly,' I responded; 'so long as the man speaks English.'

"'That should be no problem,' said Mr. Wade. 'His letter is written in perfect English.'

"I must say I felt thrilled and honoured to be in charge of this business. I had spoken to clients of ours before – and some most important ones, too – but only ever in the company of my cousin, Sir George. I had never before conducted such an interview on my own. Nevertheless, I told myself, of those that were there that day, I was undoubtedly the best qualified to deal with the matter. Old Mr. Wade is red-hot on legal issues and the like, but knows as much about bridge abutments as I know about solicitors' deed-boxes. It is the same with Mr. Goreham, the chief accountant: he is, I am told, a veritable wizard with figures, but knows practically nothing of engineering. Only Mr. Troughton, the senior draughtsman, is my superior in engineering knowledge, and he is a man of such gloomy aspect and manner that his involvement with any prospective client would be highly likely to lose us the business altogether. When I returned from Mr. Wade's office, Mr. Troughton asked me what was afoot, and as I described the matter to him, in as careless a manner as I could muster, I confess that I had difficulty keeping the excitement from my voice. I seemed to detect in his eyes a look of annoyance that I had been given charge of the matter, and I don't mind admitting that I was not entirely displeased to see him discomfited for once.

"'If you get into difficulties with the client,' said he, 'or feel that you are getting out of your depth, you can always ask me to join the discussion.'

"'Thank you, Mr. Troughton, I shall remember it,' I returned, in a tone which I hoped conveyed that I had no intention whatever of taking up his offer.

"At half past three, I was informed that Señor Rodriguez had arrived and had been shown into the conference-room, on the top floor. We generally see important clients there, for the room has a large table in it, which is useful for spreading out maps and plans. I hurried upstairs to meet him, and found him already seated at the table, sorting through a sheaf of papers that he had taken from a large leather valise. He rose to his feet as I entered, and I saw that he was a short, stocky man, with a very swarthy complexion, and a large dark moustache. He was elegantly clad in a light-grey suit, and upon the table lay a low-crowned, broad-brimmed hat of the same hue.

"'Señor Rodriguez?' said I, extending my hand.

"He shook my hand, but there was an expression of surprise upon his features.

"'You are somewhat younger than I had expected, Mr. Elder,' said he, in a very strong foreign accent.

"'Our principal, Sir George Elder, is unfortunately abroad at present,' said I. 'I am Michael Elder. I have been deputed to act for him in his absence.'

"Señor Rodriguez's eyes narrowed under his bushy eyebrows.

"'You are a member of the Elder family?' said he in a suspicious tone.

"'Certainly.'

"'A close member?'

"'I am Sir George Elder's cousin, his only relation in the firm, and have his full confidence.'

"For a moment he hesitated, then he nodded his head. 'Very well,' said he. 'You must excuse my caution, Mr. Elder, but the matter is an extremely confidential one, and I have found it wise to deal only with the heads of business. I represent the very highest interests in my country, and although my presence in London has not been generally advertised, we suspect that our enemies may have got wind of it, nevertheless. There are those who would stop at nothing to thwart our plans. Peru, for one, has spies everywhere. Do you understand?'

"'I believe so. You need have no fear as to my discretion, Señor Rodriguez.'

"Again he nodded his head. 'You are no doubt aware that the state of Chile has in recent years extended its territory to the north?'

"'I am not fully conversant with the details of the situation there,' I admitted.

"'No matter,' said he with a little smile. 'Why should you be? What is Antofagasta to you, eh? Or you to Antofagasta?'

"'Quite so.'

"'Suffice it to say, Mr. Elder, that it is desired to connect these newly occupied northern territories with the rest of the country, by a continuous line of rail. The terrain through which such a railway must pass is, in places, very severe, and will require considerable engineering works, including at least two very substantial bridges near Antofagasta. Do I make myself clear?'

"'Perfectly so.'

"There had been some slight noise behind me as Señor Rodriguez had been speaking. Not wishing to appear rude, I had not turned my head away from him, but he seemed to sense my distraction.

"'I take it you have no objection to my wife's being present?' said he.

"I turned now, and saw to my very great surprise that a lady was seated, in perfect stillness and silence, on a chair by the wall behind me. The chair was immediately behind the door, and as I had entered, and greeted Señor Rodriguez, I had closed the door behind me without looking, which is why I had not observed her. Although she was seated, I had the impression that she was somewhat taller than her husband. She was of a slim figure, dressed all in black, with a black bonnet upon her head, and a heavy veil covering her face. Señor Rodriguez explained to me that his wife was of a very nervous disposition. She did not speak English, and was unfamiliar with London, as a consequence of which she suffered great anxiety if ever he left her alone for any length of time. I assured him that his wife's presence occasioned no difficulty, and our interview proceeded. He explained to me at the outset that he had no technical knowledge of engineering matters, and would be guided by my opinions on the various difficulties likely to be encountered in the construction of the proposed railway line. This lessened the anxiety I had been feeling lest the limitations of my own technical knowledge became too evident to our client, and the consultation proceeded without difficulty for some time.

"All the while we were in discussion, I was conscious of the dark, silent figure of Señora Rodriguez behind my back. She never spoke, but occasionally coughed, or shuffled her feet on the floor. After a time, however, there came a strange, low moaning noise from behind me. I looked round in surprise. Señor Rodriguez stood up and went across to his wife. Then, leaning down close to her, he spoke softly in her ear. She, in return, whispered something back to him. So soft was her voice that no words were audible. Only the sibilance of her whisper carried to my ears.

"'My wife has abnormally sensitive faculties,' said Señor Rodriguez to me, coming to the table and leaning over in a confidential manner. 'In many ways, this is a rare gift; but sometimes – alas! – it is a curse. She is suffering at present from a very bad headache, Mr. Elder, a condition to which she is, regrettably, somewhat prone, and our conversation is, I fear, making her condition worse. When she has such attacks, the only effective cure is complete silence. Is there another room in which she could sit while we talk?'

"'Certainly,' said I. I should explain that on the top floor of the building are two large rooms, side by side, the conference-room, in which we had been sitting, and the boardroom, between which there is an interconnecting door. The boardroom was not in use at the time, so I opened the door and gestured to Señora Rodriguez, but she did not move. 'Your wife may sit undisturbed in here,' I suggested to her husband, 'if she does not object to the solitude.'

"'On the contrary,' said he, 'the solitude will be to her as balm to a wound. She will know that we are close at hand, and will not be anxious.' He took his wife's arm, and escorted her into the other room. Then he closed the door and rejoined me at the table, and we resumed the consultation.

"Barely five more minutes had passed, however, before our conversation was again interrupted. Out of the corner of my eye, I saw the door from the boardroom open slowly and quietly. I turned and saw Señora Rodriguez, standing perfectly still in the doorway, her veiled face turned in our direction. Señor Rodriguez stood up and conversed very softly with her again for a few moments.

"'Señora Rodriguez craves pardon for troubling you, but finds the air in the other room somewhat dank and still,' said he to me. 'Would it be possible for the window to be opened a little?'

"'Certainly,' said I. This interruption wasted a further five minutes, for the windows at Elder's have locking metal gates upon the inside, composed of vertical iron rods, and the casement windows cannot themselves be opened until the metal gates are open. I was thus obliged to hunt about for the key for a time, but eventually the iron gates and the window were open to the lady's satisfaction, and Señor Rodriguez and I resumed our discussion.

"It was becoming increasingly clear to me that his proposals were of a very ambitious nature indeed. If our firm could secure but a quarter of the engineering work involved it would still be a very good piece of business for us. One feature of the route in particular appeared to concern Señor Rodriguez above the rest, where the railway line was to cross a broad, canyon-like river-valley, a few miles south of Antofagasta. The river was practically dry for much of the year, he explained to me, but could become a raging torrent after heavy rainfall, or when the snows upon the mountains melted in the spring. A particular difficulty for any bridge constructed across this valley was that although one bank of the river was composed of very hard and stable rock, the other was chiefly composed of unstable shales, which could not support the weight of a bridge pier with any safety, and which were, in any case, at constant risk of landslip. By chance, our firm has been recently drawing up plans for a bridge across the Muchty Firth in the West Highlands of Scotland, the design of which has had to overcome a very similar problem. When I mentioned this to Señor Rodriguez, he showed great interest, and asked if he might see the plans. The matter is a highly confidential one, as we are in competition with several other firms for the contract, including our keen rivals, Gibbs and Wakefield of Birmingham, but I could see no objection to showing the plans to Señor Rodriguez. I hurried downstairs to the drawing-office, and explained the matter to Mr. Troughton. He was somewhat reluctant to release the papers at first, but I at length persuaded him.

"When I returned to the conference-room, Señor Rodriguez was pacing about the floor in an impatient manner, and as I spread out the papers on the conference-table he pounced upon them eagerly. Scarcely had I been able to point out to him the chief topographical features of the Muchty Firth, however, when we were interrupted yet again. The door from the boardroom opened slowly once more, and once again Señora Rodriguez stood there in silent entreaty. Her husband turned, and the professional enthusiasm quite vanished from his features and was replaced instead by a soft, husbandly tenderness. I could only marvel at the respect and solicitude shown by this man towards his wife. What might perhaps in another man have produced irritation, evoked in Señor Rodriguez only tender concern. Again he spoke to her in low tones, again she answered him in a soft sibilant whisper. Then he turned to me once more.

"'My wife bitterly regrets the inconvenience she is causing you,' said he, 'but wonders if it would be possible for her to have a glass of water. She unfortunately suffers from dryness of the mouth. Many medical men have investigated the case and made suggestions, but all – alas! – have been unavailing.'

"'Kindly inform Señora Rodriguez that she occasions no inconvenience whatever,' I returned as I hurried off to fetch the water, wondering to myself if there were any complaint that the lady did *not* suffer from.

"When I returned, Señor Rodriguez was poring over the maps and plans of the Muchty Firth bridge, making very copious notes.

"'This is very interesting, Mr. Elder,' said he, when he had passed the glass of water to his wife.

"'Of course,' I observed, as I looked over the notes he had made, 'some of the figures you have noted down are specific to the Muchty Firth bridge. The calculations for the Antofagasta bridge might be quite different.'

"'I appreciate that fact,' returned he, 'but these figures will enable me to understand more fully the mechanical principles involved, which will be the same for both bridges.'

"Thus we discussed the matter further, for another twenty minutes or so. Then Señor Rodriguez declared himself satisfied, and said that he would report back favourably to his superiors, and write to us again when the matter had been thoroughly discussed by them. With that he prepared to take his leave.

"I glanced at the clock. The afternoon had flown by, and it was almost time for us all to be leaving. I knew that Sir George's carriage would be waiting for me downstairs, so I offered to take Señor Rodriguez and his wife to wherever they were going.

"'We are staying in Eaton Square at present,' said he. 'It is kind of you to offer, Mr. Elder, but quite unnecessary. We can easily take a cab.'

"'Not at all,' I insisted. 'I pass close by Eaton Square on my way home. It will be no trouble at all to take you there.'

"It was certainly an odd little journey. Señor Rodriguez was very animated, crying out with a visitor's delight at the Houses of Parliament, Westminster Abbey and other notable buildings that we passed on our way. His strange, veiled wife, meanwhile, sat in perfect silence the whole way, scarcely moving her head an inch, and giving no indication that she was conscious of anything beyond the confines of the carriage.

"Presently we reached Eaton Square, and our driver drew the carriage to a halt at the address Señor Rodriguez had given him, a large house near the corner of Belgrave Place. Señor Rodriguez and I shook hands warmly as he and his wife alighted, and as the carriage drew away he waved to me from the doorstep of the house, his wife standing silently beside him. I sat back in my seat with some satisfaction, then, I don't mind admitting, for I was confident that I had laid the groundwork for a very good piece of business for our firm. I had, I felt, dealt in a professional and assured manner with all the questions Señor Rodriguez had put to me, and had persuaded him, I felt certain, of the unrivalled skill and experience which Elder and Kemp could bring to the various problems the proposed railway was likely to encounter. Already, I began to imagine the discussion I would have with Sir George Elder on the matter, and to imagine, too, his beaming face and words of praise for me.

"We were passing along the side of Belgrave Square, which is very little distance from Eaton Square, and I was reflecting in this fashion, when I noticed one of Señor Rodriguez's gloves on the floor of the carriage. It was yellow, and made of soft kid leather. I picked it up. It was undoubtedly his. He must have dropped it when alighting, probably when picking up his valise, which had stood on the floor beside his seat. I called to the coachman, and instructed him to return to Eaton Square.

"'I shall only be a moment,' I called to him as I sprang from the carriage, ran up the front doorsteps, and pulled at the bell. A moment later the door was opened by the imposing figure of a large, bald-headed butler.

"'Yes, sir?' said he, looking somewhat down his nose at me.

"I held up the yellow glove. 'Señor Rodriguez dropped this in my carriage,' I explained.

"'Did he, sir? How very unfortunate!'

"His tone puzzled me. 'Well, it's not so unfortunate now,' said I, 'as I have found it.'

"'Quite so, sir,' said he. 'I am sure that Señor Rodriguez will be most relieved.'

"'Right-ho, then,' said I, proffering the glove; but he made no move to take it from me. 'Are you not going to take it?' I asked in surprise.

"'No, sir.'

"'Why ever not?' I queried. 'Señor Rodriguez will be very glad to have it back.'

"'Then may I suggest that you give it to him, sir?'

"'Why can you not give it to him, may I ask?'

"'Because, sir, I am not acquainted with the gentleman to whom you refer.'

"'But he lives here,' I protested.

"'I can assure you, sir, that he does not.'

"I stepped back to verify that I had come to the right house. Yes, there could be no doubting it; this was the door at which I had last seen Señor Rodriguez and his wife. Then it occurred to me that their presence here might be a closely guarded secret, and that the butler might be on his guard for enemy agents trying by a ruse to learn their whereabouts. I leaned closer to him and lowered my voice.

"'I am not a Peruvian spy, you know,' said I.

"'I never supposed for one moment that you were, sir,' returned he.

"'Señor Rodriguez has been consulting me in confidence about the construction of a railway line,' I explained.

"'Has he indeed, sir? How very interesting for you!'

"It was clear that I was not going to get anywhere by such an approach. I offered the glove once more, the butler again declined it, and as a last attempt I tried a different tack.

"'Although you say that you don't know Señor Rodriguez,' said I, 'he should, nevertheless, be informed that his glove is in the possession of Michael Elder. He will recognize the name.'

"'I am sure he will, sir. Should I ever be introduced to the gentleman in question, the news that you have his glove will be the first information upon my lips.'

"With that, I gave it up. My day's work, which I had shortly before deemed such a triumphant success, seemed tarnished somewhat by this surprising and unsatisfactory codicil. I said nothing about it to anyone, and hoped that the next day would bring an explanation of some kind. Perhaps my conjecture had been correct, and the household in Eaton Square had been warned of possible enemy agents and instructed to deny all knowledge of Rodriguez. Perhaps I had, after all, approached the wrong house upon my return with the glove; or, more likely, I thought, perhaps Señor Rodriguez himself, being unfamiliar with his surroundings, had inadvertently mounted the wrong front steps as I left him, and, realising his mistake, had repaired to the correct house whilst I was driving up through Belgravia. At any event, I hoped to hear something from him the next day. In this hope, however, I was disappointed.

"It was then that I recalled the great care with which my visitor had copied down the figures from the plan of the Muchty Firth bridge, figures which related to our own unique solution to the engineering problems that the bridge presented. A cold, clammy hand seemed all at once to grip my vitals, as I realised that I had shown these highly confidential calculations to a man whom I had never met before, and of whose antecedents I really knew nothing. Gone from my imagination in a flash was the beaming figure of Sir George Elder, showering me with praise; replaced now by a stern and vindictive Sir George Elder, kicking me out into the street.

"I asked Mr. Wade if I might see Señor Rodriguez's letter. The address at the top of the sheet was indeed that of the house at which I had called the day before. But the address was only hand-written, not printed on the sheet, and I thought it possible that he had made a mistake as to the house number. In a state of some anxiety, I left work early, and took myself over to Eaton Square once more. There I knocked at every door, and at each asked the same three questions: Did Señor Rodriguez reside there? If he did not, did they know what his address might be? If they did not, had they observed anyone in the area answering to his description? I lost count of the number of doors I called at, and the answers I received, but it was of no consequence, for all the answers were 'no.' I then called in at Scotland Yard, to enquire if anything was known there of Señor Rodriguez. It had occurred to me that as a foreigner resident in London, he might perhaps be known to the authorities."

"Did you make any progress?" asked Holmes.

Michael Elder shook his head. "No. They had never heard of him. I saw a detective inspector named Lestrade, but I wasn't able to give him such a detailed account of the matter as I have given to you, as he was a little impatient for me to finish, and kept interrupting me."

"What was his response?"

"He said that he would make a note of it all, and if anything turned up he would let me know."

Holmes laughed. "I regret to have to disabuse you of any hopes in that regard, Mr. Elder," said he, "but the response you received is something of a stereotype, I am afraid. Translated into everyday English, it means Lestrade will put the paper containing your details into a deep drawer, and forget all about it!"

"So I suspected. He informed me that he was extremely busy, and did not have the time to pursue every trivial matter that was presented to him."

"They are certainly very busy at Scotland Yard; although I sometimes feel they do themselves no service by failing so signally to distinguish the important from the unimportant. Did Inspector Lestrade have any suggestion to make?"

"None whatever. Indeed, he gave me the distinct impression that he thought I was possibly unhinged, and had made the whole thing up myself."

Holmes chuckled. "Do not be discouraged by that response, Mr. Elder! It is the natural tendency of mediocre minds to dismiss as untrue that which they do not understand. Do you have the glove with you?"

"Here it is," responded Elder, pulling a folded glove from his pocket. It was of a dull egg-yolk colour, made of soft, expensive-looking leather, with a little pearl button at the cuff.

"Broad fitting," remarked Holmes as he tried the glove on his hand. "Hum! There is a label on the inside. Let us see: 'Thomas Grove and Son, Gentlemen's Outfitters of Colchester.' Hum! Did Inspector Lestrade see this glove?"

Elder shook his head. "He expressed no interest in it, so I did not show it to him."

"I see," said Holmes. Then, without a further word, he leaned back in his chair, his fingertips pressed together like a church steeple, and his eyes closed. A look of surprise passed over our visitor's features, and he made as if to speak; but I put my finger to my lips, and he remained silent, although his eyebrow was raised in an expression of curiosity at what he no doubt considered my friend's eccentric manner.

For five minutes we remained in complete silence, then Holmes opened his eyes, and reached for his pipe.

"Very well," said he, striking a match, and putting it to his pipe. "You mentioned earlier that Señor Rodriguez had a swarthy complexion and a large moustache. Could you now picture that gentleman once more, and give me a slightly fuller description?"

"Certainly," responded Elder. "He was a touch below medium height," he continued after a moment; "but was powerfully built, with a very broad chest, and large, strong-looking hands. There was something powerful about his features, too, and I seemed to read in them great strength of purpose. His eyes were dark and piercing, he had a sharp, hooked nose, somewhat like a bird of prey, and beneath his left eye was a large, curving scar."

"Thank you," said Holmes in a tone of contemplation. "That information should prove very useful."

"What do you think about it all?" enquired Elder after a moment.

"I think," returned Holmes, "that I should very much like to see the premises of Elder and Kemp for myself. Would that be possible?"

"By all means. We can go along there now, if you wish."

Holmes shook his head. "I should prefer to make my examination when there is no one else there," said he. "I do not wish to be disturbed, nor do I wish to excite any curiosity. Could that be arranged?"

"Certainly. I have a key, and can conduct you round the premises myself."

"That would be ideal. Drop by later, then, when you are certain that everyone at Elder and Kemp has gone home for the day, and we can go along there together. Until then, not a word of this to anyone!"

At a little after six o'clock, we were in a cab with Michael Elder, rattling through the dense traffic towards Southwark. It was a pleasant evening, and as we crossed the river, the low sun emerged from behind a bank of clouds and sparkled like diamonds upon the rippled surface of the water.

"As you will see when we reach Elder and Kemp's," said our companion, "the building has four floors. On the ground floor and the first floor above that are the general offices for the clerks and draughtsmen. On the next floor up are the offices of most of the senior men, including Mr. Wade and Mr. Goreham, and also the main store-rooms. On the top floor is Sir George Elder's private chamber, and that which old Mr. Kemp occupied before his retirement. There are also a couple of smaller, empty rooms, but most of the floor is taken up by the two large rooms I mentioned to you earlier, the conference-room and the boardroom. But you will be able to see it for yourselves in a moment, for we are almost there."

Our cab had turned off the main road into a quieter and narrower street, although even here the pavements were busy with crowds of men hurrying along to the railway station. It was a shadowed, somewhat gloomy street, lined on both sides by tall, flat-fronted buildings. Behind those on our left, as I could see through occasional gaps between them, stood a tall, grimy-looking railway viaduct. A train was passing, sending up an enormous plume of smoke, which drifted lazily over the roofs of the buildings in front. Elder called to the cabbie, and we drew up before one of these gaunt brick buildings.

Our young companion unlocked the door and led us inside and up the narrow, oilcloth-covered staircase, until we reached the top floor. There, a corridor stretched the width of the building, on the right of which were four doors, leading to chambers overlooking the street outside. On the left side, there were just two doorways, each with a pair of double doors. Our guide threw open the first of these, and we followed him into a large room. In the far wall was a broad window, covered with a metal grille, through which the parapet at the top of the viaduct was visible. In the centre of the room was a very large rectangular table, with a dozen or more chairs about it, and against the right-hand wall stood a large mahogany bureau.

"This is the conference-room," said Elder.

"And this, I take it, is where Señora Rodriguez was sitting the other day, when you entered," said Holmes, indicating a chair that stood against the wall behind the open door. "Hum! This door, presumably, leads to the boardroom," he continued, indicating a door at the near end of the right-hand wall. "Let us take a look in there."

The boardroom was an almost exact duplicate of the conference-room. In the centre stood a large oval table, somewhat more ornate and highly polished than that in the conference-room, and about it stood a dozen chairs. The window at the far end was, like that in the conference-room, protected on the inside by a grille of vertical iron bars. Against the side-wall opposite the door by which we had entered was a large, dark green safe, which stood about five feet high and four feet wide.

"It was at this table that Señora Rodriguez was sitting when her husband passed her the glass of water, I take it," said Holmes to Elder.

"That is correct. At this near end."

"And this is the window she wished you to open? Where is the key now?"

"I will get it for you," said Elder. "It is in a box in the bureau in the other room."

We followed him back into the conference-room, where he pulled open the deep bottom drawer of the bureau. From the back of this he took out a wooden cigar-box which he opened on the table. Inside was a miscellaneous assortment of keys, pens and pencils.

"Does the same key open the windows in both these chambers?" asked Holmes.

Elder shook his head. "Every window in the building has a different key." He selected a key from the box, and held it out on the palm of his hand. Attached to it was a small piece of tape, on which the word "boardroom" was written in indelible pencil.

Holmes took the key and examined it closely. "Did you bring the key back here when you had opened the window, or leave it in the lock?" he asked.

"The latter; for I knew that I should shortly have to close up the grille again."

"Has the key been used since then?"

"I do not believe so."

Holmes nodded, then he held the key to his nose and sniffed, like a bloodhound seeking a scent. In an instant, I saw a spark of excitement light up his eye. From his pocket he took a powerful lens, with the aid of which he examined the key very carefully. At length, evidently satisfied, he led us back into the boardroom, where he unlocked the grille which covered the window, then pulled both it and the window open.

"It is a long way down from here," said he, as we leaned out of the window.

"It is a fearsome drop," I concurred, gazing down into the narrow lane which ran behind the building. Although the sun had not yet set – indeed, even as I leaned from the window, its last, yellowed rays were gilding the pinnacles of a church in the distance – the narrow alley below, hemmed in so tightly between the building and the railway viaduct, was already in deep shade. The vertiginous appearance of this awesome, man-made chasm was made the greater by its very narrowness, for the parapet of the railway viaduct was barely a dozen feet from the window, and the characteristic railway smells of soot, tar and oil came distinctly to my nostrils.

"It is to be wondered what Señora Rodriguez thought of the fresh air she had sought, when you had opened this window for her!" remarked Holmes with a chuckle.

At that moment, with a thunderous roar and the sharp hiss of steam, a train passed along the viaduct at high speed, belching great clouds of thick, dark smoke about it. Quickly, we closed the windows.

"Do you not find the frequent passage of trains disturbing to your work?" I asked Elder, as he closed and locked the window-grille.

He shook his head. "You become accustomed to it," said he. "Besides, it is only on the top floor of the building that the noise is as loud as this. On the lower floors, it is scarcely audible. The engineers involved in constructing this railway line through such a crowded area faced immense difficulties, as you will imagine, which is why it is, unfortunately, so close to so many buildings. Per yard, as you are perhaps aware, it is the most expensive length of line ever built, a distinction which is unlikely to be challenged in the foreseeable future. But, with regard to the noise, the design of the viaduct – its height, the shape and size of the parapets, and so on – ensures that most of the noise rises away from the buildings. If noise were visible, like that smoke you see swirling about in the breeze, you would observe it rising upwards in the shape of an inverted cone. Civil engineering has brought knowledge of such matters to a very high degree!"

"Fascinating though it is to hear an expert speak on his own subject," remarked Holmes, "we must return from engineering to the matter in hand. Is there generally much of value kept in this safe?"

"There are some highly confidential papers, and the company's books, of course; but no great amount of cash, if that is what you mean."

"The wages of the staff?"

"The amount is calculated weekly by Mr. Jenkins, under the supervision of Mr. Goreham. It is then ordered every Thursday from the bank, the Southwark branch of the London and Home Counties, and delivered here on Friday."

"Who has a key to the safe?"

"There are four. Sir George Elder, of course, has one. Our secretary, Mr. Wade, has another; and our accountant, Mr. Goreham, a third. The fourth key is spare, and is kept in the little box from which I took the window key."

Holmes's eyebrow went up in surprise. "That does not seem the safest of repositories for such an important key," he observed.

"It is thought unlikely that anyone would come upon it by chance," responded Elder; "or would recognize it for what it was if he did so. It is disguised. If we return to the other room, I will show you."

We followed our companion back into the conference-room, where the wooden cigar-box lay open upon the table. He replaced the window-key in it, and took out another, which he held out for us to see. On the little slip of tape attached to the key I read the words "map cupboard".

"This is, despite its label, the key to the safe," said Elder.

Holmes chuckled. "And the real key to the map-cupboard?"

"There isn't one. The map-cupboard does not have a lock."

"How charmingly eccentric!" exclaimed Holmes in delight, as he took the key in his hand. "How refreshingly *outré!* Henceforth, I shall certainly regard engineers in a new light! Who is aware of this little subterfuge?"

"All the senior men in the company," returned Elder: "Sir George, Mr. Wade, Mr. Goreham, Mr. Troughton and myself."

"And is the key very often used?"

Elder shook his head. "Of course, Mr. Wade and Mr. Goreham have frequent occasion to open the safe in the course of their duties, but as they both have a key of their own, they would not need to use this one."

"I see," said Holmes. He raised the key to his nose, as he had done with the window-key, and sniffed carefully at it, a frown of concentration upon his face. Then he took out his lens once more and examined the key closely for several minutes. Finally, he replaced the key in the box, and turned once more to Elder.

"You stated that during Sir George's present visit to Russia he is to formally hand over the bridge to the authorities, and receive final payment for the work."

"That is correct."

"How is the payment to be made?"

"In gold."

"Through the London branch of the St Petersburg Bank?"

"No, in bullion and specie. This arrangement is not so unusual as people might imagine, for these foreign contracts. Sir

George is travelling with the gold from St Petersburg to London."

Holmes clapped his hand to his head. "And his ship docks on Saturday!" he cried. "The case is complete! I now know everything."

"Everything?" cried Elder in surprise.

"Well, I know the who, the why, the where, the when and the how. If there are any aspects of the matter not comprehended under those headings, my knowledge may not be complete."

"What will you do?" asked Elder in a tone of bewilderment.

"I shall go to see Inspector Lestrade at once, and explain to him why he should have paid somewhat more attention to your account. I confidently predict that when he hears what I have to tell him, the piece of paper on which he wrote your details will come back out of the deep drawer I mentioned earlier. I shall communicate with you later in the week, Mr. Elder. Until then, you must say nothing of this matter to anyone. Do you understand?"

"Certainly."

For a moment, Holmes regarded his young client, a look of doubt upon his face.

"Your story of Señor Rodriguez, his strange, silent wife, the Antofagasta railway, the yellow glove and all the rest of it, is certainly an interesting one," said Holmes at length. "You might feel tempted to speak of it to someone."

"Yes."

"But you must not."

"No."

"Believe me when I tell you, Mr. Elder, that not merely the security and prosperity of this company, but the entire future course of your own life may depend upon your adhering to this instruction. If anyone should ask you about Señor Rodriguez or the proposed railway in South America, speak freely and enthusiastically about it, just as you might have done on the day of his visit to you. But do not, under any circumstances whatever, mention the incident of the glove, nor your visit to me."

"I understand," responded Elder, clearly impressed by the gravity of Holmes's manner.

We drove at once then to Scotland Yard, but my friend was destined to be disappointed that evening, for Lestrade was not on duty. With a sigh of frustration, he made an appointment to see the policeman in the morning, and we returned to our chambers in Baker Street. There, Holmes sat smoking in silence for almost two hours, impatiently brushing aside all the questions I put to him, before retiring early to his bed.

In the morning my friend had taken his breakfast and gone out before I was up, and I did not see him all day. He returned late in the evening, in a state of extreme fatigue. He had evidently spoken to the landlady before coming upstairs, for she appeared a minute or two later with a large glass of milk and a plate of gingerbread. These he consumed in silence, then, begging forgiveness for what he termed his uncivil manner, he retired once more to his bed.

The next day he had again risen and left the house before I was awake, and I was left once more to conjecture as to the direction in which his enquiries were taking him. About four o'clock, however, I had fallen into a brown study with an open book in my hand when I was roused from my reverie by the sound of footsteps upon the stair. I assumed that it was Holmes, and I was considering what questions I would put to him, when all at once the sitting-room door was flung open, and a dirty-looking ruffian, with a greasy, straggling beard, burst into the room without knocking. Above his eyebrow was an ugly gash, encrusted with blood.

"Halloa!" I cried, springing to my feet. "How you gained access to this house I do not know; but unless you have an adequate explanation, you will certainly leave it as swiftly as you entered!"

"My dear fellow!" came a well-known voice. "I must beg a thousand pardons for startling you in this way! I have been in these disreputable-looking garments for so long that I had quite forgotten I had them on, and that my friends would not recognize me!"

"Holmes!" I cried. "Whatever is the purpose of assuming such an appearance?"

"You see before you, Watson, Mr. Jervis Jones, newly arrived in London from Cardiff, seeking work," returned my friend, affecting a soft Welsh accent. "I have been in search of information, and judged that I should be more likely to acquire it in this guise, rather than as myself."

"You have acquired a wound, anyhow!"

He put his hand up to his forehead, and gingerly touched the cut there. "It bled rather freely at first," said he; "but it is not very deep, and probably appears worse to your professionally honed concern than it really is. I was in a pub down Limehouse way when a drunken buffoon took a dislike to me. Unfortunately, considering the guise I had adopted, he declared in unequivocal terms his abiding dislike of the Welsh, and then, suiting the action to the word, as it were, hit me over the head with a beer-bottle. I responded somewhat more classically – if I may be allowed to be judge in my own cause – with a left uppercut to the jaw, and the upshot was that we were both ejected from the premises!"

"You never cease to amaze me!" I cried with a chuckle. "I am glad, at least, that you have returned relatively unharmed, Holmes! Were you able to acquire any of the information you sought?"

"I picked up the scent of a couple of rumours, but nothing of great value. To be frank, I had had only faint hopes of success when first I set out, so I am not especially disappointed." He glanced at the clock. "If you would be so good as to order us some tea, Watson, I shall give you a full account of the Elder case, and of how it came to take me down to Limehouse, once I have completed some very vigorous ablutions! You might also put a match to that fire, for there is a distinct chill in the air this afternoon, and I fear it will be a cold evening." In the doorway he paused. "The nights are drawing in, Watson. Summer is almost over, and giving way to the season of mist and fog. Suitable weather for a little adventure, would you not say? The game is afoot, my friend, and if you are up to the rigours of the chase, I think I can promise you an adventure tomorrow night which you will not quickly forget!"

An hour later, Sherlock Holmes and I were seated on either side of a blazing fire, drinking tea and smoking our pipes. Outside, the daylight was fading into the grey twilight of early evening. Inside, with his old mouse-coloured dressing-gown wrapped about him, my friend explained to me his analysis of the strange events that his young client had described to us so vividly earlier in the week.

"To begin with," said Holmes, "it was difficult to judge whether Señor Fernando Rodriguez was an honest gentleman, who spoke nothing but the truth, or a fraud, whose purpose in calling upon our client earlier in the week was not as he represented it."

"The latter, surely!" I cried, laughing; but my friend held up his hand.

"Do not be too quick to jump to conclusions." said he. "It cannot be denied that the events of the other day had a suspicious quality to them, but I have known men condemned before on account of the suspicious manner of their actions, who were in reality perfectly innocent. It was just possible, I considered, that, despite the odd circumstances, Señor Rodriguez was a sincere and genuine man, who happened to have an unusual wife and a powerful desire to conceal his true address from everyone, even from the man with whom he was proposing to do business. A man in very great fear for his safety – or that of his wife – might well have acted as Señor Rodriguez did."

"I suppose it is possible," I concurred, but without much conviction.

"However, the glove he left behind him rather settled the matter."

"Why so?"

"Because it had been purchased from a shop in Colchester. It seems highly unlikely, to say the least, that a South American gentleman, recently arrived in this country, would travel fifty miles into the Essex countryside to purchase gloves. Nor does it seem likely that a man described by Elder as elegantly dressed, and giving all the appearance of a man of means, would have purchased the gloves second-hand in London. It seems probable, therefore, that Rodriguez was being less than fully honest about his antecedents. But if he were lying to that extent, then he might also be lying about anything else, including the name he had given and his purpose in calling at Elder and Kemp. Now, it is always a sound rule when dealing with liars to ignore completely what they say, and to concentrate instead upon what they do. If we therefore leave aside the discussion of South American railways which took place the other day, what then remains?"

"Señor Rodriguez contrived to get sight of the confidential plans for the Scottish bridge that Elder mentioned to us."

"That is true; and yet it is difficult to believe that that was the real purpose of the charade that was played out earlier in the week. As an explanation it fails to account for the presence of the wife, and her unusual behaviour. You must remember that if the man calling himself Rodriguez had been speaking the truth, then it might just have been the case that he had an odd, nervous wife; but if he were lying, then the whole explanation given for her presence with him at Elder's falls to the ground, and we must presume that, so far from her presence there being an incidental and unimportant matter, the consequence, simply, of her not wishing to be left alone, it was, rather, of central importance to their scheme. In other words, if their purpose was a dishonest one, then she must have accompanied her husband there for a specific reason. What could that reason be?"

"I cannot imagine."

"Well, then, consider the woman's actions. What, precisely, did she do?"

"She complained of a headache, and went to sit in the boardroom by herself. She then asked for a window to be opened, and later requested a glass of water."

"Precisely!"

"I do not follow you. None of these things seems very significant."

"In themselves, perhaps not; but if the purpose of this couple was a dishonest one, then we must assume an ulterior motive for all their actions. The request for a glass of water, for instance, we must suppose was a planned ruse to get Elder out of the way for a few minutes. In fact, by the time the plan was implemented, it may no longer have been necessary, as Elder had already been absent for some time, bringing the plans of the Muchty bridge, but the woman, who had been in the other room, may not have known that. Now, why would they want Elder out of the way? Clearly, so that they could examine something in his absence. What could that something be? The woman's request that the window be opened might have seemed of little significance had the window been an ordinary one. But it is unusual: it is protected by an iron grille, which must be unlocked with a key. Perhaps, then, I conjectured, it was this key that was the focus of their attention."

"I observed that you held the key to your nose when Elder showed it to you," I interjected, "although I could not imagine why."

"I wished to know if there were any lingering scent of soap upon it," returned Holmes. "For if they had wanted to make a copy of the key for some reason, the easiest way would have been to press it into a bar of soap and use the impress later as a mould to make an exact duplicate. I was gratified to discover that my surmise was correct: the key bore a faint but unmistakable odour of soap. A close examination of the key with the aid of a lens confirmed the matter, revealing as it did minute traces of soap adhering to the metal. Clearly, these people wished to gain access to the premises of Elder and Kemp at some later time. It still remained to discover what their purpose might be, but the presence in the boardroom of the company safe suggested a likely motive. When Elder showed us the spare key to the safe, which was also kept in the little wooden box, the question was settled beyond doubt, for my examination of it revealed similar traces of soap to those I had found on the window-key.

"The purpose of the charade played out by these villains was thus laid bare. They wished to provide themselves with duplicate keys so that they could re-enter the premises later, when no one was about, and open the safe. But what was it they sought there? For Elder informed us that there was not usually much of value kept in the safe. It was only when he revealed to us the details of the Russian payment that this aspect of the matter became clear. On Saturday afternoon, Sir George Elder arrives back in London with a quantity of gold. You perceive the significance of the day, no doubt?"

I considered the question for a moment. "Of course!" I cried at last. "On Saturday afternoon, all London banks will be closed, and he will not be able to deposit his gold safely until Monday morning!"

"Precisely, Watson! The gold will thus have to be stored on the firm's premises in Southwark from Saturday afternoon until Monday morning. These villains have got wind of this fact, and have concocted a charmingly complex scheme to obtain access to the premises whilst the gold is being stored there."

"But who are these people?" I asked.

"There, if I am correct," Holmes responded, "my knowledge of the criminal classes gives me an advantage. You recall Elder's description of Señor Rodriguez?"

"He described him as very swarthy, with a large dark moustache, a hooked nose and a curving scar beneath his left eye."

"If we set aside the swarthiness and the moustache, both of which could be assumed for the role being played, we are left with the hooked nose and the large, distinctive scar. Now, as it happens, I know of someone whose appearance precisely matches that description. He is, moreover, just the sort of person who might interest himself in Sir George Elder's Russian gold. Have you ever heard me speak of Albert Foulger or his gang?"

I shook my head.

"He is a highly resourceful criminal, Watson, as cunning as he is ruthless, and has the distinction of being the third most sought-after villain in the country. You do not recollect his name, but you may be familiar with his work. Do you remember the Hatton Garden diamond robbery, of three years ago?"

"Certainly. It was a daring raid, in the middle of the night. The gang got away with a small fortune in diamonds, and was never caught."

"Those, indeed, are the chief facts of the matter. Several senior policemen were assigned to the case, including our old friend, Inspector Lestrade. Their enquiries eventually led them to believe that the Foulger gang was responsible, but conclusive evidence was lacking. Albert Foulger, the head of the gang, could not be questioned, for he had disappeared without trace. There were rumours that he was somewhere on the south coast, in Southampton, or Portsmouth, or Brighton; but if he was, the police could never find him, and after a while the trail went cold. The official view, which I think is probably correct, is that the gang made such a profit from their haul of diamonds that they have since found it unnecessary to engage in their usual nefarious work.

"Now, as you have no doubt surmised, Watson, Albert Foulger is the gentleman I referred to, as having the hooked nose and scar that Mr. Elder described. The scar is a souvenir he carries of the murderous war for superiority which was fought between the Foulgers and the Maynard gang at the end of the 'seventies. This ended in complete victory for the Foulgers, and the death of the rival gang-leader, Tobit Maynard, and one of his sons. All this was known for a fact to the police, but, of course, as is the way with these things, nothing could ever be proved against anyone.

"However, to return to the present: Albert Foulger has two sons, Patrick and Jimmy, and, unless I am much mistaken, tomorrow night will see all three of them making an attempt upon Sir George Elder's gold. It is just such a prize as could tempt Albert Foulger out of retirement, and lead to the reconstituting of his gang. It also represents the best, indeed, perhaps the only opportunity for Lestrade to collar the lot of them, as I succeeded in convincing him yesterday. He has, I trust, been making his preparations today, while I have been touring the pubs of the East End, in the faint hope of picking up a little more information. It was a delicate business, despite what you might think," added my friend with a chuckle; "for it was, of course, vital that I gave no hint to the Foulgers or their associates that we were on their trail."

"I don't know about 'delicate'," I remarked, laughing; "it sounds a simply hopeless task to me! Why, there are thousands of pubs at that end of London! You could probably spend a month going round them, and not see them all!"

"I did have the advantage of knowing some of Albert Foulger's old haunts," my friend responded; "but your estimate of the task as fairly hopeless is probably correct, nevertheless. I learned little which related to the Foulgers or their plans. Still," he added with a dry chuckle, "the day was not entirely devoid of interest, and had at least the merit of novelty!"

"What of the woman?" I asked, as my thoughts returned to young Elder's tale. "Do you have any idea of her true identity?"

My companion paused, in the act of knocking his pipe out on the hearth, and burst out laughing.

"I very much fancy," said he after a moment, "that our Señora Rodriguez is in reality Jimmy Foulger."

"What!"

"He has played a similar part before, in a fraud the gang attempted down in Kent, five years ago."

"Well, I never!" I exclaimed.

"It will no doubt discomfit our young client to learn that he has been taken in by such an imposture; but he should not consider himself too great a fool, for Jimmy Foulger undoubtedly plays the part with great conviction! And now," my friend continued after a moment, "I think, if you have no objection, Watson, that I shall distract myself with a little soothing music, to drive what has been a rather fatiguing day from my mind!"

So saying, he picked up his violin, and after adjusting the strings for a few moments, began to play a series of the most languid and haunting melodies. I lay back in my chair, and closed my eyes to listen, reflecting as I did so on what a singularly assorted fellow I shared chambers with.

The following day, Holmes went out shortly after breakfast, and did not return until late in the afternoon, and then only briefly.

"You have had a successful day, I trust?" I enquired, as he bustled about the room.

"Satisfactory enough," said he in a brisk tone. "I have seen Sir George Elder and his young cousin, and also Inspector Lestrade. Everything is now in place, Watson. If you do wish to accompany me this evening," he added, "you had best make ready, for it would be safest to get there before dark. It is essential that we are in position when our quarry turns up at the water-hole, as it were. Our night's expedition should, I think, be an exhilarating one!"

My experience of camp life in India had made me a quick and ready traveller, and in a few minutes we had left the house and were hurrying up Baker Street. The streets were choked with traffic, so Holmes proposed that we travel by the Metropolitan Railway to the nearest point and proceed from there on foot. Thus it was that, some forty minutes later, we made our way down from Mansion House station to the river, and so across Southwark Bridge. From there, my companion led me into a maze of narrow, shady streets, which passed this way and that between tall, flat-fronted industrial buildings and warehouses, until we at last reached a lane which lay in the shadow of a towering railway viaduct. This we followed a little way, then Holmes turned into a narrow alley which passed through one of the arches beneath the viaduct. This brought us into another shaded lane, over which the viaduct on the one side, and the buildings on the other seemed to loom and glower as if they might meet together high above us, close off the sky, and plunge the lane into total blackness.

"Why!" I cried, as I looked about me. "This is the lane at the back of Elder and Kemp's building!"

Even as I spoke, my companion gave a sharp rat-a-tat-tat with his knuckles on an unmarked brown door. It was opened at once by a uniformed policeman, and we passed inside. A thin, sharp-nosed man in a grey overcoat came forward out of the shadows to meet us, and I recognized our old friend, Inspector Lestrade.

"Good evening, Dr. Watson," said he to me as we shook hands. "It is good to see you out on the hunt with us again!"

"I hope the night will be a successful one," said I.

"So do we all, I'm sure," returned the policeman. "I've waited a long time to get my derbies on old Foulger, I can tell you!"

"Is Sir George here?" asked Holmes.

"Yes; he is upstairs with his cousin."

"Splendid!" said Holmes. "Any further developments to report, Lestrade?"

The policeman nodded his head enthusiastically.

"There are indeed!" said he. "Acting on the information I gave them, as to the shop from which the lost glove had been purchased, my colleagues in Colchester were able to discover the address of everyone who had bought such gloves there in the last year. Enquiries in the district have now eliminated all of those purchasers save one, and that one – a man going under the name of Henshaw, who has been resident in the town about three years – is, they are certain, Albert Foulger. He is away from home at present, but there are men watching his house day and night, ready to seize him the moment he shows his face."

"Excellent!" cried Holmes. "And Troughton's house?"

"That, too, is being watched. Every move he makes is being marked down."

"Troughton?" I interrupted. "What! Mr. Troughton, the chief draughtsman of Elder and Kemp? What has he to do with these criminals?"

"Surely it was apparent," returned Holmes, "that before the Foulgers visited here, in the guise of Señor Rodriguez and his wife, they must already have known that the spare key to the safe was kept somewhere on the top floor of the building, along with the key to the window-grille. We cannot imagine that they lit upon these keys by chance. The obvious conclusion, therefore, is that someone here told them of the keys. Yet, according to Elder's account, of those that do not have a key of their own to the safe, only Troughton knew of the spare key and its whereabouts. The inference that Troughton is in league with these villains is inescapable."

"Why did you not mention this inference to your client?"

"I gave him, if you recall, a general warning against speaking of the matter to anyone. I did not specifically mention Troughton's name, because I feared that, if I did so, Elder's manner towards him might be altered, and he might thus be alerted to our suspicions."

"Is it not possible that someone else at Elder's might know of the keys kept on the top floor?" I queried. "In which case, Troughton might, after all, be innocent."

"It is just possible that one of the senior men may have mentioned to one of the junior clerks that the spare safe-key was kept on the top floor, but it seems unlikely."

"Such speculation is no longer necessary," interrupted Lestrade. "I now have definite information that Troughton is in league with the Foulger gang."

"How did you establish the connection between them?" asked Holmes.

"Ah!" responded the policeman. "You can't beat an old dog, when all is said and done! After you had stumbled on the clue concerning Troughton's possible involvement in the matter, Mr. Holmes, I mentioned Troughton's name to my colleague, Inspector Barker, who has made something of a speciality of the criminal gangs of the East End. He recognized it at once. 'Why!' says he; 'there is a man of that very name who runs a shop in the Mile End Road, selling jewellery and other articles of value. We have often suspected that he is also involved with criminal gangs, and is one of the chief agents in London for the disposal of stolen goods'. Well, I need hardly tell you, Mr. Holmes, that all I need is the scent of such a clue and I am on the trail at once, and don't give up until I find what I am looking for. You can't beat the methods of the official force, you know! To cut a long story short, I have established that the Thomas Troughton that works in this building is the cousin of Ezra Troughton, the shopkeeper of the Mile End Road. Furthermore, Thomas Troughton was yesterday evening followed by one of my smartest men from his house near the Elephant and Castle to his cousin's shop. The two men are thus not merely related, but intimately acquainted."

"That is good work!" cried Holmes, clapping the policeman on the shoulder. "So, our traps are all set, and now we must wait for the game to emerge from the shadows and take the bait! Have you reconsidered the disposition of your men, Lestrade?"

The policeman shook his head. "My mind is made up on the point," said he.

"Very well. The decision is yours. Now we must see how the Elders are faring, Watson. The daylight will begin fading shortly, and Sir George might light a lamp, which would be fatal to our plans."

We left the Scotland Yard man beaming, and ascended the steep stairs.

"'Stumbled on the clue' indeed!" said Holmes to me in an indignant tone. "The cheek of the fellow! Were it not for the information I have given him, he would be as far from apprehending the Foulger gang as he has ever been! As it is, his stubbornness threatens to ruin everything!"

"What do you mean?"

"He insists upon keeping most of his men downstairs. I have told him that it is a waste of time. The copying of the window-key indicates beyond doubt that it is through the window that the criminals intend to enter the building. Within reach of that window, therefore, is where Lestrade's men should be. His argument is that his men must be able to get out of the building at a moment's notice, in order to apprehend the criminals, and thus must remain on the ground floor. I have told him he is making a mistake, but he will not listen. Having accepted my analysis of the matter, he declines to accept the conclusion which that analysis necessitates. That, I suggest, is as good a definition of pig-headedness as one could imagine! I am inclined, Watson, to wash my hands entirely of the affair. After all, I have already fulfilled my own particular commission. I have solved young Elder's little mystery, and have ensured that his eminent cousin's gold will not be stolen. But here is Mr. Elder now; and Sir George, who appears less than entirely happy!"

Holmes's client had emerged from the conference-room as we reached the head of the stairs, followed by a large, stout man, whose expression was one of irritated annoyance. Holmes introduced us, and we all shook hands.

"I shall feel happier when this night is over," said Sir George Elder.

"Have no fear!" returned Holmes in a cheery voice. "Your gold could scarcely be safer were it in the Bank of England! Inspector Lestrade appears to have half the division deployed downstairs!"

"No doubt," said Sir George, a sceptical note in his voice; "but these criminals are desperate men, so I understand."

"Indeed they are; but our trap is laid; now all we have to do is wait for our quarry to put in an appearance! One of these rooms which face the front of the building will probably be best for our vigil."

Sir George Elder opened a door. "This is old Mr. Kemp's private chamber," said he. "We can sit in here. I imagine we shall have a long wait."

"It may not be so long as you suppose," returned Holmes, as we followed Sir George into the office. "They will not, of course, make a move until after dark. But once the daylight has gone, they may not wait very long. It must be remembered that from the criminals' point of view there are two problems which must be overcome. Their first problem is to gain entry to these premises and seize the gold. But their second problem is to transport the gold across the centre of London without attracting attention to themselves. They will probably judge that they are more likely to achieve that successfully in the evening, when there are still plenty of people about, than later in the night, when the streets will be practically deserted."

So the four of us sat in that small chamber and waited. And what a wait it was! Slowly the light faded, until the sky outside was a deep, inky blue and the first stars appeared, by which time my companions were but vague shadows in the gloom. At Holmes's request, Sir George Elder entertained us for a while with an account of his time in Russia; but, in truth, I missed much of it, for my attention wandered constantly, as faint sounds from without set my senses alert.

We had been sitting in the dark for about an hour when there came the sound of a footstep upon the stair, and we heard the voice of Inspector Lestrade. Holmes called softly, to guide him to where we were sitting, for it was by now almost pitch black within the building, and he made his way slowly to the doorway of our room.

"Is all in order up here?" asked he in a low tone.

"Perfectly," returned Holmes. "Both of the doors into the boardroom, from the corridor and from the adjoining conference-room, are slightly ajar, so that we shall be able to see and hear anything that goes on in there."

For a few moments, they discussed the matter further, then Holmes announced that he was going to take a look from the window of the conference-room, and I said I would accompany him. Slowly and with great care, we made our way across the corridor and into the large conference-room. My sense of touch was of necessity my chief guide, for it was now so dark that one could not see one's hand before one's face. Ahead of us, the wide window showed up faintly as a grey blur.

"It should be safe enough to take a look from here," murmured my companion, as we positioned ourselves by the window. "It is almost as dark out there as it is in here. It is a cold night," he continued. "It is clear enough now, but I'll wager the fog will thicken as the evening wears on."

"We may be above the fog at present," I remarked, craning my neck in an effort to see into the dark alley below. "It appears to be thicker down in the lane."

At that moment, with a tremendous throb and roar, a train passed on the viaduct, opposite the window. For an instant, the dark shape of the driver and fireman were visible, lit by the glow from the locomotive firebox, then the engine was past, and was succeeded by a line of swaying, rattling carriages, their compartments illuminated by the yellow glow of oil-lamps. In another instant, the carriages, too, had passed, and the scene before us had returned once more to one of Stygian blackness.

It was some time after the lighted train had passed us before my eyes became accustomed again to the darkness. Then I could once more make out some of the taller features atop the railway viaduct – a telegraph pole or two and a signal mast with a ladder leaning against it at an angle, all wreathed in thin wisps of fog. So close was the viaduct, that when a gang of railway workers passed along it, carrying between them a long plank of some sort, I could hear their voices quite clearly, although I could not make out what they were saying. Then another train approached, making for the centre of London, which slowed down as it passed us, until it drew to a halt exactly opposite to where we were crouching by the window. For a minute, as it stood there, we had a clear view into the compartments, where some of the passengers were standing up, and beginning to gather their belongings together, ready to alight when the train reached the terminus. Presently, with a hiss and a clank, the train began to move slowly forward once more, until, at length, it had passed beyond our view. A few moments later, the gang of workmen returned from wherever they had been. They put down their plank and exchanged a few words. It had just struck me that they appeared to be staring across at our window, when I felt Holmes's hand on my arm, pulling me slowly back from the window.

"Careful!" said he in a whisper. "Don't let them see you! Wait here, and I shall bring the others!"

I lowered my head a little, so that my eyes were just above the window-sill, and watched as the men on the viaduct continued their discussion, several times pointing across to the Elder and Kemp building. Then, as Holmes returned, and Lestrade, Elder and Sir George crouched down beside me, the workmen picked up their plank once more and placed one end of it on top of the viaduct parapet, so that it projected outwards two or three feet. For a moment, it remained there, and I saw the men look about them cautiously, then, slowly and carefully, they pushed it forward, across the gap between the viaduct and our building.

"Magnificent!" murmured Holmes appreciatively, in a soft tone. "What enterprise! What bold imagination!"

"What the devil are they doing?" interrupted Sir George in a sharp whisper.

"It is something in your own line, Sir George," returned Holmes. "They are attempting to throw a bridge across the chasm between the railway viaduct and this building. They will hope to locate this end of the bridge upon the outside window-sill of the boardroom."

"By Jove!" exclaimed Sir George hoarsely. "Whatever next!"

"Once they are confident that their bridge is secure, one of their party will be sent across to attempt to open the window," said Holmes. He paused as a dull thud indicated that the heavy plank had reached the window-sill. For a few moments the men on the viaduct stared along their bridge, no doubt endeavouring to be certain that the far end was securely located on the window-sill. One of them leaned over and thumped the plank several times with his fist, then, a moment later, climbed onto the parapet, and so onto the plank. Crouching down, and proceeding in an infinitely careful manner, he then began to make his way slowly across.

"He will smash the glass in the window," whispered Holmes. "Do not be startled by the noise, Sir George. He will probably use a small hammer. He will then put his hand through the broken pane and between the bars of the grille, and unlock the grille with the duplicate key they have had made. He will then push the grille open, and reach up and unlatch the window."

Holmes paused again, as there came a sharp tap on the boardroom window. After a moment, there came a second tap, slightly louder, accompanied by the tinkling sound of breaking glass. I held my breath. Through the open door that communicated between the boardroom and the conference-room came the sound of furtive activity. A few seconds later, a low metallic creak indicated that the grille was being pushed open, then came a sharp snick as the window-latch was unfastened. By this time, I judged that all my unseen companions were holding their breath, for there was utter silence in the building, so that one might have heard the fall of a pin. A few moments later, I heard soft footfalls in the adjoining room, and the slight creaking of a floorboard. Then came a slight metallic click, and a dull yellow light showed through the open doorway, as the intruder opened a shutter on a small lantern. A second click, and the light vanished as abruptly as it had appeared, then I heard the intruder call softly across to his companions on the viaduct.

"All right, Jimmy! Come on!"

I turned my attention to the viaduct once more. A second man, no more than a dark blurred shape, was climbing onto the parapet and making his way onto the plank. I had the impression that there was a third man behind him on the viaduct, wearing a cap of some sort, but I could not be certain, for the fog was thicker now, and swirled like the sea before one's eyes.

The second man had almost reached the windowsill, in the same crouching posture as the first, when there came a sudden surprising interruption. From somewhere in the building below us, there came a momentary clattering noise, as if someone had lost his footing upon the stair. It was not a loud noise; in normal circumstances it would probably have passed unremarked. But in the still silence of that dark night it captured all one's attention, as a faint and distant gunshot might catch the ear of the night watch at an army camp. It was followed by a moment of utter stillness, as if the whole world had, for an instant, ceased to move, then the man in the next room slid open the shutter of his lantern once more, and it was clear from the movement of the light through the door-crack, and upon our ceiling, that he was making his way towards the far end of the boardroom. The yellow spread of light around the half-open door became gradually brighter. Then, all at once, I saw an arm push the door between the two rooms fully open. The next moment, the intruder had stepped through the doorway and was playing the light of his lantern about the conference-room. In less time than it takes to record it, the light moved from the dark recesses at the far end of the room to where we crouched by the window, and the dazzling light was fully in my eyes.

There was a moment of silence, then rapid footsteps, as the lantern and the man carrying it vanished from the room.

"Get back, Jimmy!" we heard him call out. "It's a trap! Get back!"

Holmes and Lestrade sprang forward, and there came a piercing blast from a police-whistle, close to my ear. I hurried after them as fast as I could. In the boardroom, a violent scuffle was taking place on the floor by the window, but I could not make out clearly who was involved. Then a constable pushed open the door from the corridor behind me, and asked what he should do.

"Over here, Timpson!" called out Lestrade in an urgent tone, and the constable pushed past me to lend his weight to the struggle. A moment later, I saw Holmes's dark silhouette show up before the grey blur of the window, as he stood up.

"Are your men in position on the viaduct, Lestrade?" said he in an urgent tone.

"They are there somewhere," returned Lestrade's voice from the darkness.

I heard Holmes groan with annoyance.

"I told you that this is how they would do the job," cried he. "I said that unless you had more men on the viaduct, you would not land your catch. What is the use of fishing with a net full of holes! Is that you there, Watson? Good! Come on! We must try to stop them!"

In an instant he had climbed onto the window-sill and was making his way along the wooden plank. "Hold it firmly on the sill!" he called back when he was half-way across.

I should never have described my friend as foolhardy or reckless – he was much too thoughtful and intelligent a man to warrant such a description – but there was, in his otherwise severely rational nature, a spark of romance and adventure which could be kindled to a blaze by his own enthusiasm, or by the excitement of the chase. Then the intensity of his desire to bring some matter to a successful conclusion would drive him on, heedless of his own safety. These thoughts flashed through my mind in an instant, as, with some trepidation, I watched as he made his way along the plank to the viaduct.

Reaching the other end, he sprang down from the parapet onto the level of the railway tracks and turned.

"Come on, Watson!" he called. "Quickly! It is not far! The plank is a thick one," he added, evidently perceiving my hesitation; "it bends very little. You need not fear – I'll hold it firmly against the window-sill!"

For a moment longer I hesitated; but I was conscious that any further delay would only make the criminals' escape more likely, and I did not wish to be held responsible for that. So, perhaps foolishly, and certainly with a knotted sensation in my stomach, I put my foot onto the window-sill, and, stepping onto the plank, began to inch my way forwards.

I looked down at my feet, and my gaze was irresistibly drawn further, beyond the wooden plank, to where the dense fog swirled and drifted like a dark sea, far below.

"Don't look down!" came my friend's voice, containing an unmistakable note of concern. "Look forward, to where you are stepping!"

I raised my eyes for a moment, saw Holmes leaning his whole weight against the end of the plank, and made to resume my cautious progress. But in looking up, and through the wraiths of fog that drifted sideways before my eyes, I had somehow lost my sense of the vertical. At one and the same time, I had the conflicting impressions that I was standing upright and that I was slowly slipping sideways. My mind reeled in confusion. I had no idea which way I should lean to prevent myself tumbling from the narrow plank into the abyss. Then, through the mist, came Holmes's firm voice.

"Crouch down on the board," said he.

I leaned forward, bent my knees and touched the plank with my finger-tips. This last action restored some, at least, of my sense of balance, and after a moment in that position, I was able to push myself up with my extended fingers, and move forward once more.

"Here!" called Holmes, holding out his hand to guide me. "If such things are to be done, they are best done quickly," said he, as I reached the end of the plank.

I had my hand on my friend's shoulder, and was about to lower myself down onto the level of the railway tracks, and reply to his observation, when there came a sudden sharp cry from behind me. Almost at the same instant, I felt the board beneath my feet quiver and move. I sprang down at once, and turned.

Lestrade's prisoner had evidently broken free, for he was running pell-mell across the board towards us. But his flight was too vigorous, and was bending and shaking the narrow bridge. In an instant, the far end of it had bounced and slipped from its narrow purchase on the windowsill. I saw it go, and grabbed for the near end, but it was no use; the plank was too heavy for me to hold it in position. At the same instant, I saw the man before me, his eyes wild and staring, stretch out his arms in a vain effort to reach the parapet wall.

I lunged forward and seized his sleeve, then had both hands upon his arm; but the effort had almost pulled me over the parapet, and I knew I could not long hold him unless he could gain some purchase with his other hand. Then, in an instant, as I heard the plank crash to the ground, far below, Holmes was leaning over the wall beside me and had seized the man's other arm, and between us we hauled him up, over the parapet-top, and to safety.

As our prisoner lay by the wall, panting and shaking, Holmes leaned down and snapped a pair of handcuffs onto his wrists.

"Now," said he, "for the others."

At that moment, however, two large police-constables appeared out of the fog a short distance along the tracks. Between them they held a slighter figure, who bore a striking resemblance to the young man who lay at our feet.

"Here is Jimmy, come to join Patrick!" said Holmes. "Have you seen anyone else?" he asked the policemen as they approached.

"No, sir!" one of them returned. "No one, save only a railway official."

"In a peaked cap?"

"Yes, sir; of course! It was he that told us to get along this way."

"Where is he now?"

"Gone to alert the station authorities, he said."

"A short man?" Holmes asked; "with a sharp, hooked nose, like that of an eagle, and a deep scar below his left eye?"

"Why! That is the man exactly!" returned the policeman in a surprised tone. "How can you know?"

"That man was Albert Foulger," said Holmes, "the chief of this daring little gang. I think, Watson," he continued, turning to me, "that unless the authorities manage to take him at his hidey-hole in Colchester, this is the last we shall see of Mr. Foulger for a while!"

My friend's words were to prove prophetic. Troughton and his cousin were arrested and later convicted for their part in the matter, along with Patrick and James Foulger; but of Albert Foulger himself no trace was to be found. Although a watch was kept for some time upon his house in Colchester, and upon his known haunts in London, he was never seen. Once again he had succeeded in disappearing completely.

Two days after the dramatic events I have described above, there was a full account of the affair in the *Standard*, which I read aloud to Holmes as we sat at the breakfast-table. The paper also devoted an editorial to the subject, which concluded with the following words:

Thanks to the alertness of the police officers concerned, especially Inspector G. Lestrade of Scotland Yard, a daring attempt at robbery was foiled, and most of the gang arrested. In this case, it is certainly no exaggeration to declare that by their prompt actions, the police have earned the gratitude of the whole of London.

"It does not mention your name at all," I observed, as I finished reading.

"For which I am very relieved," returned my companion in a dry tone. "It is not a case with which I should choose to be associated."

"But without your intervention," I protested, "the gold would certainly have been stolen, and the gang would have escaped scot free. It is you, Holmes, who has earned the gratitude of the whole of London, and the newspaper should acknowledge that fact! I have a good mind to write to the editor and apprise him of the true facts of the matter!"

My friend shook his head.

"The point of Saturday night's little exercise was not to save Sir George Elder's gold, Watson," said he. "Had that been our purpose we could have achieved it with considerably less trouble by simply moving the gold elsewhere, or by changing the lock upon the window. The whole point of our efforts was, rather, to trap Albert Foulger. This we did not succeed in doing, and he remains still, regrettably, the third most sought-after villain in England. I therefore consider the exercise a failure, and the fact that Foulger is a very cunning man does not lessen my mortification at being beaten by him. It may be that one day we shall once more have within our grasp this enemy of all honest citizens, but until that time, I should be obliged if you would suppress your letter-writing impulses, my dear fellow. Any further attention drawn to the matter will, I fear, serve only to reveal that it was somewhat less of a success than is supposed, and can only diminish what little reputation I now possess!"

THE THIRTEENTH STEP

I NEED NO RECOURSE to my notebooks to recall that it was a pleasant, balmy day in late spring when Lady Temperley, wife of the former under-secretary at the Foreign Office, called at our chambers in Baker Street to consult Sherlock Holmes. For several weeks the buds on the trees in the park had been slowly swelling. Now, following a period of bright, sunny weather, the trees had burst forth into the most beautiful display of blossom. I remember this particularly, as Lady Temperley herself, although no longer young, had, nevertheless, something of the freshness of the spring about her. A handsome woman of late middle age, she was dressed in a smart blossom-pink walking costume and seemed to bring a welcome breath of the English countryside to the brick-built fastness of London.

She had travelled up from Derbyshire the previous evening, she informed us, and had stayed the night at the Midland Hotel.

"I received the telegram you sent," said Sherlock Holmes. "There is, I understand, some problem or puzzle on which you wish to consult me, but your message gave no indication as to the nature of the problem."

Lady Temperley frowned. "It is difficult to describe," said she at length. "Indeed, you may think me foolish for coming all this way to consult you over such a vague, indeterminate business. But it has been troubling me greatly in recent days, Mr. Holmes, and I have been unable to sleep at night. Last night, at the hotel, I lay awake for several hours."

Sherlock Holmes eyed his visitor keenly. "Have you spoken to anyone else about the matter?" he asked.

"I have mentioned some aspects of it to Ralph – my husband, Lord Temperley – or have tried to, at least, but he believes I am troubling myself unnecessarily. Even he admits, however, that recent events have not been quite as one would have wished, although he describes it as a series of unfortunate coincidences. But it is all so vague, Mr. Holmes, that I scarcely know where to begin."

"It is apparent that you are suffering from great anxiety, Lady Temperley. Do not trouble yourself over getting matters in perfect order before you begin. Simply recount the relevant facts as they occur to you. We can sort out the order of events later."

"Very well," said our visitor. "You should perhaps know first that we live, my husband and I, at Hardshaw Hall in Derbyshire, where his family has resided for many generations. Our life there is, generally speaking, a quiet and uneventful one. Our son, Michael, is no longer at home, being posted to India at present with his regiment. We frequently have visitors, however, sometimes for very extended periods, and it is the great pleasure of our lives to do so. My husband, I know, is very proud of the reputation for hospitality which Hardshaw enjoys throughout the length and breadth of the country, and he is always ready to accommodate anyone who wishes to come.

"Last autumn, for example, at the request of the Prime Minister, we put up Prince Balkovsky and his family from Russia for several weeks, and, more recently, for a similar period of time, Sir John Meacham and his wife. He had, as you may be aware, just returned from several years in the West Indies, where he had been governor of the island of St. Stephen. At the same time, for almost a year now, we have been putting up an old friend of my husband's, Major Thomas Lockhart. He and my husband were comrades-in-arms in their army days, although they had been out of touch for several years until they happened to run across each other in London, one day last summer. When Major Lockhart left the army he had knocked about the world for some time – Australia, India, Africa and so on. I think my husband was rather envious of that: when he left the army, he had had to return immediately to Hardshaw to take up his duties there, as his late father was becoming old and frail. Major Lockhart was under no such constraints, and had set his heart upon a farm in Australia. He had expected to come into a considerable inheritance, which would have made this possible, but there was some delay about it, so he had been kicking his heels in London for some time when my husband ran across him. Ralph was so pleased to see him that he invited him to come and stay with us at Hardshaw until the inheritance business was sorted out. And there, save occasional trips up to London to consult his solicitor, he has been ever since.

"I think that Major Lockhart was very grateful for Ralph's offer of hospitality, but, really, my husband benefits from the arrangement just as much as the major does. I think he had been finding Hardshaw rather dull before, and Major Lockhart's presence has brightened the old place up considerably. He and my husband share a taste for riding, shooting and fishing, and when they are not so engaged, they spend hours on end discussing horse-breeding, farming methods and the like. In the course of his travels, Major Lockhart had stayed with various people, including several connections of my husband's – his cousin, Wilfred Docking, who farms in South Africa; an old Army friend, Maurice Foster, who now lives in New Zealand; and numerous others – and Ralph very much enjoyed hearing the latest news of all these people. I suppose it is inevitable that Major Lockhart will eventually leave us, but when he does so, it will be something of a wrench for u We have become so used to his presence at Hardshaw that I am sure we shall miss him greatly when he goes.

"That, then, is the background to the present events," said Lady Temperley after a moment, "and you will appreciate, then, why I said that our life at Hardshaw has generally been a placid and uneventful one. I come now to more recent events:

"Towards the end of last year, my husband received a letter from a distant cousin of his, the Wilfred Docking I mentioned, who lives in South Africa. The gist of this was that Docking hoped that his son, Edward, who was nineteen years old, would be able to enter All Saints' College of Oxford University this coming autumn. This possibility had first been raised when Major Lockhart had been in South Africa, and his opinion had been sought as to whether Edward should seek a commission in the Army or try for a place at Oxford. The major had favoured the latter course, pointing out that once Edward had completed his studies at Oxford, it would still be possible for him to then apply for a commission should he wish to do so.

"Wilfred Docking had agreed with this view, and they had therefore made a preliminary application to All Saints' College, with which Docking's family had some previous connection. This preliminary application had been favourably received, and now Docking wondered if it might be possible for us to put his son up for a few months beforehand, perhaps help him with any correspondence that was necessary, make sure he was prepared and so on. Of course, we said we should be delighted to do so. There then followed various delays while arrangements were made, during which, I understand, Edward, with the careless irresponsibility of youth, took the opportunity to travel all over South Africa, bidding fond farewells to various cronies of his. He eventually ended up in Cape Town, where he stayed for a few days with an old school-fellow, Andrew Cotter, while he waited for the boat, and at last set sail and arrived in England in the middle of February this year."

Lady Temperley paused. "I mention Edward's friend, Andrew Cotter, particularly," she continued after a moment, "as I shall have cause to refer to him again later. However, to continue my account: Shortly after Edward's arrival, we learned that his application to All Saints' had been finally accepted, subject only to his proving satisfactory in an entrance examination for which he would be required to sit in July.

"This may all sound fairly straightforward," Lady Temperley continued with a shake of the head, "but, although neither my husband nor I are experts on the matriculation requirements of an Oxford college, it soon became apparent to us that Edward was likely to fall short of them. I don't doubt that his heart is in the right place, but he is wild and boisterous, like a gale blowing into a house through an open window and disturbing the order within. He is a very good horseman – in fact he is good at all outdoor sports and any activity requiring physical strength – but his general level of education, although adequate for most purposes, is not, we felt, up to the required level for a scholar at Oxford. We therefore thought it wise to employ a tutor to coach him in all those branches of learning in which he seemed deficient. This tutor – a man by the name of Philip Sowerby – has therefore also been staying with us for several months, although he goes home to Derby at the end of each week and returns to Hardshaw each Monday morning.

"I understand from Mr. Sowerby that Edward is making progress, and he is confident that the young man will perform satisfactorily in the forthcoming examination. I must say I am glad that he has expressed that opinion, as I should not myself have drawn that conclusion from appearances. Sometimes the coaching seems the other way about, with Edward introducing Mr. Sowerby to riding, shooting and other outdoor pursuits, of which, I understand, the tutor had had little previous experience. Neither my husband nor I have raised any objection to this, so long as the schoolwork is not neglected, which Mr. Sowerby insists it has not been. Meanwhile, in his free time, Edward soon struck up a friendship with Stephen James, a boy of about his own age who is the son of a neighbouring farmer. In fact, the two boys already knew each other, by letter at least, for, coincidentally, when my husband happened to hear some years ago from Matthew James, Stephen's father, that his son was looking for a boy of his own age with whom he could correspond, preferably someone from overseas, he had suggested that Stephen write to his cousin's son, Edward, in South Africa. This he did, and the two boys exchanged letters for two or three years in their schooldays, so I understand, although I don't think they had been in touch for the last year or two.

"Edward and Stephen have spent an enormous lot of time riding pell-mell across the countryside. Whenever I have chanced to see them, they always seemed to be leaping recklessly over hedges and stone walls without a thought for safety or caution, and I have been constantly worried that they would break their necks one day. At the same time, Edward has made the acquaintance of the James boy's sister, Agnes, a sweet and delightful girl, a little younger than her brother, and I have been just as anxious about that, fearing constantly that Edward's impetuosity would lead him to do or say something inappropriate or unseemly and cause a breach between the James family and us."

Lady Temperley paused then, and asked if she might have a glass of water. More than ever now, her features appeared to indicate that she was under a great strain, and it was some time before she continued her account. Holmes, meanwhile, passed no remark, but I could see that he was watching her closely.

"I come now," said she at length, "to the most recent events. Sometime after Easter, there was a spring fair in the local village. It is a traditional event, and takes place at the same time every year. My husband and I always contribute something to the festivities, and invariably put in an appearance on the Saturday afternoon. This year we attended with Edward, who had never seen anything quite like it and was enjoying it immensely.

"In one tent was a fortune-teller who called herself 'Rose Spindle, Spinner of Destiny'. I don't really care for such things, and don't usually bother with them, but Edward badgered me to try it, and insisted it would be fun. Eventually I gave in to the lad, much against my better judgment. I very much wish now that I had not. There was an odd smell in the fortune-teller's tent, and the air was thick with some sort of cloying incense. The fortune-teller greeted me cordially enough and examined the lines on my hand, then spread some cards on the table between us. After she had studied these for a few moments in silence, she looked up at me with her dark, penetrating eyes.

"'I almost wish that you had not come,' said she in a deep voice. 'But, still, it is best to know the truth.'

"'Whatever do you mean?' I asked.

"'I see some misfortune,' she replied. 'I see a great loss – perhaps even a death.'

"'Death?' I cried in a state of shock. 'My death?'

"'No, no,' said she quickly with a shake of the head. 'I do not think so, but it might be the death of someone close to you.'

"'A relation of mine?'

"'No, not a relation, but someone very close to you. That is strange,' she added, as she continued to study the cards: 'you will receive a warning of some kind, but for some reason you will do nothing. Perhaps there is nothing you can do.'

"I did not wait to hear any more, but staggered from that dark tent to the bright afternoon outside, desperate to get some fresh air into my lungs. I can scarcely convey to you how I felt; it was as if a great weight had been placed upon my shoulders and I could not shake it off. I know you will think me foolish, but–"

"Did you recognize the woman?" Holmes interrupted. "Was it anyone you had seen about in the village?"

Lady Temperley shook her head. "She was wearing a heavy veil and I could not see her face very clearly. There were some Gipsies camped at the end of the village that week – perhaps it was one of them. I made a few enquiries at the time, but could not learn who it was."

"Did you mention to your husband, or anyone else, what the woman had told you?"

"Not at first. When I was asked about it, I made up some trifling matter on the spur of the moment, and dismissed it as nonsense. Later, I did relate some of it to my husband, but he refused to take it seriously. I have never given anyone a full account of it before today."

"Very well. Pray, continue."

"A couple of weeks later, my husband, Major Lockhart and I were chatting over breakfast one morning. Edward had already finished and gone out somewhere. It was a bright, sunny day, and the French windows to the terrace were standing open.

All at once, our conversation was interrupted by the rapid clatter of Edward's feet on the steps outside, which lead from the lawn up to the terrace. A moment later, he burst into the room like a whirlwind, flopped onto a chair and helped himself to a cup of tea.

"'Do you know how many steps there are supposed to be, up to the terrace, Uncle Ralph?' he asked.

"'There are twelve,' replied my husband. 'Why do you ask?'

"'That's the funny thing,' said Edward in a puzzled tone. 'I always count the steps when I'm running up them, and it usually comes to twelve, but today it came to thirteen.'

"'Oh, you must have made a mistake, Edward,' I said quickly.

"'No, Aunt Felicity, I didn't,' he insisted. 'Or, if I did, it was a very odd one.'

"We let the matter drop then. A few moments later, my husband left the room, and shortly afterwards Major Lockhart and I did the same. The subject was not raised again until late that evening, when my husband and I were alone.

"'What was that young fool playing at this morning, talking about the steps like that?' my husband demanded in an angry voice. I could see that he was terrifically upset.

"'Don't be too hard on the boy,' I responded. 'It's not his fault, Ralph. He doesn't know about it. You know what he's like – he approaches everything like a bull at a gate. It can't be helped.'

"My husband shook his head, snorted loudly and took himself off to bed without another word. It was clear that the matter had been preying on his mind all day. You see, Mr. Holmes, what Edward didn't know, as it is scarcely ever mentioned, is that there is an old tradition at Hardshaw Hall, associated with those very steps he had run up so gaily, an unpleasant and sinister tradition. It goes back nearly two centuries, to when one of Ralph's ancestors, Sir John Temperley, walked up those same steps, counting them off absent-mindedly as he went. On that occasion, too, instead of counting twelve, as usual, he counted to thirteen, which is traditionally regarded, of course, as an unlucky number. Now, Sir John Temperley was not at all superstitious, and simply assumed he had made a mistake. In fact, it amused him so much that he told everyone he knew about it, although some, it seemed, chided him for what they thought inappropriate levity. Less than two weeks later, their caution seemed justified: Sir John's wife was dead, killed in a riding accident.

"Such a terrible misfortune, and the circumstances surrounding it, made a very great impression upon everyone, especially those of a superstitious cast of mind, and, as the years passed, the tragedy became firmly embedded in local folk-lore, and known to everyone in the district. Even so, one might have expected that such an incident would at length pass, forgotten, into the pages of history, but occasional little mishaps at Hardshaw, real or imagined, which could in any way be connected to the steps, served to keep the matter fresh in the general mind. Then, twenty-odd years later, there occurred another serious incident which sealed forever the place in superstitious history of the garden-steps at Hardshaw Hall. A visitor to the house, all unaware of the tradition, commented in amusement on what he described as 'the surprising fact' that there were thirteen steps leading from the lawn up to the terrace. Within a week, this visitor was dead, having fallen from his bedroom window in circumstances which could never be fully explained. Thus, you see, 'the thirteenth step at Hardshaw Hall' is taken, with good reason, as a forewarning of death or disaster. There is even a little verse on the subject, although I don't know when it was written."

Lady Temperley unfastened the small embroidered bag she had been holding, and took from it a folded sheet of paper which she passed to Holmes. He studied it for a moment, then passed it to me and I read the following:

Beware the steps at Hardshaw Hall
If your life you wish to save
Take twelve steps only from lawn to wall
The thirteenth step is to the grave.

Holmes sat in silence for several minutes, his brows drawn down into a frown as he considered the matter. "And has anything untoward occurred yet?" he queried at length in a sceptical tone.

"Indeed," replied his visitor. "Something far worse than you could possibly imagine."

"Surely there has not been a death?" said Holmes sharply, a note of surprise in his voice.

Lady Temperley nodded her head. "It is worse than that," said she. "Not one, but two deaths have occurred, one at Hardshaw, one elsewhere but directly connected to Hardshaw. One is the result of a dreadful, tragic accident, but the other may well be murder."

Holmes frowned again. "The details, please," said he.

"I have described to you how Edward and the neighbours' boy, Stephen James, have spent a great deal of their time in recent months galloping back and forth wildly across the local countryside. On the Monday of the week before last, they were setting off as usual when they decided to make a race of it, a steeplechase, in fact. They began in the field beside the Hardshaw stables, their destination being the church at Boarsley. That is about five miles away, although the church spire can be seen far in the distance as soon as one breasts the first hill on the Hardshaw estate.

"They set off together, but after the first half-mile or so they parted, the two boys each choosing a different route to their destination. Edward eventually reached Boarsley, and as there was no sign of Stephen there, he assumed he had won the race. He waited some considerable time, but Stephen never appeared. At length Edward concluded that his rival must have met with an accident, so he set off back to try and find him.

"He was just approaching Blackwood Copse, which stands in an area of rough heathland, when he saw his tutor, Mr. Sowerby, trotting away from the copse in the direction of the Hall. Edward called out to him, he turned his horse, and the two of them met up by the wood. Mr. Sowerby informed Edward that he had seen Stephen's mount wandering about, but had seen no sign of Stephen himself. The two of them then dismounted and searched the wood on foot. It did not take them long to make a most melancholy discovery – the body of the unfortunate James boy, stone dead. He had suffered a grievous wound to the head, and they could only conclude that his mount had stumbled on the rough, broken ground and flung him off. This was also the official verdict of the inquest which was convened to consider the matter two days later.

"Of course, Edward was devastated. He told me that it had been his suggestion that they should have a race, and he kept blaming himself for what had happened, although I told him he shouldn't. And it was not just Stephen he felt terribly sorry for, but also Stephen's sister, Agnes. As I mentioned earlier, Edward had become very fond of Agnes and he was mortified that he should have been at least partly responsible for causing her such anguish. I don't think he was able to sleep for several days, and he kept muttering over and over to himself that he must try to make it up to her somehow.

"Three days after this terrible misfortune, we received a letter from South Africa, from Edward's father, informing us that it was his intention to come to England in about three weeks' time. I had mentioned to him in a previous letter about Edward's coaching with Mr. Sowerby, and he referred to that and said he was very much looking forward to hearing how Edward was progressing. After this cheering information, however, he mentioned that he had, unfortunately, some bad news for Edward. A close friend and former school-fellow of Edward's, the Andrew Cotter I mentioned before, who had been working away from home in Cape Town and had been out of touch with his family for some considerable time, had been found dead in a wild, uncultivated area, a mile or two outside the town. It was not known how long his body had lain in the place in which it was found, but the surgeon who conducted the examination gave it as his opinion that he had certainly been dead for at least six weeks, and probably longer. Indeed, but for a signet ring he was wearing and some papers in his jacket pocket, it was thought unlikely that the body would ever have been identified. It was all terribly sad, for it seemed from what Mr. Docking said that this boy, Cotter, had fallen in with vicious, criminally-inclined companions in Cape Town and was in fact being sought by the police there in connection with a robbery. Furthermore, from the location of the body and marks visible upon it, the police thought it very likely that Cotter had been murdered.

"I have never seen anyone so completely shocked and distraught by anything as Edward was by this news. All the blood seemed to drain from his face as I read the letter out to him, and I thought that, strong lad though he is, he was going to faint. My husband gave him a tot of brandy, which seemed to steady him a little, but he remained sitting in a dazed stupor for some time. I suppose it was not very surprising, considering that this dreadful news had come so hard on the heels of the death of poor Stephen James. I tried to imagine how I would feel if two of my closest friends had been found dead within a few days of each other, but I couldn't bear to even think about it."

Lady Temperley shook her head. Her gaze had been cast down to the floor as she recounted these disturbing events, but now she raised her eyes to Holmes, a pathetic, pleading expression on her features.

"That is where we are, Mr. Holmes," said she, her voice trembling with emotion, "in a waking nightmare of death and predictions of disaster, made low by what has happened, and with no idea what might happen next. All I know is that there is something wrong – I feel it in my bones – and if there is anything – anything at all – that you can do or say to help me, I shall be eternally in your debt."

Sherlock Holmes did not reply at once, but sat with his eyes closed, his brow furrowed with intense concentration. For myself, I confess I could make no sense of what Lady Temperley had told us, and did not know what to think of it, other than that she and her relations had been the victims of the most atrocious misfortune. I could not really believe that there was any connection between the doom-laden prophecies of a Gipsy fortune-teller and the deaths of two young men, many thousands of miles apart, nor that the old tradition of "the thirteenth step at Hardshaw Hall" could really foretell misfortunes to come. And yet, try as I might to dismiss what must surely be mere superstition, I could not quite shake off the disturbing effect of our visitor's account. Round and round these strange and melancholy facts my thoughts circled, unable to reduce them to something rational, something that was not simply an incomprehensible enigma. Glad I was, then, when Holmes at last spoke. But if I had hoped that a keener intellect than my own might perceive some clear way through the puzzle, my hopes were not entirely satisfied by his opening remarks.

"It is possible," said he in a measured tone, "that some of the incidents you have described to us are, indeed, simply coincidental. One must always allow for that possibility."

"Does that mean that you have no hope of ever bringing light into the darkness?" asked Lady Temperley, a clear note of disappointment in her voice.

"Not at all. You misunderstand me. My remark about coincidences is not a negative one, an admission of defeat, but a positive one, pointing out to you that we may be able to shed light on some of the facts you have mentioned by setting some of the others aside for the moment. It can sometimes be an error to try to explain every single thing that puzzles you by one over-arching theory. All it takes then is one aberrant fact, one fact which your theory cannot justifiably explain, to destroy the theory and leave you with nothing. Do you understand the point?"

"I think so," said Lady Temperley in a doubtful tone. "Is there anything else you wish to know, or anything I have not made clear?"

Holmes nodded his head. "I have two questions for you, Lady Temperley. First, am I correct in believing that you and your family are the owners of the famous Temperley Emeralds, and that these are kept at Hardshaw Hall?"

"Yes, that is so. They have been in my husband's family for generations."

"Second, do you intend to return to Derbyshire this afternoon?"

"Yes. I feel my place is there, at Hardshaw, and I would wish to get back there as soon as possible."

"Very well. If I accept your case, I take it you give me *carte blanche* to make any enquiries I wish, and to take any steps I consider necessary?"

"Certainly, by all means."

"Then I shall meet you at St. Pancras station before your train departs, and accompany you back to Hardshaw this afternoon."

When Lady Temperley had left us, Holmes sat for some minutes in silence, with his eyes closed, evidently going over again in his mind all that our visitor had told us. Then, as if he had reached a decision, he sprang to his feet, opened the top drawer of his desk and took out his revolver.

"Will you come?" he asked me, as he examined the chambers of the gun.

"If I can be of any assistance to you."

"Then I should be obliged if you would bring your own pistol."

"Are you expecting trouble?" I asked in surprise.

"I sense that the matter is coming to a head," said he, "and it is always as well to be prepared for the worst."

Our train had passed St. Albans and was well on the way to Bedford before Holmes alluded once more to the business which was taking us to the North.

"I wish to know a little more about the Temperley Emeralds," said he, addressing Lady Temperley. "Are they in the form of a necklace?"

"Partly. There is indeed a very large and ornate necklace, but also an elaborate matching bracelet and a pair of ear-rings."

"Do you wear these jewels very often?"

Lady Temperley shook her head. "They may be fabulously valuable, as seems to be widely known, but, personally, I do not care for them. The setting of the stones is heavy and old-fashioned, and they are, of course, bright green. I do not think that the colour suits me at all. The last time I wore them was about two years ago, at a grand ball thrown by the Duke of Holdernesse."

"Where are they usually kept?"

"Inside a locked case, in a locked drawer in my bedroom."

"Have you had any reason to take them out of the drawer recently?"

"Only once in the last two months, as far as I can recall. Edward and his tutor, Mr. Sowerby, expressed an interest in the emeralds, so I got them out to show them one day. But why are you asking me all these questions about the Temperley Emeralds, Mr. Holmes?"

"Such valuable gemstones are not infrequently the focus for crime, Lady Temperley. As I am considering all the events which have so disturbed you recently, and all the circumstances surrounding those events, it would, I feel, be remiss of me to omit consideration, too, of so famous a prize as your emeralds. Tell me, Lady Temperley, how did you come to select Mr. Sowerby as tutor for Edward Docking? Was he recommended to you by someone?"

"I do not believe so. I cannot be certain, as my husband dealt with the matter, but I believe he simply advertised the position in the Derby evening newspaper. I understand that Mr. Sowerby had been a schoolteacher of many years' experience, but had recently retired. He is very scholarly and bookish in appearance, and he evidently struck my husband as the most suitable of the candidates. I think that Mr. Sowerby himself was very pleased to get the position, as he is not, I understand, very well off."

Holmes nodded his head at this information, but made no response, and lapsed then into thoughtful silence. Save to reply in the most perfunctory manner to odd remarks of mine or Lady Temperley's, he scarcely spoke another word until our train reached Bakewell, in the Peak District of Derbyshire. Lady Temperley had wired ahead the time of our arrival, and a carriage was waiting for us in the station yard.

As we rattled slowly up the narrow, hilly roads, between the ever-present grey stone walls which divide up the countryside in those parts, I was struck by the wild beauty of the landscape. Flocks of sheep were busily grazing the short, springy turf in the fields, moorland birds wheeled high above us, buffeted by the strong, capricious winds, and, over all, the sun was shining brightly. It was hard to imagine that anything very sinister could occur in such fresh and open countryside.

After about twenty minutes, we turned off the road, passed between two lichen-blotched stone gateposts, and followed a track through a dense stand of trees, emerging at length before the ancient stone manor house which was Hardshaw Hall. It was a solid-looking, square-edged sort of building, early Tudor in origin, I judged, with no pretensions to unnecessary architectural refinement, but built rather, it appeared, to withstand the strong Peak District winds and the annual assault of the elements.

As we drew up before the front of the building, a door opened and a butler descended the steps and opened the door of the carriage. He informed us, in answer to a query from Lady Temperley, that her husband was taking tea in the drawing-room with Major Lockhart and Mr. Sowerby.

"Is Edward not with them?" asked Lady Temperley.

"Mr. Docking went for a ride with Mr. Sowerby shortly after luncheon, milady. Mr. Sowerby has now returned; Mr. Docking has not yet done so."

The three men in the drawing-room rose to their feet as we were announced. The first, a distinguished-looking man with grizzled grey hair and moustache, I recognized, from photographs I had seen in the illustrated press, as Lord Temperley. The second, a large, broad-shouldered man with dark hair and a waxed black moustache, I took, from his military bearing, to be Major Lockhart, and the third, a scholarly-looking man with a bald head and a slight stoop, I knew must be the tutor, Mr. Sowerby.

"My dear," said Lord Temperley to his wife, "It is good to see you safely back home again. I trust that your visit to London was satisfactory."

"Yes," said she. "This is Mr. Sherlock Holmes and his colleague, Dr. Watson," she continued, introducing us, as Holmes had suggested to her earlier, as historians of old tales and traditions, who were going to look into the business of the thirteenth step for her. "I thought," she added, "that we could put them up for a few days while they conduct their researches in the old family papers."

"By all means," said Lord Temperley affably. "Come and take a seat, gentlemen, and we can all have some tea."

As she sat down next to her husband, Lady Temperley enquired after Edward Docking, and it was clear that she was concerned at his absence.

"Mr. Sowerby was just telling us where they got to earlier this afternoon," said Lord Temperley.

"How came you to part company?" Lady Temperley asked the tutor.

"I am ashamed to say I was exhausted, Lady Temperley," he replied, "and could not carry on. But Edward wanted to go further, so I came back alone. I'm sure he will be all right. He is a much better rider than I am."

"I was over in that general direction myself a little later," interjected Major Lockhart, "but I didn't see anything of Edward, so I think he must have gone all the way up to Burnage Edge. If so, that's quite a long ride, so I suppose that's why he's late. I did see Agnes James up that way, out for a trot by herself, and had a little chat with her. She told me that she and Edward had arranged to meet up somewhere in that vicinity, but she hadn't seen anything of him either. No doubt he will be back soon."

"I certainly hope he is," said Lady Temperley. "I don't like him going off by himself. I worry about the boy, Ralph. He's had several bad shocks lately, and the last time I saw him he looked as pale as a ghost."

I was struck by Lady Temperley's concern for Edward Docking. She had made no reference to it during our railway journey, but it had clearly been on her mind all day. I supposed that, in the absence of her own son in India, her maternal concerns had transferred themselves to this son of her husband's cousin. There is certainly something in the recklessness of youth to cause concern in anyone's breast, and that concern must inevitably be intensified when one is placed in a position of responsibility for someone else's son or daughter. And yet, I reflected, most young men succeed in passing through their reckless youth to reach their adulthood more or less unscathed. As we sipped our tea, I observed that the men, Lord Temperley, Major Lockhart and Mr. Sowerby, did their best to assuage Lady Temperley's anxieties, and presently the conversation moved on to other topics. Sherlock Holmes was asked about his interest in the singular old tales and traditions which are to be found in the ancient manor houses of England, and did a first-rate job of making it sound like his consuming passion, citing numerous examples from all parts of the country. For myself, I was glad that I was not questioned too closely on the subject, for I doubted that my replies would have sounded either so convincing or so knowledgeable as those of my friend.

Sometime later, I was in my room, sitting on the side of the bed and staring out of the window, wondering if our presence at Hardshaw Hall would really serve any purpose, when I heard noises from outside. I rose to my feet and looked down into the drive. A man on horseback had just arrived. I watched as he sprang from the saddle, ran up the steps to the front door and thundered on the door-knocker. As he did so, a low farm-cart appeared round the corner of the building behind him and drew to a halt by the steps. In the back of the cart was a bundle of some sort, covered with a tarpaulin. There seemed to be a sense of urgency about these people, whoever they were, and I wondered idly what their business might be. As for our own business, I could not imagine where we would begin, and I lay on the bed to ponder the question.

Ten minutes had passed, and my aimless thoughts had given way to drowsiness, when I was rendered fully awake by a loud knock at my bedroom door. I opened it to find one of the young housemaids there, who informed me in a breathless tone that Sherlock Holmes required my presence downstairs without delay.

I followed the girl downstairs, and ran across Holmes as he crossed the hallway. He took my arm and led me towards the back of the house.

"It's bad news, Watson," said he in a low tone, as he pulled open a door and we passed into a narrow corridor beyond. "It's Edward Docking."

"What has he done?" I asked.

"He is dead, Watson."

I stopped abruptly. "Good God!" I cried. "Surely not!"

"I'm afraid so. He appears to have been flung from his horse, just as Stephen James was. That is what everyone supposes, anyway. He was found in a copse by some of the estate workers. Lady Temperley almost passed out at the news. She is now lying down in her bedroom."

We passed through a doorway, across a small yard and into one of the numerous outbuildings there. Inside, a still figure lay on a stone table, and several men stood around, among whom I recognized the three gentlemen we had been speaking to in the drawing-room just a short time previously.

"My colleague is a medical man," said Holmes to Lord Temperley. "The local doctor has been sent for, Watson," he continued, turning to me, "but if you would care to give us your opinion, it might be helpful."

"Of course," I said, and stepped forward to examine the body. The front of the skull had been smashed in, as if by a severe impact against a large stone. There were no other marks on the body that I could see, and I gave it as my opinion that the blow to the head was undoubtedly the cause of death.

As I finished my examination, Sherlock Holmes stepped forward and began to rummage in the dead youth's pockets.

"What on earth are you doing, Mr. Holmes?" asked Lord Temperley, a note of disapproval in his voice.

"I am just seeing if there is anything of interest in these pockets," returned Holmes without looking up. "Ah! What is this?"

As he spoke he drew forth from an inside pocket what appeared to be a large string of green gems. There were gasps of amazement all around me, and as he held it up and it caught the light, I saw that it was an elaborate necklace, consisting of intertwined gold chains set with a great many green stones.

"The Temperley Emeralds!" cried Lord Temperley in astonishment. "I cannot believe it! Why in Heaven's name did Edward have the emeralds in his possession? And how did he get hold of them?"

Holmes pushed open the door and carried the necklace out to the yard. There, he took a small lens from his pocket and began to examine the necklace closely. "You had better have the jewel-case brought down to the drawing-room," he said after a moment to Lord Temperley, who had followed him out to the yard. "Then we can see if the bracelet and earrings are still there."

"I'll get it myself," returned Lord Temperley. "It's locked in a drawer in my wife's room, to which the servants don't have access. What about the necklace?"

"I'll hold onto that for the moment," replied Holmes. "I'll take it into the drawing-room."

For a fraction of a second, Lord Temperley hesitated and looked at Holmes, but there was something in the latter's manner which inspired confidence and trust, even in those to whom he was a perfect stranger. "Very well," said Lord Temperley, then turned away to return to the house. As he did so, however, three men came round the corner of an outbuilding, into the yard. The first, who was carrying a leather case, looked every inch the country medical practitioner in his tweed suit and gaiters, but the other two were policemen, the first in the braided uniform of an inspector, the second a very large, burly constable.

"Hello, Dr. Horrocks," said Lord Temperley. "Grim business here, I'm afraid. The young man we've been putting up for the last three months has had a bad riding accident. But what brings these policemen here?"

"We happened to be all together when your message reached us," returned the doctor. "Inspector Waltham thought he'd better come along and see what's happened."

"I don't think there's anything here in your line, Inspector," said Temperley with a shake of the head.

"Perhaps not, sir," said Inspector Waltham, "but this is the second such accident in just a few weeks, so I thought I'd better verify the matter for myself. Might I enquire who all these gentlemen are, sir?"

"This is Major Lockhart, whom I think you may know," replied Temperley. "He's been staying with us all year. This is Mr. Sowerby, the unfortunate boy's tutor. And these gentlemen, who arrived with my wife just a short time ago this afternoon, are Mr. Sherlock Holmes and Dr. Watson."

The policeman turned to Holmes, an expression of recognition on his features at the name he had been given.

"Excuse me, sir," said he, "but might you be Mr. Holmes the London criminal expert?"

"Among other things," returned Holmes in a dismissive tone. "I am here because Lady Temperley asked me to look into some matter for her."

"A crime?" asked Inspector Waltham.

"Not exactly," said Holmes.

"Might it be anything to do with that jewellery you are holding?"

Before Holmes could reply, Lord Temperley stepped forward. "No, it isn't," said he in a testy voice. "Look, Inspector, there's no point our standing out here discussing the matter. When you've finished here, come through to the drawing-room and we can sort it all out then. I'll send someone to show you the way." With that, he turned on his heel and was gone.

Major Lockhart and Mr. Sowerby followed Lord Temperley through the doorway into the house, but as I made to do the same, Holmes tweaked my sleeve and drew me back, out of earshot of the others. "I take it, Watson," said he in a low tone, "that you observed the oddity of Edward Docking's hands."

"I saw nothing unusual about his hands," I responded in surprise.

"Yes," said Homes. "That was the oddity."

A few minutes later, Lord Temperley joined us in the drawing-room. He was carrying in his hand a large flat jewel-case, covered in pale pink velvet.

"The bracelet and earrings are still in the case," said he.

"If you would bring them over to the window," said Holmes, "we can examine all the pieces together."

I watched with interest as they held up the various items of jewellery by the window, examining them carefully. The daylight was beginning to fade now, but the sinking sun cast its vivid beams through the tall window and sparkled on the green stones.

"I am no expert on gemstones," said Holmes after a few moments, "but I am not at all sure that these stones in the necklace are genuine. They seem to me to be distinctly duller and less vivid than the stones in the bracelet and ear-rings."

"But that is impossible," cried Lord Temperley. "Here, let me see." There followed several minutes of silence, then at length he cried out. "You are quite right, Mr. Holmes. I am certain of it. Even in this poor light, you can see that the colour of the stones in the necklace is nowhere near as vivid as the others. And, now I look carefully, I can see that the setting of the stones is not as it should be, either. It is somewhat cruder than I remember. What the devil does it mean?" he cried in a tone of despair. "If these are not the Temperley Emeralds, what are they? Where are the real emeralds, and why did Edward have this imitation in his pocket? Come over here a moment, gentlemen," he said, turning to where I was sitting with Sowerby and Lockhart, "and give us your opinion."

For several minutes we examined the jewellery in silence. At length I ventured the opinion that the stones in the necklace seemed to me a little dull compared to those in the bracelet and ear-rings. Sowerby's opinion concurred with mine; he thought that the emerald necklace did not appear so vivid as on the previous occasion he had been shown it, a month or two previously. Major Lockhart's opinion of the necklace was the same, although his grounds for saying so were slightly different. In demonstration of his view, he held up the necklace to the window and looked through one of the larger stones directly at the setting sun. He then did the same with one of the ear-rings, and declared that whereas the stone in the ear-ring was undoubtedly genuine, the stones in the necklace were not.

"We are all in agreement, then, gentlemen," said Temperley. "The stones in the necklace are false. In fact, I believe the whole necklace is false."

"But how can that be?" cried Sowerby. "And why should Edward have been carrying an imitation of the Temperley Emeralds about with him?"

"Yes, it doesn't make much sense, Temperley," said Major Lockhart. "Unless," he added, "Edward had given the real necklace to someone and received the imitation in return – but what possible reason could he have for doing that? And, in any case, how could he have extracted the real necklace from where it was securely locked up?"

"I think I can get to the bottom of the matter," said Holmes, "but first I need to ask Lady Temperley a question."

"What question?" demanded Temperley.

"I should rather not say until I have asked Lady Temperley herself."

"But she is utterly prostrated by what has happened this afternoon," said Temperley, "and cannot be disturbed,"

"She does not yet know all that has happened," returned Holmes. "She will answer my question – that I can promise you."

"Oh, very well," said Temperley in a tone of resignation, "if you insist. I will call for her maid to show you up there."

A few moments later, the maid entered and she and Holmes left. The discussion in the drawing-room continued in a desultory fashion for a little while, but reached no conclusion, as no one could suggest what had become of the real emeralds, nor why Docking should have been carrying with him a duplicate set. The whole business seemed utterly inexplicable. As the minutes ticked by and Holmes did not return, I began to wonder where he had gone, and what he was doing. At length I could stand the tension no longer and, making some excuse, I left the drawing-room and went up to my bedroom. There, I sat on the bed, but left the door ajar, so that I might hear anyone passing in the corridor outside.

For several minutes, all was silent, then I heard footsteps on the stairs and the sound of voices approaching, which I recognized as those of Lord Temperley and Major Lockhart.

"I'll go and see how Felicity is getting on," said Temperley, "and see what Mr. Holmes is up to. Do you know where Sowerby has gone?"

"No, I've no idea," replied Lockhart. "Anyway, I'll be in my room if you want me."

I heard them move off, and, for a few moments, silence descended again on the upper floor of Hardshaw Hall. My mind had wandered once more to speculation as to what Holmes might be doing, when all at once, I heard a cry of surprise, followed by a cry of anger from the same voice, then the sound of a scuffle. I had not the faintest idea what was happening, but I sprang from my bed, seized my revolver and hurried out into the corridor.

For an instant I paused. Then I heard further cries, among which I thought I recognized Holmes's voice, which seemed to come from a doorway a little further down the corridor. I hurried that way and, finding the door ajar, pushed it wide open. As I did so, I almost cried out in astonishment at the scene which met my eyes. The room was in utter chaos, with drawers pulled out and furniture overturned, and, in the centre of the room, two men grappling fiercely. One was Sherlock Holmes, the other Major Lockhart. At the very moment I pushed the door open, the two of them overbalanced and tumbled to the floor. Lockhart stretched out his hand, picked up a poker from the fireplace and raised it up to strike a blow. I sprang forward at once and clapped the pistol to the side of his head.

"Put that down or I fire," I cried. There was a moment of stillness, then, as I pressed the muzzle into his temple, he threw the poker into the hearth with a clatter. "Now get to your feet and don't try anything."

I took a step back, keeping the pistol pointed at Lockhart, as he and Holmes scrambled to their feet. A voice from behind me made me half turn. In the corridor stood Lord Temperley and Inspector Waltham.

"What the devil is going on here?" demanded Lord Temperley.

"I have been looking for your emeralds," said Holmes. "Here they are," he added, holding up a large ornate necklace, set with vivid green stones. "They were in the bottom of Lockhart's trunk, as I'd suspected they would be."

"It's a lie!" cried Lockhart. "I don't know what your game is, Mr. Holmes – you and that crony of yours – but you'll have to do better than that!"

"How can you possibly justify such a serious accusation, Mr. Holmes?" demanded Temperley in an angry voice.

"Because, Lord Temperley, it is true," replied Holmes. "It has been Major Lockhart's plan all along to steal the emeralds. Everything that has happened has been with that one aim in view, since long before he ever came to stay here."

"I find that very hard to believe," said Temperley in a tone of stupefaction. "Why, Major Lockhart has been staying with us for nearly a year now. If he had really wished to steal the emeralds, I am sure he could have done so long ago. In any case, how, if at all, does this relate to the poor boy lying dead downstairs? Why did he have the duplicate necklace in his pocket, and where did it come from?"

"I fancy Major Lockhart could shed some light on that subject, considering that it was he who had the duplicate necklace made," returned Holmes. As he spoke he dipped his hand into Lockhart's trunk and brought out a folded sheet of paper. "I have here a letter addressed to Lockhart from Holland and Westwood, jewellery manufacturers of Hatton Garden in London, discussing the details of the manufacture of the imitation necklace."

"You devil!" cried Lockhart in a wild, hoarse tone, his eyes bulging with rage. "How dare you make free with my private correspondence!" Abruptly, with no warning, he sprang forward and clamped his large, powerful hands round Holmes's throat, as if he would strangle the life out of him. "You fiend!" he cried. "You damned, interfering fiend! I'll swing for you, so help me!"

I stepped forward quickly and raised my revolver, but as I did so I saw Holmes bring his hands up swiftly, grasp hold of his assailant's fingers and slowly pull them away from his throat. There was a cry of pain from Lockhart, as Holmes pressed his fingers backwards and forced him down to the floor.

"Let's get the bracelets on him and get him downstairs," said Inspector Waltham in a brisk tone, producing a pair of handcuffs from within his jacket.

As Lockhart and the policeman left the room, Temperley turned to Holmes.

"If Lockhart had the duplicate necklace made," said he in a weak, trembling voice, as if he could scarcely believe the words he himself was uttering, "how came it into Edward's pocket, Mr. Holmes? Do you believe that Lockhart somehow managed to slip it in there?"

"I think not," replied Holmes. "I fancy that Lockhart was just as surprised as everyone else when the imitation emeralds turned up where they did – although not for the same reasons."

"Do you believe there is anything suspicious about poor Edward's death?"

"I am certain of it," said Holmes. "There is not a doubt in my mind that he was murdered. But, come. Let us go downstairs, Lord Temperley, and I will explain to you my view of the matter. It is a more complex business than you perhaps realise."

Two hours had passed. Major Lockhart had been taken away in a police van, but Inspector Waltham had at length returned by himself to discuss the case with Sherlock Holmes and Lord Temperley. Holmes, meanwhile, had had a long private discussion with Lady Temperley and seemed to have succeeded in calming and reassuring her, so that she had taken her place at the dinner-table with the rest of us. It had been a strange meal, with very little conversation. The tutor, in particular, had seemed very uncomfortable to be there at all, but, in truth, I think that none of us could concentrate on anything, so keen were we all to hear Holmes's analysis of the surprising and puzzling events which had recently disturbed the historic calm of Hardshaw Hall.

Now, our meal finished, we had repaired to the large drawing-room. A fire had been lit, for the evening had brought a chill with it, and its familiar friendly crackle was as comforting to the mind as its warmth was comforting to the body. Inspector Waltham had joined us as we sat, sipping our coffee, and, at last, in response to a request from the policeman, Sherlock Holmes prepared to begin.

"The first thing that caused me concern," said he, "was Lady Temperley's account of her visit to the fortune-teller at the village fair, and what she was told there."

This remark elicited cries of surprise from all present.

"I have always understood that you were highly sceptical of such superstitions," I interjected, "and your remarks to Lady Temperley this morning gave no indication that you attached any credence to the fortune-teller's predictions."

"Yes, of course that is so. You misunderstand me, Watson. My train of thought was simply this: that such fortune-tellers generally predict good things for those that consult them, or, at the very least, a mixture of good and bad. They do, after all, wish their customers to leave the tent feeling glad that they have paid a visit, so that they will recommend the experience to their friends. But Lady Temperley was given only bad, gloomy predictions, which upset her profoundly. I felt sure there must be some reason for this, and I wondered if the Gipsy fortune-teller had been bribed to say what she did. If so, that certainly threw suspicion in my mind onto Edward Docking, without whose insistence Lady Temperley would probably not have visited the fortune-teller at all.

"We then come to the incident of the thirteenth step. Lady Temperley believed that it was simply Edward's ignorance of the old Hardshaw tradition which had led him to speak so light-heartedly of counting the steps, and, despite his irritation over the matter, I imagine that that was also the view of Lord Temperley. But as I listened to Lady Temperley's account, suspicious as I already was of Docking, I could not help but think that this seemed of the same pattern as the fortune-teller business, and I wondered if he were quite so ignorant of the old tradition as he pretended to be. It seemed to me, rather, that the stage was being deliberately set for some misfortune to befall the family, but what might this be? I at once thought of the famous Temperley Emeralds, which I knew were fabulously valuable.

"As to the purpose of these superstitious warnings of misfortune, I could think of no specific reason for them, and thought it possible that they might be intended simply to confuse the issue, so that when the 'misfortune' occurred, rational consideration of the matter would be hampered. Incidents which appear to fulfil a 'prophecy' tend to strike the mind differently from incidents which occur 'out of the blue,' as it were. This seemed to me the most likely purpose of these warnings of impending doom. But why should a young man who was hoping to enter the University of Oxford in the autumn, and who was being very kindly put up and tutored in the meantime by distant relatives of his father, have been plotting against his generous benefactors in this way? It seemed to me that such deep plotting would only be entered into by someone who had no real intention of taking up a place at Oxford at all, and who did not really care a fig for Lord and Lady Temperley.

"As my thoughts circled round Edward Docking in this fashion, it occurred to me that as he had been brought up in South Africa, and Lord and Lady Temperley had never met him before, they had no way of knowing that he really was who he said he was. It was therefore perfectly possible, as far as I could see, that he was not really Edward Docking at all, but someone else entirely."

There were cries of incredulity from Holmes's audience at this suggestion, but he waved his hand to still their protests.

"I realise that that may strike you as fantastically improbable," he continued, "but it can scarcely be denied that the whole state of affairs was a very singular one, so the explanation for it was always likely to be a singular one, too. Indeed, Lady Temperley herself was convinced that something was very seriously amiss, even if she could not quite put her finger on what it was that troubled her so much."

"That is true," said Lady Temperley, "but I should never have considered such a wild and extraordinary speculation as you are suggesting, Mr. Holmes."

"I imagine not," responded Holmes. "That is perfectly understandable. You had accepted what you had been told by others, and you were in the very midst of all these disturbing events. In such circumstances it is always difficult to free your mind from what you have implicitly taken to be the truth for so long. In my professional life, however, I have generally found it worthwhile to consider all possibilities, however improbable they may seem at first.

"Now," he continued after a moment, "Lady Temperley had mentioned to me that although Edward Docking and the neighbour's boy, Stephen James, had never met, they had corresponded with each other some years ago, in their schooldays. Bearing that in mind, it seemed to me that if the young man staying here were not really Edward Docking, then if anyone was likely to see through the deception, either because of something the supposed Docking said, or something he might have been expected to say but didn't, that person would be Stephen James. Of course, if the James boy did harbour such doubts about his riding companion, and was unwise enough to give any indication that he did, then, if there were any truth to this theory, he would undoubtedly be putting himself in very great peril. When Lady Temperley then described to us how Stephen James had been killed while out riding with the young man taken to be Docking, I very much feared that it was murder, and that what might be termed the 'improbable possibility,' if not entirely confirmed, had at least become somewhat less improbable. So it seemed to me, at least, and I decided to follow this theory as far as it would take me.

"Now, if the young man purporting to be Edward Docking was in reality someone else, who might that someone else be? It could, of course, be someone that nobody had ever heard of, but most likely, I considered, was that it was the Andrew Cotter who had been mentioned to me by Lady

Temperley. He was said to be a former school-friend of Docking's, and Docking had gone to stay with him in Cape Town immediately before sailing for England. He would probably have been familiar enough with Docking's habits to succeed with the imposture, and was probably also sufficiently familiar with Docking's handwriting to imitate it successfully when he was obliged to write to Docking's family from England. But if it were really Andrew Cotter you have been putting up for the last three months, where, then, was the real Edward Docking? On this question, I feared the worst, and thought it very likely that he had been done to death by Cotter, in or around Cape Town.

"When the letter from Docking's father arrived recently, bringing news of the discovery of the body believed to be that of Andrew Cotter, Lady Temperley noted that the young man she took to be Docking appeared terribly shocked and upset at the news. Of course, it was always possible, even if my theory were correct, that Cotter might be shocked and anxious at the discovery of the body of the young man he himself had murdered, but I rather fancied that what really shocked him was the other item of news in the letter, that Edward Docking's father was coming to England in just a few weeks' time, for this would mean that his exposure as both an imposter and a murderer was imminent.

"As I considered the matter in this way, I was aware that there was yet another issue which must be taken into consideration, and that is this: although Lord and Lady Temperley had never met Edward Docking before the young man they believed to be he had arrived in England in February, Major Lockhart certainly had. He had stayed with the Dockings for a while during the time he spent in South Africa. Now, according to my theory, the young man who came to stay here at Hardshaw Hall was an imposter – probably Andrew Cotter – yet when he arrived here, calling himself Edward Docking, Lockhart said nothing. I gave this question a lot of consideration, but could think of no convincing reason why Lockhart should have remained silent on the matter if he were an honest man, and I was obliged to conclude then that he was not, and that his intentions here were dishonourable. If that were so, then what appeared to have been a chance meeting between Lockhart and Lord Temperley last year in London, which led to Lockhart's coming to stay here, might well not have been so accidental as it seemed. It is not too difficult to deliberately contrive a supposedly 'chance encounter' with someone if you really wish to do so, as I am sure countless young men would attest each time they recall how they first struck up a conversation with some young lady or other who happened to be the object of their admiration."

Lord Temperley nodded his head. "Incredible though it seems to be saying this," he remarked, "I am sure now that you must be right. There have been one or two odd little incidents in the last few months which have made me wonder about Lockhart and his supposed plans for the future. No, I didn't mention any of these things to you, Felicity," he added, as his wife made to speak: "they were all very trivial and might have meant nothing, and you had enough to worry about as it was. I'll give you a couple of examples, Mr. Holmes, so you can see what I mean: I chanced to notice one morning that Lockhart had had a letter from those jewellers you mentioned, although I had no idea, of course, what it was about. When curiosity got the better of me and I asked him about it, he said it was to do with an old ring which had belonged to his mother, which he was having reset. I remember I had the distinct impression from his manner as he said this that he was not telling me the truth. I explained this oddity away to myself afterwards by conjecturing that he was perhaps short of funds and was selling the ring to raise a little money but did not want to admit it, so I gave it no further thought. On another occasion, a couple of months ago, Lockhart and I were talking. We had been discussing Edward's impressive horsemanship, and Lockhart referred to him in passing as 'Andrew.' Of course, he corrected himself at once, and I thought it was just an unimportant slip of the tongue, and didn't give it any more thought. Lockhart even made a joke of it, I recall, and deliberately referred to the boy subsequently as 'Benjamin' and 'Bertie,' laughing heartily at his own jest. But now that I recall the incident, it does seem to me that Lockhart appeared inordinately bothered and embarrassed about it, much more so than one might expect if it had really been simply a trivial slip of the tongue."

Holmes nodded. "I believe that Lockhart and Cotter had plotted the whole business together, their ultimate aim being the theft of the Temperley Emeralds, after which, no doubt, they both intended to disappear, probably to Australia or somewhere else far away, where they would hope to avoid all attempts to find them. But if it had been Lockhart's intention all along to steal the emeralds, as I believe, why should he have involved Cotter in his criminal plan? The likeliest explanation, as I see it, is that Lockhart knew that he himself had no talent for opening locks and closing them up again in a way which could not be detected, and he knew that Cotter, with his criminal experience in South Africa, did have this skill. This in turn suggests that the plan was first hatched when the two of them met during Lockhart's time in South Africa. Cotter's ability to pick locks was no doubt his chief contribution to the scheme, Lockhart's being the ordering of the imitation necklace. It must, I imagine, have been during those periodic trips to London which I understand he took that Lockhart arranged to have the duplicate necklace made. When was the last time he went up to London, Lord Temperley?"

"Just last week. He went on the Wednesday and came back on the Friday."

"Then that was probably when he collected the completed duplicate necklace from the jeweller. It must have been their intention to leave the duplicate necklace in place of the genuine one, to prevent – or, at least, delay – the discovery of the theft, but this of course meant that they could do nothing until the duplicate necklace was ready. And now, having at last got the duplicate necklace, they would wish to put their plan into operation at the earliest opportunity, for with Docking's father due to arrive in just a couple of weeks – by which time they must both have hoped to have left Hardshaw completely – the time available to them was rapidly running out.

"As to what happened in the last twenty-four hours, we can only speculate. One thing, however, seems certain, which is that Cotter was murdered. He is supposed to have been flung from his horse, and to have struck his forehead on a stone. That means that he must have fallen forwards, in which case he would naturally use his hands to try to break his fall. And yet, despite the fact that he was not wearing gloves, his hands are completely unmarked. I have never known such an accident in which the victim's hands were not at least dirty and grazed, if not cut and bruised. I therefore think that Cotter had dismounted when he was attacked, and that he was deliberately struck down by someone. That someone must have been Lockhart. They had probably arranged to meet in the copse where Cotter's body was subsequently found, in order for Cotter to hand the necklace over to Lockhart. No doubt Cotter had taken the necklace from Lady Temperley's room this morning. Her absence in London for the day would, of course, have provided him with an ideal opportunity. But if both Lockhart and Cotter were intending to leave Hardshaw very soon, Lockhart, it seems, also had his own separate plan, which was to rid himself of his partner-in-crime forever, by murdering him. We can only speculate as to when Lockhart decided on this course of action. It may have been a recent decision, or it may be that he had intended all along to get rid of Cotter in this way, once the younger man had served his purpose and the robbery had been accomplished. This would, of course, save Lockhart having to share the spoils with him. However that may be, it is clear that things did not go quite as Lockhart had planned.

"The fact that he had gone to the trouble and expense of having the duplicate necklace made can only mean, as I mentioned, that he intended it to be left in the jewel case, in place of the genuine necklace. But when Cotter had taken the genuine necklace from the case, he evidently decided for some reason not to leave the imitation necklace in its place, but to take it with him when he went riding. As this, of course, set at nought the whole point of their careful plan, we must suppose two things: first, that Lockhart was not party to this decision, and had no idea when he murdered Cotter that the duplicate necklace was in his pocket, and, second, that Cotter had some very compelling reason for taking the duplicate necklace with him. What I suspect is this, that having deliberately got rid of Mr. Sowerby this afternoon by riding further than he knew the tutor would wish to go, Cotter then intended, after his rendezvous with Lockhart, to meet Agnes James, as it seems they had arranged. Perhaps, then, his reason for taking the necklace with him was that he intended to offer it to the girl, in an attempt to win her favour."

"If so," interrupted Inspector Waltham, "he must have been a complete fool. She would have recognized at once that it was a part of the famous Temperley Emeralds. It is inconceivable that she would have accepted it."

"I quite agree," said Lady Temperley. "And even if he had explained to her that it was just a copy of the original, it is such a heavy-looking, old-fashioned piece of jewellery that I can't believe that a young girl such as Agnes would find it an attractive thing to wear."

"I am sure you are right," said Holmes, nodding his head. "I think, however, that Andrew Cotter must have been very much smitten with Agnes James, and it is my experience that when a young man is in thrall to a woman in that way, there are no lengths he will not go to, however troublesome, no stratagems he will not attempt, however absurd, in order to win the woman's heart. No man is spared, but passion makes a fool of every one."

"You may be right about the whole business, Mr. Holmes," said the policeman after a moment. "In fact, I don't doubt that you are. But I can see that we're going to have the devil of a job to prove it all against Major Lockhart."

"The murder charge may indeed be difficult to prove in a court of law," agreed Holmes, "even though the circumstantial evidence is compelling. But you should at least be successful with the charge of theft. The genuine necklace was in Lockhart's trunk upstairs, and we know the name of the jewellers in London who made the duplicate necklace for him, so that is a start. It should also not be too difficult to prove, with the aid of photographs from South Africa, that the young man who has been known here as Edward Docking was in reality Andrew Cotter."

Inspector Waltham nodded his head, scribbled a few lines in his note-book, then closed it up. "I'd best be getting back to the station," said he, as he slipped the note-book into his pocket and rose to his feet. "I thank you very much for your help, Mr. Holmes. I'll take the duplicate necklace with me, and the letter from the jewellers, and set enquiries in motion at once."

When the policeman had left us, we sat in silence for some time, each no doubt pondering the dreadful recent events from his own point of view. At length the silence was broken by the tutor, Mr. Sowerby.

"This may be a very trivial point," he remarked in a hesitant tone, "but I am still puzzled about one little thing, Mr. Holmes. When you left the drawing-room earlier this evening, you said that there was one question you wished to ask Lady Temperley, and you implied that her answer would shed light on the matter. I confess I have racked my brains, but I cannot think what on earth that question could have been."

Holmes chuckled. "Nothing very subtle, I'm afraid, Mr. Sowerby," he replied. "When the duplicate necklace turned up, and the genuine article was found to be missing from the jewel-case, I was convinced that my theory was correct and that Major Lockhart had the emeralds, probably hidden somewhere in his bedroom. But the discovery of the imitation emeralds in Cotter's pocket – not to mention Inspector Waltham's inadvertent revelation of my true profession as a criminal investigator –

would also have been the first warning that Lockhart had had that his plans had gone awry, and I thought it likely that he would take the earliest opportunity to move the emeralds to somewhere where they would be much more difficult to find. It was therefore my intention to search his bedroom for the necklace without delay, the only problem being that I had no idea which of the rooms was his. The simplest solution to this difficulty, it seemed to me, was to ask Lady Temperley, which, as she was alone in her room, I could do without anyone else overhearing. That is therefore precisely what I did. It is a singular fact, but sometimes the dullest, most banal little question can yet be the most important!"

Little remains for me to tell of what had been a singularly strange, unpredictable and dreadful case. Subsequent enquiries proved beyond all doubt that the surprising theory which Sherlock Holmes had expounded to us in the drawing-room at Hardshaw Hall was indeed correct in every detail. As Holmes had predicted, Major Lockhart was acquitted of the murder of Andrew Cotter due to a lack of evidence, but was convicted of the theft of the Temperley Emeralds, and of conspiring to conceal the death of the real Edward Docking, for which he received a lengthy prison sentence. As Holmes and I journeyed back to London, the day after the surprising and dramatic events I have described above, an odd and striking thought occurred to me. Although Cotter had cynically tried to use the old tradition of "the thirteenth step of Hardshaw Hall" for his own ends, without, presumably, giving it any real credence, it had, nevertheless, once again correctly predicted a death at Hardshaw. But this was a death which that villain could never have expected, the death being his own.

Also from MX Publishing

MX Publishing is the world's largest specialist Sherlock Holmes publisher, with over a hundred titles and fifty authors creating the latest in Sherlock Holmes fiction and non-fiction.

From traditional short stories and novels to travel guides and quiz books, MX Publishing cater for all Holmes fans.

The collection includes leading titles such as *Benedict Cumberbatch In Transition* and *The Norwood Author* which won the 2011 Howlett Award (Sherlock Holmes Book of the Year).

MX Publishing also has one of the largest communities of Holmes fans on Facebook with regular contributions from dozens of authors.

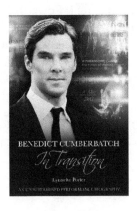

www.mxpublishing.com

Also from MX Publishing

"Phil Growick's, 'The Secret Journal of Dr Watson', is an adventure which takes place in the latter part of Holmes and Watson's lives. They are entrusted by HM Government (although not officially) and the King no less to undertake a rescue mission to save the Romanovs, Russia's Royal family from a grisly end at the hand of the Bolsheviks. There is a wealth of detail in the story but not so much as would detract us from the enjoyment of the story. Espionage, counter-espionage, the ace of spies himself, double-agents, double-crossers...all these flit across the pages in a realistic and exciting way. All the characters are extremely well-drawn and Mr Growick, most importantly, does not falter with a very good ear for Holmesian dialogue indeed. Highly recommended. A five-star effort."
The Baker Street Society

www.mxpublishing.com

Also from MX Publishing

The American Literati Series

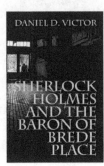

The Final Page of Baker Street
The Baron of Brede Place
Seventeen Minutes To Baker Street

"The really amazing thing about this book is the author's ability to call up the 'essence' of both the Baker Street 'digs' of Holmes and Watson as well as that of the 'mean streets' of Marlowe's Los Angeles. Although none of the action takes place in either place, Holmes and Watson share a sense of camaraderie and self-confidence in facing threats and problems that also pervades many of the later tales in the Canon. Following their conversations and banter is a return to Edwardian England and its certainties and hope for the future. This is definitely the world before The Great War."
Philip K Jones

www.mxpublishing.com

Also from MX Publishing

The Detective and The Woman Series

The Detective and The Woman
The Detective, The Woman and The Winking Tree
The Detective, The Woman and The Silent Hive

"The book is entertaining, puzzling and a lot of fun. I believe the author has hit on the only type of long-term relationship possible for Sherlock Holmes and Irene Adler. The details of the narrative only add force to the romantic defects we expect in both of them and their growth and development are truly marvelous to watch. This is not a love story. Instead, it is a coming-of-age tale starring two of our favorite characters."
Philip K Jones

www.mxpublishing.com

CPSIA information can be obtained
at www.ICGtesting.com
Printed in the USA
LVHW021828081118
596437LV00009B/670